PRAISE FOR

"Sasha has done it again! I devou... them to come out because I kno... should be on your must-read author list if you are into sports romance."

"You want a sizzling soccer romance??! This is for you! I could not put this book down! I was hooked from the second I started reading!!"

"Sasha Lace has fast become one of my favorite authors! The world she exposes, the world she builds, has me glued to my screen from the first word to the very last!"

"This is everything that I love about contemporary romance: strong male and female main characters, romance with instant chemistry."

"A witty, flirty, and a little bit of everything else romantic story. The sizzle was awesome too. Read it in one sitting, it was such an easy read."

"30% in and Sasha Lace became a one-click author."

"I am loving that an author is giving women their shot in the world of sports romance!"

"Gabe needs to be added to your list of book boyfriends, he is handsome, knows what he wants and my heaven, knows his way around a woman. The spice in this was beautiful and fun. It was delicious."

"I left each chapter wanting more and more and MORE. Well-written, fast read that gives readers everything they are looking for."

"As with any book by Sasha there was a point where I was reduced to a crying mess and wanted to throw my Kindle at a wall . . . which led to having to stay up all night to get to the HEA."

"Would I recommend this book? Yes! Would I recommend everything written by Sasha Lace? Yes!"

Playing to Win

TITLES BY SASHA LACE

Playing the Field series

Playing to Win

SASHA LACE

Text copyright © 2023, 2024 by Sasha Lace

Published by Montlake, Seattle

First published as *Melting the Mountain Man* by Sasha Lace in 2023. This edition contains editorial revisions.

www.apub.com

Amazon, the Amazon logo, and Montlake are trademarks of Amazon.com, Inc., or its affiliates.

ISBN-13: 9781662526183
eISBN: 9781662526176

Cover design by The Brewster Project
Cover image: © LadadikArt/ Getty Images; © DG FotoStock © Oleksii Sidorov © Chris Sargent © Taiga / Shutterstock

Printed in the United States of America

*For my lovely ARC team, readers, and everyone
who took the time to review and support me when
this series was first published. It meant the world.
Thank you so much.*

PRONUNCIATION GUIDE

Bara brith: (*barrah breeth*) *Traditional Welsh bread flavored with tea, dried fruits and spices.* (*Bara = bread. Brith = speckled*).

Bore da (*boh-ray dah*) *Good morning.*

Caerphilly (*Care-filly*) *A kind of mild white cheese, originally made in Caerphilly, Wales.*

Cariad (*ka-ree-ad*) *Darling.*

Cawl (*cow-al*) *A traditional hearty Welsh stew that typically includes meat and vegetables.*

Cwtch (pronounced "kutch", to rhyme with "butch") *A hug that is also a cubbyhole. There is no real direct translation into English. You'll have to find your own sexy Welsh ex-rugby player and ask him to demonstrate.*

Ewan (*Yoo-in*)

Geraint (*Guh-RAHNT*) *Sexy Welsh Lumberdaddy*

Nadolig Llawen (*Nah-doll-lig llah-when*) *Merry Christmas. For the "ll", place your tongue behind your teeth and blow gently.*

Nos da (*Noss dah*) *Goodnight.*

Sir Tom Jones OBE *If you don't know, there is no helping you.*

Wassail (*Wahs-uhl*) *Spiced ale or mulled wine drunk during celebrations for Christmas Eve and Twelfth Night. There is some controversy over whether it's actually of Welsh or Old English origin. For the purposes of this story, it's Welsh.*

Chapter 1

Dad surveyed the dirt track ahead and flexed his fingers on the huge steering wheel. "You're sure about this? It's not too late to back out."

His tone was light, but I didn't miss the shadow that crossed his work-hardened face. My family had never warmed to Bryce. They were always polite—their Southern manners wouldn't allow them to be anything else—but I wasn't blind to the way they looked at us together.

I took a deep breath and smoothed my clammy palms over layers of scratchy organza and lace. "Yes. I'm sure. Of course I'm sure."

Dad's jaw tensed, but he held his silence as we rumbled over wide-open countryside in his beat-up old tractor. It was an unlikely wedding car, but Dad's face had lit up like a Christmas tree when he'd suggested it. It would likely horrify Bryce's fancy LA relatives when we rocked up outside the church, juddering and spewing fumes. They'd hear us coming a mile off. No doubt that's why Dad had been set on the idea.

We hit another bump in the dirt track. I snapped my hand to my veil to stop it flying off. Dad flashed me a glance and chuckled. I couldn't help but laugh with him. My family thought it was too fast. I got it. Bryce was so different from the guys I'd brought home in high school. He was LA to the core, dazzling and full of charm. I always got so nervous at the fancy events PR insisted I attend, but none of it fazed Bryce. When the cameras appeared, he'd grip my hand and whisper in my ear, and it grounded me. This wasn't who my parents had envisioned for me, but this is what I wanted. A heavy weight pressed down on my shoulders. I had one life to live. I had to do it my way, even if it meant disappointing my family. Maybe with time, they'd come to love Bryce as much as I did—probably around the same time pigs sprouted wings and took to the skies. Still, I wouldn't lose hope.

The tractor rumbled to a halt. A cardinal's song rang out in the bracing silence. The bright-red bird perched on a branch in one of the many trees that lined the shady path to the church. I'd loved that sound as a kid. Now the low whistle jangled in my ears. A rush of anxiety gripped me. What if the table arrangements got messed up and my warring cousins got seated together? What if I stumbled over my vows and couldn't get my words out? What if Bryce's creepy uncle with the dairy intolerance got served the crème brûlée?

What if this whole thing is one gigantic mistake?

Sweat prickled my top lip in the awful heat, but I took a calming breath. By the end of today, I would start my life as Mrs. Bryce Muller. Everything could begin. After years of pressure, grind, and picking up a dozen injuries, I'd finally get to announce my retirement from soccer and start a family. A thrill of excitement went through me.

"This is it. Ready, darlin'?" Dad's voice was thick with emotion. *This is it.*

The low whistle from the little red bird increased in pitch. My heart pounded along with its staccato trill. Dad opened the cab door and held out a hand to help me down. My heels clanked on the rusted metal steps. So much for an elegant entrance. If I could have gotten married in cleats, I would have. Assuming the tractor wasn't enough to knock Bryce's family into a tailspin, the cleats would have sent them over the edge. I fought to take a full breath against the press of my tight dress.

Dad's rough hand closed around mine. "Just breathe and take it all in."

My parents had been married for thirty years. They adored each other. If Bryce and I could be half as happy as my parents, we'd be doing great. Smiling, I closed my eyes and lifted my face to the sun's warmth.

Just breathe and take it all in.

Diesel fumes filled my nose and made me cough. I opened my eyes to see Anna, my maid of honor. She gripped my elbows. Her face was gray and grim. An alarm bell rang in my head. We'd been friends since elementary school. I knew this look. It was the one she'd worn the time she'd taken home the ill-fated school hamster. Poor little Hamilton, God rest his soul.

What had gone wrong? The catering? The band? My crazy cousins in a brawl?

"I'm sorry, Maddie." Tears filled my best friend's eyes. "It's Bryce. He ran. I don't think he's coming back."

Chapter 2

MADISON

A soft knock sounded on my bedroom door. "You've got a visitor."

I groaned and slipped lower underneath the comforter.

Another knock. "Maddie? I know you said you didn't want to see anyone, but you should come. This man says he's flown all the way from England."

England? Weird. I didn't know anyone from England. Reluctantly, I threw back the blankets and stood. Crumbs flew from the black pajamas I'd worn for the past week. I crossed the dark bedroom and opened the door a crack. Mom's concerned gaze moved from my bird's-nest hair to my bare feet before she fixed a breezy smile in place. Guilt made my shoulders heavy. I was so tired of that expression. Living at home with my parents was getting old. They worried about me. If I had the energy for it, I'd be worried about me too.

Pink tinged Mom's cheekbones, and her eyes sparkled. "He's very . . . nice. His eyes are very . . . green."

I tapped her chin. "Put your tongue back in, Mom."

"Are you coming down?" Her smile faltered. She couldn't hide the desperation in her voice. "He *has* come all the way from England."

Whoop de doo. England. Let's have a parade. I couldn't care less if he'd come from the moon in a little silver rocket. Mom clasped her hands together. Her eyes pleaded with me. How could I say no? She had to be sick inside at the prospect of being rude to a guest.

I sighed. "Sure. I'll be down in a minute."

Mom's shoulders relaxed. She smoothed the collar of my pajamas. "You're going to get dressed first?"

"Yes, Mom. I'm going to get dressed." My voice sounded flat and lifeless.

I pushed the door closed. Glaring at the mirror, I tried to pinch some color into my gaunt cheeks. I threw some clothes on and dragged a hairbrush through my knotty hair. My jeans, which had once fit snugly, felt baggy around my waist, but I couldn't find a belt. Whoever he was, why wouldn't he call first? With each step down the stairs, the sweet smell of Mom's butter cake twisted my gut. My appetite had vanished along with my groom.

In the kitchen, a smartly dressed man sat at the island. Something was familiar about him, but I couldn't place it.

He stood and flashed an easy smile. "Well. Madison Thorner. The 'Thornado' in the flesh." His crisp, clipped British accent sounded strange in my kitchen. "What an honor."

I cringed to hear the nickname the press had given me spoken out loud. The man's cool, smooth palm met mine. Mom was right. He was very pretty. His eyes shimmered with emeralds. I had no time for pretty boys. Bryce had been pretty. He was also full of crap.

"I'm Gabe Rivers, the director of the Calverdale Ladies."

I tried to smile, but I'm sure he could see the confusion on my face. Gabe Rivers? I knew that name. Wasn't he some British soccer bigwig?

"Can I get you a drink? Some iced tea or—"

"I'm fine, thank you." Gabe turned his dazzling smile on Mom. "Pam has been looking after me."

Mom's blush deepened, and she smoothed her hands over her apron. "It's lovely of you to drop by, Gabe."

Good job playing it cool, Mom. I would have laughed if I had any humor left in me. Mom was clearly a sucker for a pretty face and a British accent. I guided her to the door.

"You can leave us to it. Thanks, Mom."

Disappointment flickered in her eyes, but she left, closing the door behind her. No doubt she'd be outside listening in. I turned my attention to our visitor. Why did I have a random British man who looked like he'd stepped off the cover of *Vogue* standing in my parents' kitchen on a Monday morning? There could only be one reason for a visit from a soccer club boss. Whatever this dude was selling, I had zero interest in buying.

"I'm staying in Lexington. It never hurts to get out of the city and explore further afield when you travel. I thought I could drop in and meet a local soccer star while I'm in the area." Gabe flicked an imaginary spot of dust from his immaculate suit. "I've always felt very . . . at home in the countryside."

Somehow, I kept a straight face. This guy looked as out of his element out here as Bryce always had. "You thought you'd *drop* in? What are you doing in Lexington? Are you here for a tour of the Ale-8-One factory or the Bluegrass Railroad Museum?"

A small smile pulled at his lips. "Both things sound . . . delightful." His voice was casual, but his green eyes blazed with purpose. "While I'm here, I wanted to talk to you about the possibility of—"

I held my hand up to stop him. "If you're here to talk about soccer, you should know I've retired. I don't want you to waste any time on your vacation."

Gabe snapped his mouth shut. I hadn't meant to interrupt, but the thought of going back to my old life made my guts churn. At least Mom wasn't here to witness me being rude to our smart British guest. I just wanted to be left alone. My old teammates still called me. Everybody begged me to come back. Nobody understood that I couldn't. Soccer didn't interest me anymore. Nothing did.

Gabe cleared his throat. "You can't retire. You're too good to retire."

I snorted. Who the hell was this British guy to stand in my kitchen and tell me whether I should be retired? Twenty-eight was young to retire but not unheard of.

A knot welled in my throat, but I bit back my angry retort and turned my face to the window to watch Dad chopping wood. The rhythmic thuds of the axe ricocheted in my head. My nieces played over by the swing. Brooke had suffered through round after round of IVF before the triplets. My sister had fought so hard for her happy ending. I was thrilled for her, but still the knot in my throat tightened. Jealousy was an ugly thing. I couldn't help it if I'd always wanted to be a mother. Now I'd have to settle for being the bitter old aunt with a dusty wedding dress in the attic, like a character in some crusty old English novel. Bryce had ruined everything. I'd never forgive him.

Gabe sauntered around my kitchen as if he owned it. I was sure I'd read something weird about this guy once. Wasn't he on some true crime podcast?

"I'm taking my team to the top of the Women's Super League. If we're going to be a world-class team, we need world-class players. I know we don't have the LA weather—"

"I'm never going back to play for the Halos. I don't care about that."

The silence thickened. Bryce was in LA. I'd never set foot anywhere near him again.

Gabe flashed a smile that had probably charmed the panties off a thousand women but only cemented my irritation. How could I get him out of here without making Mom mad?

"I've watched every one of your games. I'll pay you whatever you want, but I've learned these things aren't always about money. Tell me what you need to consider coming out of retirement, and I'll make it happen."

I sighed. This man was annoying. "I have no plans to come out of retirement."

"Nobody tackles the way you do. You're fearless. You're at the peak of your game. It's no time to quit."

"You don't give up, do you?"

"No. I definitely don't do that." His eyes flashed with humor, and his smile widened.

I couldn't help my incredulous snort. This guy reminded me so much of Bryce. Another smooth-talking narcissist with a pretty mouth full of empty promises. I'd never fall for anything a man like this spouted ever again.

"Come for dinner tonight with my family. My wife is our striker. She can tell you about the team."

"I'll have to pass, but thanks for dropping by."

I moved to the window to watch Mom gossiping over the fence with our neighbors, likely about our fancy guest. This area had a small-town feel, and I was a local girl who had done well and made it as a pro athlete. Everybody had been in the church that day. Now, people treated me like an unexploded land mine they'd stumbled across and didn't have the expertise to defuse. It was why I hardly left the house. A heavy weight pressed on me. I just wanted to go back upstairs. Time to wrap this up.

I crossed to the door and prayed he'd get the hint. "I hope you enjoy the rest of your tour. You should visit the Natural Bridge while you're here. It's a pleasant hike."

Gabe studied my face and inclined his head in a nod. "I apologize. I've clearly caught you at a bad time. The offer stays open. If you change your mind, call me." He slipped a business card from his pocket and placed it on the table. "I can see myself out."

My parents had brought me up better than to be rude to a guest. I didn't want to be like this. My daily mood was PMS on steroids, and as much as I tried, I couldn't paste on a smile and get on with life.

Children's laughter drifted through the kitchen window. A pang pulled at my heart.

Gabe stopped mid-stride to the door. He turned on his heel to face me. "Actually, fuck it. My wife told me not to lay it on thick. She knows I like to get my own way, but Miri's not here and I don't do *softly softly*. I heard what happened to you. I get it. You thought your life was going one way, and now it's not. A bad breakup is rough. It fucks you up. You know what's worse? Throwing away the thing you were born to do over a man who is clearly a piece of shit. I've watched your tapes. You own that midfield. I have a team full of technical players, but I need more aggression. I need a box-to-box midfielder to drive this team forward. Every team wants a player like you. You win that ball every single time, and you run with it. You need to be on a pitch, not hiding away up here in BFE. I'm offering you a fresh start, but if you're not up for the challenge . . ."

"BFE? You said you'd always wanted to visit."

"I'm here for you, not a tour around a fizzy drink factory." A wry smile lifted his lips. "Although since you mention it, we did that tour, and it was very interesting. The point is, I promised my wife I'd take our team to the top. My wife has given me everything I've ever wanted, and now I'm going to give her that dream.

"I inherited this team, and honestly, I wasn't thrilled. I would have done anything to trade and direct the men's team, but these women changed my mind. Nobody thought we'd earn promotion to the Women's Super League, but we've fought hard, and my wife has amazed me at every turn." A smile touched his lips and it looked genuine. "The entire team has amazed me. I owe them their spot at the top. We're going to show everyone that Calverdale Ladies are every bit as good, if not better, than the men's team. To do that, I need world-class players. I'm not going home without you."

No one had dared speak to me frankly in a long time. The stuff about the wife was touching, even if I didn't buy it. He was probably screwing around behind her back. I wouldn't trust a man who looked like this as far as I could throw him.

He cocked his head, his gaze shrewd. "You look angry. I get it. Come and be angry on my pitch. We need you."

No. You don't get it. Women aren't allowed to be angry. Not this angry. Not in this house. Not with my family.

He stepped close enough for his spicy cologne to invade my nostrils. He smelled of money and entitlement. Just like Bryce. "You're not done yet. I watched your tapes, and I know it. You were born to play. This is your calling. Don't stand there and tell me you're done because I don't believe you. Deep down, I don't think you believe it either."

I stared at Mom talking with the neighbors. It was me who had put those dark shadows under her eyes. Me and that flouncy dress in the attic. It was Mom's wedding dress. It's not like we could get rid of it.

Maybe leaving isn't the worst idea in the world.

At least I could be angry and not feel guilty about it all the time. At least I could breathe. The tiniest glimmer of something buoyant flared inside.

A fresh start.

No more pitying glances. No more casseroles on the doorstep and deathly silence the minute I stepped into a room. An entire ocean between me and Bryce. Mars wouldn't be enough distance, but England was pretty far. It was a chance to stop dragging everyone I cared about down with me.

Gabe peered out the window at my mom. "I know England is a long way from home, but these women will welcome you with open arms. The team is a family. We'll look after you, and help you settle. Anything you need, just ask and you'll have it."

I sighed. Mom and Dad had always talked about the UK. They'd fallen in love with Wales on a school trip, and they'd gone back to get married. I could talk to this guy, at least. It was flattering, really. He'd come a long way. The smallest of smiles found my lips, and for the first time in a long while, it wasn't false. England wasn't my plan, but sometimes plans got scattered and dirty, like old confetti.

I folded my arms across my chest. "Fine."

"Fine?" He looked a little bemused.

"You're right. I'm angry. Where are you taking me for dinner?"

Chapter 3

GERAINT

PRESENT DAY

WALES, UNITED KINGDOM

I surveyed the dimly lit pub lounge, and my heart sank. We had three customers—two, if you didn't count Simon, the border collie. Not good. Today, of all days, we needed to look good. A crash rang out from behind the bar. Young Aled grabbed the base of his spine and groaned as he bent to pick up the shattered pint glass. Young Aled was seventy-eight years old, but still the youngest of the Aleds at the pub.

"Don't worry, I've got it." I moved behind the bar to help him.

Young Aled's hands shook as he retrieved a dustpan and brush from under the bar. "It's fine. I'll get a mop when I change the barrel."

"No, you won't." Last time Young Aled had attempted to change the barrel, I'd found him in agony on the basement floor with a slipped disc.

I held him back with a hand on his arm. "Don't touch those barrels."

A burning smell drifted from the kitchen. My jaw tensed. Ewan, one of the local lads, helped me out when things got busy, but he wasn't a trained commis chef. I'd taken him on as an apprentice as a favor to his grandfather. He could barely get through a shift without chopping his finger off or incinerating the kitchen. I glanced at the clock and my breath quickened. The brewery guy should be here any minute.

Bryn, one of the regulars, rolled up his sleeves and moved behind the bar to pull himself a pint.

I put a hand out to stop him. "What are you doing?"

"Getting myself another pint."

"Not today. We've got to look professional. Get back in your seat, and I'll serve you."

Chuckling to himself, Bryn rolled his eyes and continued pouring his pint. I glanced down the bar to find an empty space where Young Aled had been. Damn it. He must have gone down to the basement to change the barrel.

Ewan appeared from the kitchen, wiping greasy handprints down his apron. He swiped his straight curtains of jet-black hair to the side of his forehead. "Have you heard about Young Aled and Mrs. Ackwright?"

"Aren't you supposed to be in the kitchen? What is the beef looking like?"

Amusement sparkled in his eyes. "It's on."

"What's on? The beef?"

Ewan raised a suggestive brow. "Young Aled and Mrs. Ackwright."

Not another one. My elderly barman was always romancing some old widow from the village.

"I hope I'm still a randy old bastard in my seventies." Ewan chuckled and poured himself a pint of mild. "God bless him. You have to admire the man's efforts."

I waited until he'd filled his glass and then took it out of his hand. "Not today. No drinking on the job. We need to look professional. Get back in the kitchen. Don't cremate that beef, whatever you do."

Ewan's jaw dropped. I followed his gaze to the door. A woman had stepped inside the pub. She looked to be in her mid-fifties. Her blonde hair fell in neat face-framing waves. A smart pale-blue shift dress hugged her slim frame.

Ewan slid me a glance and spoke under his breath. "They sent a woman. Did you know she'd be a woman?"

"Does it matter?" I whispered back.

A thoughtful expression crossed Ewan's face, and he put out a hand to hold me back. "You'd better let me handle this. You're going to say the wrong thing and put your foot in it."

That was highly likely. Still, as the landlord, this had to be me. "I'll be fine."

Ewan blew out a breath, unconvinced. "Maybe it's good. She might be one of those cougars on the lookout for a younger man. This should be a doddle for a big handsome bastard like you." Humor laced Ewan's tone, and he nudged me in the ribs. "Say as little as possible. Just look all square-jawed and broody."

I couldn't help my laugh. There wouldn't be any charming the brewery. The Dragon Inn had been losing money hand over fist since I'd inherited the lease from Dad. Now we just had a handful of locals and a few hikers in the season. Dad had wanted to keep it up and running for the community. The locals had been his best friends. I did everything I could to honor his wishes.

The woman surveyed the pub lounge and headed toward the bar. "Hello. I'm looking for Geraint Madoc."

My brain turned over the English words, processing. It had been a while since I'd spoken English. Always easier to express myself in Welsh.

I held out my hand. "That's me. This is my commis chef, Ewan."

Ewan inclined his head. "Hello."

The woman flashed a tight smile. "I'm Jill, the rep from Mason and Cartwright Brewery."

"It's a pleasure. Can I get you a drink?"

"No, thank you." She glanced at the watch on her slim wrist. "I have another meeting after this."

Good. Let's get this over and done with.

"Right." I inclined my head to the pub lounge. "Follow me."

Heat from the crackling fire blasted my face as I ducked under an arch to exit the bar. The designers of seventeenth-century coaching inns hadn't had six-foot-six ex-rugby players in mind when they'd decided on the height of the roof. I pulled out a chair at one of the small tables scattered about the lounge. Jill sat. She surveyed the lounge, taking in the stone floor, the exposed brickwork walls, the oak beams, and the border collie curled in the armchair by the inglenook fire.

I knew what this place looked like. I'd kept on top of basic maintenance, but we were long overdue for a refurbishment. Black-and-white mountaineering photos from the seventies cluttered the walls. The green velvet booths were frayed and past their best. The place was fading and falling apart at the seams, not through lack of love, just lack of funds.

I cleared my throat. "It's not normally this quiet."

Lies. Three customers were our equivalent of rush hour, and yes, I was including Simon the border collie in the count. You couldn't find a more loyal customer than Simon.

"You're in an excellent location. You should get hikers in the season."

I didn't miss the emphasis on the word *should*. We sat on the Llanberis Pass, one of the routes to the summit of Snowdon, the highest mountain in Wales. In warmer months, the pub attracted the odd hiker seeking a pint of real ale and home-made Welsh cakes. We lost custom to trendier places. Business had been slow for a while.

Jill pulled out her briefcase. "I was sorry to hear about your father."

A heavy weight pressed down on me. "Thanks. He always spoke highly of the brewery."

Another lie. Dad might have leased the pub from them, but he'd hated their guts. Mason and Cartwright was a soulless chain that only cared about profit. It was the kind of gastropub that classed chicken Kiev and chips as haute cuisine.

Jill's eyes drifted over my head, and she peered at my old rugby photos on the wall.

Her gaze riveted on my face before it moved slowly over my body. A strange, faintly eager look flashed in her eyes. "I used to watch you play."

I should have taken those photos down. Dad had insisted upon displaying them, and the locals knew better than to ask me about it.

"About this lease—"

"I went to a lot of rugby matches with my husband." She leaned back in her chair, relaxing. "We're divorced. I'm living the single life."

She gave a significant lift of her brow. Slowly, her gaze slid down my body again. The smile on her lips held a hint of flirtation. We needed to get back on track. This meeting was making me stressed enough without introducing flirting into the equation. There had always been women back in the rugby days. The team had attracted rugby groupies. I'd had plenty of offers, but I'd never strayed from Jess. Pity she'd dropped me after the injury. It turned out my ex-wife was the biggest rugby groupie of them all.

I cleared my throat. "About the lease . . . I know the figures for the past year don't look great, but I've been working on a way to—"

"A rugby player and a trained chef. You're multitalented. Why don't you play anymore?"

She sat forward and gazed at me intently, waiting for an answer. I opened my mouth and closed it again. Even after all this time, the injury was my least favorite topic of conversation. "I'm keen to renew the lease."

"You're very isolated out here. Is it just you? You must get lonely."

Her bold, appraising stare made a muscle jump in my jaw. Yes, it was lonely, but I had no choice. It had been Dad's dream to hold on to this place. He'd made me promise I wouldn't let it go. "I suppose . . . Sometimes . . ."

She pressed her lips together and smoothed her tight skirt over her thighs. "The brewery is thinking of selling. They've had an offer from a wellness firm. Yoga. Gong baths. Wild swimming. That kind of thing."

Ice laced my stomach. "Gong baths?"

"It's an ideal location." She gazed out of the window at the lofty peak of Snowdon in the distance. "Peace and quiet. Very . . . zen."

They couldn't be serious. The Dragon wasn't just my livelihood, it was my home and a hub for the local community. Sure, we only had a few customers, but they were regulars—locals from the farms around here who had been coming for years.

My heart pounded, but I kept my voice level. "The Dragon has been a pub since the seventeenth century. This is a piece of history. People still come here—"

"Not enough people to turn a profit. Any decision the brewery makes will be a business decision. This can't come as a shock." She traced circles on the wooden table with a sharp crimson fingernail. "You haven't turned a profit all year."

No, it shouldn't have shocked me, but I hadn't allowed myself to contemplate the worst possible scenario of losing the pub. My gaze drifted to the bar, where Aled and Ewan had their heads bowed in conversation. What would happen to my staff? Who would employ an elderly barman who broke more pint glasses than he poured lager into, and a chef who could burn scrambled eggs? Keeping these two in work drained any profit, but I couldn't leave them in the lurch.

I straightened in my chair. "What do I need to do?"

Jill wore an indulgent smile. It was a smile you'd give a toddler when they showed you their finest dried pasta art project. "This is just business, Geraint."

"Please. I can turn a profit. I'll make it better. Whatever it takes."

Blood pounded in my temples. Gong baths? What the heck was a gong bath? The idea alone would have horrified Dad.

"Maybe I could talk to the board. It seems a shame when you've been here for so long." Jill tapped her nail on the table thoughtfully. "Perhaps I can persuade them to give you time to come up with something."

A flirtatious smile played on her ruby-red lips, and I noticed for the first time how thickly she wore her makeup. A visible orange tidemark circled her throat. She gave an exaggerated flip of her hair. Her perfume hit my nose, and the cloying smell made me faintly nauseated. Under the table, a hand landed on my leg. Jill held my gaze with a brazen look as she squeezed my thigh tight enough for her sharp nails to dig in through my jeans. Surprise flew through me, but I held perfectly still.

"It would be a favor, but since we're getting on so well, I don't mind helping you out." Slowly, her hand slid up my leg.

It took every instinct not to physically recoil. I clamped my palm down, halting her before she got any higher.

Her face darkened, and she measured me with a calculating gaze. "We should discuss it over dinner."

Once again, I didn't miss the emphasis on the word *should*. Did I have a choice?

"I . . . dinner . . . right . . . Yes . . . no . . . I don't know . . ." Gently, I peeled Jill's hand away. My voice came out thick and awkward. "Let me see what I can come up with. What if I put together a plan?"

She raised an unimpressed eyebrow. "Maybe the board won't be interested. It all depends."

"Depends on what?"

"On you, Geraint. It depends on you." She packed her briefcase and stood. Her condescending gaze lingered too long. "I'll be in touch. Call me about dinner."

Chapter 4

MADISON

I blinked and missed the sunshine. Apparently, that's how summer goes in England. We had a few blue skies and then a drizzly season playing in unrelenting gray. Rain never bothered me. Worse to be miserable in blazing sunshine. My limbs ached after practice. Mud laced my tongue, and sweat plastered my hair to my neck. I needed to shower, but the moment I got into the locker room, I did the thing I couldn't stop doing. The thing I hated myself for most. I pulled out my phone and scrolled Bryce's Instagram feed.

English accents echoed all around—a constant reminder that this wasn't my home. I stared at my screen. No new updates. The latest picture was still a glossy spaghetti carbonara. Bryce had a habit of photographing his food in fancy restaurants. At least someone was enjoying meals out. Food held no joy for me anymore. Eating had become functional, something I had to do to play soccer, like putting gas in a car.

"Shame about the yellow card, but great job out there."

Miri planted a neon-orange cleat on a wooden bench and tugged at the mud-encrusted laces. I shoved my phone back in my locker. Miri was just being nice. I'd played well enough back home, but so much of playing at this level was mindset, and my head was scrambled.

Gabe had brought me here to help his team win, but in the handful of matches we'd played, all I'd done was fumble a few passes and give away a penalty. There were kids in the Junior Academy who would have done a better job. The girls had been sympathetic, and so had Gabe, but they had to be expecting more from me. I was lucky they hadn't just put me on the bench and been done with it.

"Thanks. You had a great game."

Miri yanked off her cleat. "Are you coming out with us tonight?"

My shoulders tensed. I had to join in, but the team socials grated on me. No matter how much I tried to let my hair down, I couldn't shift the constant ache in my heart. The girls were welcoming, but so much here was different. Despite sharing a common language, sometimes I could hardly follow a conversation. England might not be as far away as the moon, but it still felt alien.

"I can't tonight."

"What about next week? You're coming to the Christmas party, right?"

"I won't be able to make it. Sorry."

I hid my face behind my locker, busying myself with my shower bag. I'd been pushing Christmas out of my mind. My parents had been disappointed that I hadn't booked tickets to come home, but I couldn't face it. This should have been my first Christmas as Mrs. Bryce Muller. Instead, I'd be eating pizza alone in my shoebox apartment.

I shut my locker, to find Miri watching me. Her voice was tentative. "What about Christmas Day? Will you come to ours for dinner? You'll have to excuse my family. They are all kind of annoying, but my brother is a decent cook. It's all casual, but we have fun. Skylar will be there too, we'd really love to have you."

The last thing I needed was to play happy families with the team I was failing. I'd been avoiding Gabe as much as possible, and the captain, Skylar, was always trying to corner me for a chat. They were just being nice, but this season had been one humiliating failure after the next. I couldn't sit across from these people for a whole day eating and making small talk. Christmas was just another shitty day like any other. I wanted to be alone.

"Thanks for the offer, but I'm fine."

Miri's face dropped. "Gabe said you're not going home for Christmas. You're not spending the day on your own, are you? We'd really love you to—"

"I won't be alone. I have plans for Christmas. I'm going to . . ." My mouth went dry as I scrambled to think of an excuse. I blurted the first thing that flew into my head. ". . . Wales. Snowdonia."

"Oh. That's . . ." Miri hesitated, a bemused smile pulling at her lips. "Random. Why?"

"My parents got married there. I'd like to visit the church they always talked about. Saint Dwynwen."

My pulse quickened at the lie, but a lie was more convincing when edged with the truth. My parents had always spoken fondly about Wales.

Miri nodded her approval. "Nice to get out of the city and escape the traffic."

That's what I wanted. An escape. That's why I'd come to England, only now I needed to escape my escape plan. Maybe I should go to Wales. I could disappear and wait for Christmas to blow over. Maybe I *could* even visit the little church where my parents married. Why not? What else was I going to do?

I stood taller. The idea solidified into something concrete. This is what I needed. That small glow rekindled inside, the first good feeling I'd had in a month.

"Yes, I'm spending Christmas in Wales."

Chapter 5

MADISON

I followed the GPS down another ridiculously narrow winding road through snow-capped mountains. Snow clung to the windshield, obscuring my view, despite the best efforts of the wipers to clear it. Driving in the UK was a lesson in concentration. Nobody seemed to have told these people they drive on the wrong side of the road.

I'd driven in bad weather in Lexington. The difference was I'd been driving a truck, not this rented Mini Cooper that felt like being at the wheel of a go-kart. The car slowed, losing power. I pushed the gas pedal flat, and the car dropped to a slow crawl. A little circular light with an oil can glowed on the dashboard. The engine warning symbol. Holy crap. Dad had drummed into me the basics of car mechanics when he'd taught me to drive. I hadn't paid much attention, but I knew enough to recognize this was the symbol of doom.

The wipers whined as they scraped snow away at top speed. Even with the gas pedal fully depressed, the go-kart wouldn't budge from its juddering limp. I'd have to pull over until I had some visibility. I slowed to a stop at the side of the narrow road and turned the engine off. A sudden break in the clouds revealed the sun glinting from snow-blanketed valleys and peaks in an endless panorama of dazzling white. If I wasn't stuck in the middle of nowhere, in a foreign country, with a failing go-kart, it would have been the most incredible view. I took a deep breath and turned the key in the ignition.

Nothing.

Okay. Stay calm.

I'd have to call the rental company. They'd send a tow truck. It was a pain, but I could manage this. I pulled my phone out. The phone had no reception. Bleak nothingness stretched around me. The snow closed in again, swirling in a relentless white flurry. The last remnants of the road ahead had long since disappeared beneath the furious blizzard. My mouth went dry at the gravity of my situation. I was adrift in the middle of a gigantic white ocean in a foreign land, with no heat and no phone reception.

Stay calm. It's Wales, not Jupiter.

I pressed my forehead to the steering wheel. Of course. Why not? My fiancé had ditched me on our wedding day. Why wouldn't the next logical step be me freezing to death in the Welsh mountains? How perfect.

An icy shiver ran through me. Without the heater, the car was going to get very cold, very fast. I tried the ignition again. No response. What were my options? I could sit here panicking and wait until I froze to death, or I could get out of the car and find help. It had been a while since I'd seen any road signs or evidence of people, but some way back, I'd passed a village. It would be a long walk, but I'd have to try.

I shoved the car door open past a heavy heap of snow. I cast a wary eye at the sky. The bright white was fading to gray. The thought of being caught in the mountains in the dark made my heart pound. I took another deep breath.

You've got this, Maddie.

I clutched at faith that the universe had my back, even if all signs indicated otherwise.

◆ ◆ ◆

Wet snow hit my face, so cold it burned. My teeth chattered and my body shook. My fingers would probably have to be pried from the handle of my suitcase with a wrench if I ever got indoors again. I should have left the damn thing in the trunk. I glanced at my watch. Twenty minutes of trudging through a blizzard, and I'd seen nothing but a vast expanse of white. The snow-choked sky had swallowed the sun. Soon it would be dark. A bitter laugh escaped me. How could I have gotten into such a vulnerable position?

I get it, universe. You do not have my back. Glad we cleared that up.

A faint sound rumbled in the distance. My ears pricked. Twisting, I made out a wash of headlights. A battered Ford Ranger powered through the snow, spraying up huge plumes of powder. My shoulders dropped with relief. I waved my hands high in the air until the vehicle slowed and came to a stop next to me.

An imposing dark figure loomed in the driver's seat. A huge padded coat wrapped around his broad shoulders, and a trapper hat obscured his face. A twinge of anxiety gripped me. Maybe it wasn't such a good idea to be in the middle of nowhere with a strange man so big he looked like the giant at the top of the beanstalk. Still, what could I do? My options weren't great, but I'd be better throwing my luck in with a possible psychopath than turning into a human popsicle. A potential horrible death is always preferable to a guaranteed one.

The window crept down, and my heart pounded with a sense of foreboding. I should have been delighted to find another human in this vast expanse of nothingness, but the sight of the formidable black-clad figure in the driver's seat did nothing to ease my nerves.

His dark eyes studied my face. He was a solid bear of a man, flannel clad and bearded like some kind of lumberjack. Did they have lumberjacks in the UK? They had trees, so they must have people to cut them down. Maybe he had an axe in the trunk. A shiver ran through me.

Mr. Lumberjack/potential axe murderer opened his mouth, and a stream of unintelligible words poured out. My heart sank. He didn't speak English? I couldn't offer him a smile even if I'd wanted to. My lips were too numb. Also, I *didn't* want to because he was intimidating. I didn't get easily intimidated, but for a guy this huge, I'd make an exception.

"Hi, I'm Maddie. My car broke down. Is there any chance I could hitch a ride?" I forced out the words through stiff lips.

Without another word, he got out of the truck. He slipped off his heavy coat and wrapped it around me. A malty smell and something woody, like pencil shavings, filled my nose. The coat came down to my shins. Its weight and warmth were as comforting as submerging in a hot bath.

He took off his enormous hat and plonked it on top of my head. The snow-blanketed world disappeared for a moment before I readjusted the hat so it didn't cover my eyes.

"Thanks."

"No problem."

Beneath all that dark, disheveled hair and the beard, he was strikingly handsome, in a craggy, wild way. He smiled, and somehow it brightened his whole face. Even the featherlike creases at the corners of his eyes crinkled. How could a man this big and imposing have such a disarming smile?

He inclined his head and opened the passenger door. "Well? Are you getting in?"

He had the most beautiful voice—melodic and lilting—the gentle pitch incongruous with his impressive, well-muscled profile.

Was this a good idea? I wanted to not die of hypothermia, but neither did I relish getting chopped into little pieces and buried in the woods.

Hey, sexy stranger. Thanks for rescuing me. Please don't be an axe murderer.

Screw it. I couldn't spend another minute in this cold. I handed him my suitcase. He hefted the monster over the passenger seat into the extended cab of the truck. I slid into the passenger seat, and he shut the door gently. He took his place in the battered driver's seat.

I cleared my throat. "Are we going, then?"

He shifted in his seat, and I couldn't help but notice that his thighs were as enormous and firm as tree trunks. Under his navy cable-knit sweater, his broad torso and arms bulged with muscle. He had the kind of jawline that needed to be studied.

He flashed his boyish smile. "Seat belt."

"Right."

I pulled the strap across myself, but my fingers were so numb that every time I tried to fasten it, I couldn't hit the target. He watched me for a moment before he took the metal buckle from me. His fingers were warm and rough as they touched mine. My body thrummed with the contact. Despite the cold that had seeped into my bones, warmth crept over my skin. He returned to his position and turned the key in the ignition. The thunder of the engine after all that silence in the snow made me jump.

He turned to me, easing into that broad, friendly smile. "Where to?"

The battered Ford had the same smell as Dad's truck—a musky, warm cedar scent, like the inside of a sauna. I relaxed into the seat, cozy in the fleece-lined hat and coat. "I'm trying to get to the Dragon Inn. Do you know it? Honestly, it didn't look that great on the website, but it was the only one with space at short notice."

"What was wrong with it?"

"The reviews were terrible. Someone called it a pigsty. It better not be as bad as all that. I need a hot shower and a decent bed."

A line appeared between his brows. "I know it. I'll take you."

We set off slowly, tires crunching over snow. An awkward feeling settled over me. He still hadn't introduced himself.

I tried to pinch some sensation back into my frozen cheeks. "What's your name?"

"Geraint."

I blinked, processing the reply that had sounded more like a growl than human speech. "Excuse me?"

"Geraint."

"Grant?"

"Ger-aint. 'Ger' like egg and 'aint' like white."

He flashed another grin. What was he so happy about in the middle of a blizzard? The guy had a golden retriever level of affability, and it was unnerving. It didn't guarantee he wouldn't be an axe murderer. Sociopaths probably found plotting the deaths of their next victims highly satisfying. The crunch of the tires filled the silence.

"American?"

"Yes. Kentucky."

He shot me a sidelong glance and smiled with disarming candor. "What are you doing out here, Kentucky?"

Escaping from my escape. "Freezing to death, Wales."

"I passed your car back there. It's just a lump in the snow."

I sighed and turned my face to the window to watch the blanket of white passing by. Cheerful whistling pierced the silence. I gritted my teeth. The only person I knew who whistled was my dad. He'd whistled on the way to the church. He hadn't whistled since.

"Can you not do that, please?"

"Do what?"

"Whistle."

He hesitated, measuring me for a second before turning back to the road. "You don't like whistling?"

"Does anyone?"

He grimaced in good humor. "Fine. No whistling." His hand hovered by the radio dial. "Music?"

"No, and keep your eyes on the road, please."

"Yes, ma'am. No whistling. No music." His voice filled with teasing. "What about singing? I could sing you a song."

I rolled my eyes. "Absolutely not."

He pressed his lips together thoughtfully. "What about talking? Is that allowed?"

Don't feel obligated.

I folded my arms. "I know what you're thinking: stupid tourist up here not knowing what she's doing, but how was I supposed to know I was driving into a blizzard? It was a nice day when I set off."

His voice took on a softer edge. "I don't think you're stupid. The weather is changeable up here. You weren't to know."

Irritation made my shoulder blades stiffen. "Of course I didn't know."

I'd ended up stranded without a car. None of this was supposed to be happening. I shouldn't have even been here. Not in Wales. Not totally alone. This was all Bryce's fault. It was almost worse that this man was being nice. He'd rescued me from the side of the road. He deserved gratitude and warmth, things I wasn't good at anymore.

"I'm sorry." My voice sounded thin and tired.

"What for?"

"I'm not in the best mood."

He flashed me a glance, surveying me kindly. "No problem. You're not having a great day."

Right. Or a great year. I shivered and pulled the coat tighter.

"Are you still cold?"

29

"I'll manage."

Mr. Egg-white fiddled with the heater on the dash and angled the hot air toward me. Silence smothered us again. Better to sit quietly than do more damage with my words. We rumbled through a dazzling white terrain of farmland in swirling snow until the truck ground to a halt. I drank in the ramshackle building with its whitewashed brick walls, gray slate roof, and faded blue window frames. A Welsh flag—a red dragon on a green and white background—hung limp above the frosted glass front door.

Without a word, Geraint climbed out of the truck. I got out and watched him drag my enormous suitcase to the pub entrance. He walked with a slight limp, his right foot dragging a little over the snow. I moved to take the case. "Here. You don't have to do that."

He smiled and tightened his grip on the handle. "I've got it."

"At least let me get the door."

I opened the frosted glass. A blast of warmth and malty beer hit me. Geraint dragged the case inside, and I stepped into the dimly lit pub lounge behind him. It was small and quaint compared to the bustling wine bars I'd left behind.

"Is it even open?" I peered at the old photos on the wall and ran a finger over a faded velvet couch. It came back clean rather than coated in dust, as I'd expected. I lowered my voice and whispered behind my hand, "It's not a total pigsty. That's a relief. Apparently, customer service is an issue."

His affable smile dimmed. "Right."

I slipped his coat from my shoulders and passed it back to him along with his hat. "Well, thanks for coming to my rescue. I appreciate it." I pulled out my purse and took out a twenty-pound note. "Money for the gas."

He glanced at the money but made no move to take it. "No. It's fine."

"It's not enough?"

He flashed a broad smile. "I was going this way anyway."

"Well, thank you." I put my purse away, but he didn't budge.

Why wasn't he leaving? It had been nice of him to give me a ride, but now I wanted to check in, sort out my car problem, and collapse into bed. The journey had wiped me out. My hands still ached. How long did it take for frostbite to set in? If I had to have a finger amputated, I'd be sending Bryce the bill.

Geraint straightened one of the crooked black-and-white photos on the wall. Did he expect me to buy him a drink or something? I'd said thank you and offered him money for gas. What more did he want?

"Look, no offense, but I've had a long day and I'm not really in the mood for company." My voice came out sharper than I'd intended.

He moved around the empty bar and planted himself behind the till. Confusion made my brain reel. This guy was getting weird.

"What are you doing? I don't think you're allowed back there."

He reached beneath the bar and retrieved a big red book and pen. He clicked the top of the pen, and his dark, smiling eyes met mine. "Checking in?"

Chapter 6

Geraint

The American surveyed the empty pub lounge. So this was the woman who had booked to stay here over Christmas. I hadn't expected someone so young. It was a good job I'd found her. The weather was getting worse by the minute. I volunteered whenever I could with the mountain rescue guys. Plenty could go wrong in these mountains and deep lakes when people got into situations unprepared. The terrain was wild and unforgiving. Easy for even the most experienced hiker to get into trouble.

She ran a hand over the bar and threw me a questioning glance. "You work here?"

"I'm the landlord."

She wrinkled her nose, which glowed pink with the cold. "And you didn't think to tell me that?"

Guilt made heat stroke my jaw. I'd thought it would be amusing not to tell her, but clearly she didn't see anything funny about it. I'd already annoyed her, and she hadn't spent the night here yet. This didn't bode well if she left us a review.

I smiled, trying to put her at ease. "I was enjoying your praise too much. It wasn't a pigsty, by the way. The review called us a hovel. A rancid hovel."

Red stained her cheeks, and she frowned. My stomach dropped. I was only kidding around, but I was making it worse. She wrapped her arms around her waist. The poor woman was still shivering. Everything she wore, from her ankle boots to her tight jeans, was inappropriate for the weather. Her hair hung in masses of wet curls that dripped down her back. I couldn't stop myself from drinking in her incredible figure. She looked feminine but powerful. I fought to keep my gaze from dropping to where her nipples pressed like pebbles against the thin material of her soaked white jumper.

"There are towels in your room." I moved to the vast fireplace that dominated the pub lounge. "I'll get some heat in here. You're going to catch your death."

"I apologize. I didn't mean any offense. It all looks very . . . very . . ." She frowned as her gaze drifted from the peeling wallpaper to the stained carpet. "It's fine. I don't pay attention to reviews, anyway. One woman's hovel is another woman's . . . cute, cozy inn."

I kept my mouth shut and piled the logs. Young Aled dealt with the tourists. He checked them in. He served their meals and answered their questions. I cooked and tried to stop the pipes from rattling and the building from collapsing on our heads. It was better that way. Customer service wasn't my strength. Too easy to put your foot in it. If only Aled was here instead of shacked up with Mrs. Ackwright. I'd even take Ewan if it meant I didn't have to deal with tourists.

The American's impatient gaze burned into me. "Do you have a phone? I still don't have any reception. I need to call the car company."

"In the back." I pointed to the door behind the bar.

"Thanks, Geraint. Geraint? Did I say that right?"

She said my name as if she'd read it in a book and was saying it out loud for the first time. It wasn't even close. Still, we couldn't risk more bad reviews, especially not with the brewery breathing on my balls.

"Good. You sounded like a local that time."

She slid me a dubious glance. "Really? Or are you just being nice?"

"No. It was spot on."

She folded her arms. "Don't BS me. It was terrible, wasn't it?"

"Okay. It's the worst I've ever heard, honestly. Not even close."

Her lip twitched. It was the nearest I'd seen her come to a smile since I'd found her. I had to fight to drag my eyes from her pretty mouth.

I grabbed a couple of blankets from the armchair and passed them to her. "My friends call me *G*. You can call me that if it's easier."

"G, it is." Her face was guarded as she wrapped the blankets around herself and pulled them tight. "Thank you."

"No problem."

We hadn't started off on a good foot, but now she was my guest. It was my job to help her feel at home here, especially over Christmas. Why was she here alone this time of year? The poor woman had to be freezing.

"Are you going to show me to my room?"

"It's room four. I'll take you."

We both moved to take her case at the same time. Her fingers brushed mine, and she yanked her hand away as if she'd dipped it into molten metal. Pink tinged her cheeks. My fingers tingled from the touch. I cleared my throat, pretending not to be affected by one small brush of hands. We hardly ever had women in this pub, and certainly not ones this pretty or with teeth this white. That was one thing I knew about the States—good dentists.

I reached for the case again. Irritation flashed in her eyes. "I've got it."

I held my hands up in mock surrender. She looked like she was about to fight me to the death for the honor of hauling this case up the stairs. Fine. Life is about picking your battles. My life was also about avoiding bad reviews. The customer was always right, even when they were openly hostile.

I flashed a smile. "Follow me."

Chapter 7

MADISON

The narrow winding staircase creaked underfoot. Geraint was so huge, he had to fold his body almost in half to fit. With every one of his heavy steps, an enormous crack rang out. He opened the door at the top of the stairs and stepped aside to let me into the bedroom. Orange and brown geometric patterns covered the textured walls. Gaudy orange pendant lamps hung over a huge double bed. All it was missing was a lava lamp and a disco ball. I had no idea if it was ironically retro or just old. Judging from the rest of the place, it was the latter. A clean cotton smell hung in the air. At least it wasn't dirty.

Huge French doors led onto a small balcony. Beyond, salmon pink streaked the vast white sky as the sun set over regal snow-capped mountains. I'd been battered by broken-down cars, snow, and ice, but my whole body relaxed with a sigh. The incredible view soothed me.

Geraint's intense gaze burned into me. For a moment, I'd forgotten he was there. He was as still and impressive as the mountains that surrounded us. Something about him was vaguely maddening, but I couldn't put my finger on it. Maybe because his solid, imposing presence was having a weird effect on my body. My heart pounded every time he glanced in my direction, and one brush of his fingers had made heat pulse between my thighs. This was no time for any of that nonsense. The last thing I wanted was to find a man attractive. I was done with men. Well and truly done. This place was an escape to hibernate for a fortnight and get through Christmas.

Geraint inclined his head in a nod and gave me his broad back. "I'll let you settle in."

"Wait. Aren't you going to tell me about the room?"

He paused at the door. "What about the room?"

"I don't know. You're supposed to say something, aren't you? Like how to work the shower? Or what time to order dinner?"

He walked toward a side door, beckoning me to follow. "You're right. Follow me. This is the bathroom."

I peered inside the small room with its dated maroon fixtures. He pointed at the shower. "This is the shower." He raised a questioning eyebrow. "Is that enough, or am I supposed to do a demonstration?"

"You tell me. You're the guy that checks in guests."

"I don't normally do this bit. Aled deals with tourists. What else do I need to say?"

Jeez. Did I have to do the guy's job for him? I couldn't even be irritated about it because he looked so earnest. Why didn't he know what he was doing in his own pub? I folded my arms in front of me. "What time is the evening meal?"

"What would you like to eat?"

"I don't know. What have you got? A menu might be helpful."

Confusion crossed his face. "A menu?"

It wasn't an unusual request, was it? A small flicker of amusement bubbled inside. I was too tired to be yanking this guy's chain,

37

but I couldn't stop. "Don't you have menus in Wales? It's a list of food that a person peruses and selects an item from."

He raised a brow. "I'm familiar with the concept, I just don't use them. Tell me what you want, and I'll make it."

I had no appetite. I ate these days purely because I needed the nutrition for training. "Whatever you've got is fine."

"You don't have any preferences? No favorite dishes? Dietary requirements?"

"Anything will do."

He scraped his beard with a huge palm, and his arm bulged with muscle under his navy cable-knit sweater. "Okay."

I flexed my fingers, trying to bring life back into them. I'd have to figure out the car situation, but it wasn't something I could deal with until I could move my fingers to make the call.

He swallowed. "You're going to give us a bad review, aren't you?"

The beleaguered edge to his voice made something inside me soften. I rolled my shoulders back. "Why do you say that?"

He shrugged. "We've had a lot of them lately. We're due a refurbishment soon."

"It looks fine. Don't worry about it."

I tossed my wet hair over my shoulder. I needed a boiling shower. The cold in my bones ached.

He frowned and took a step back. "Come down when you're ready. I'll have some dinner for you."

"Wonderful. I'll put on my finest gown."

"No need to dress for dinner."

"It was a joke."

His face dropped. "Oh."

Another spark of amusement lit inside. He was so easy to wind up. He towered over me, dark and formidable—all hard corded muscle, stubble, and rough edges—but he had the affability of a Labrador.

I held out my hand. "Are you leaving me the key?"

He pressed cold metal into my hand. Heat raced from where his palm met mine.

"Is this the only key?"

"No. We keep spares."

"You're not going to murder me in my sleep, are you?"

He flashed a puzzled grin. "If I wanted to hurt you, I would have left you wandering along that road by yourself. You were doing a great job of seeing to your own demise." The smile slipped from his lips to be replaced by an uneasy look. "You're not worried to be here with me, are you?"

"No. I'm not worried. I can take care of myself, and I would have been fine without you. I would have found the village."

Probably. Maybe. At some point.

I took a breath, trying to slow my racing pulse. This was ridiculous. Sure, he was a good-looking man, and he had that accent. LA was full of good-looking men. So what? I didn't have to lose my cool. He stepped back, and I took a deep breath. The less time spent with a man who made my body respond like this, the better.

"Actually, if you don't mind sending some food up, I'd rather have room service."

Chapter 8

GERAINT

The American hated me. It had been so long since we'd had a woman stay here, her presence had thrown me. Customer service was hardly my strength at the best of times. Balancing the huge tray of food in one hand, I lifted my fist to knock on the door. A scream rang out. Adrenaline shot through me.

I pushed the door open. "What is it? Are you okay?"

Madison emerged from the adjoining bathroom, wearing only a towel.

"The water is ice cold. I couldn't get the hot to come on." She bristled, her eyes flashing with indignation. "It turns out you should have done a demonstration of the shower."

I fought to keep my gaze on her face, although it was difficult. The tiny bath towel barely skimmed her thighs, revealing exceptionally pretty muscled legs. She pinned the towel tight to herself. I had to fight not to linger on the soft swell of her cleavage. I'd been trying not to notice her incredible body, but now that she was half-naked, it was difficult.

She took a step closer. She raised a skeptical brow and gripped the towel tighter. "Well? Aren't you going to call a plumber?"

"I'll fix it."

"Do you know how?"

"I'll figure it out. Let me bring your food in first. It's getting cold."

I retrieved the tray from the hallway and put it down on the dressing table. The bathroom door was shut, but I could hear her moving about inside. My gaze fell on the bed, where her clothes lay in neatly folded piles. A lacy blue bra sat on her pillow. Madison emerged from the bathroom in baggy jeans and a T-shirt. She propped a hand on her hip and scowled.

"Well? Do you want to look at the shower?"

I snapped my guilty eyes away from her underwear. "Right. The shower."

A sweet floral scent hit me as I went into the small bathroom. Cosmetics cluttered the tiny sink. A pang of loss pulled at me. This is what my bathroom had looked like once.

Madison's voice drifted from the bedroom. "What is all this food?"

"The stew is called cawl. It's meat and vegetables."

I twisted the shower lever and angled it to my hand. Freezing water hammered my palm. Sometimes these old things were temperamental.

"And what about this one?" she called. "What's the one that looks like fancy grilled cheese?"

"That'll be the Welsh rarebit."

Shock rang out in her voice. "I'm eating rabbit?"

"Rarebit is the cheese sauce. It's blended with mustard, Worcestershire sauce, and a splash of ale."

"I need absolute assurance that no rabbits were harmed in the making of this food."

"I can assure you no rabbits were harmed."

The water warmed gradually until heat seared my palm. Maybe she hadn't realized you had to wait until the water got hot in these old buildings. I turned the shower off and dried my hands on a towel.

"Wor-cest-ers-hire? How do you even say that word?"

I couldn't help but laugh at her pronunciation. "Not like that."

She appeared in the doorway. Amusement flashed across her face. It was beautiful and unexpected, like finding a cool freshwater stream running down the mountainside. So she had a sense of humor somewhere under that permanent scowl?

"Do you want me to make you something more familiar? I can do you a burger." I tried to keep my voice from sounding horrified at the idea. I drew the line at French fries. If I was cooking chips, they'd be proper ones.

"No, thank you." She returned to the dressing table and prodded the Glamorgan sausage with her fork. "What's this? Pork?"

"Glamorgan sausage is vegetarian. It's cheese and leeks rolled in breadcrumbs."

She put the tiniest amount on her fork and took a tentative bite. "This is actually . . . nice." She stared at the golden breadcrumb sausage before she took another bite. "My appetite hasn't been great lately." She gave me a questioning look. "What's a Glamorgan?"

"It's an old county in Wales."

"This is good." She nodded her approval. A sparkle lit her eye, and if I didn't know better, I'd say it was mischievous. "Looks like I'm a fan of Glamorgan sausage."

"Wait till you try the bara brith."

"The what now?"

Amusement flickered in her eyes again but disappeared just as quickly. It transformed her face into something hard to look away from. For a moment, it dazzled me. What had I done? How could I light her up like that again? It was random but addictive, like a perfect apple dropping from a tree right into my hands. A sudden windfall.

"Fruitcake. Nothing beats a nice cup of tea and some fruitcake. The shower's working now, by the way. You just have to let it run before the hot comes."

"Thanks." She sighed and put her fork down with a gentle click. "You can take the tray with you."

Sadness lurked around her eyes. Where had her smile gone? How could I bring it back? She moved to the French doors and stared off at nothing.

She blew out a breath. "I have to straighten out my car situation."

"Don't worry about it. I've dealt with it."

She twisted, her eyes snapping to mine. "What do you mean?"

"I spoke to the rental place. They've gone to collect it. They'll get a new car sent over."

Her lips parted with surprise. "You didn't need to do that. How did you even know who to call?"

"You left the card from the rental place in my truck. It's no problem."

Frowning, she studied my face for a moment, then turned back to the glass. "I just realized something. It's a week until Christmas, and you don't have a single Christmas decoration. There is no tree downstairs. No lights. You don't celebrate Christmas?"

Ewan and Aled had been on my case for the same reason. Dad had always loved Christmas in the pub. I'd been too busy trying to keep the place standing—maintaining the roof, repairing the gutter, fitting new doors. Now I had Jill and the brewery on my balls, it had slipped even further down the to-do list.

"I haven't really had time for Christmas this year."

Silence fell between us. She stared out at the mountains with a puzzled look, as though they held the answers to some unspoken

43

question. Time to go. Better to leave her be while she didn't seem as irritated by me.

"I'll let you settle in. I'll be in the bar downstairs if you need me. Come down if you fancy a drink . . ."

I was at the door before she spoke again. She kept her back to me, her voice thin and fragile. "Thank you."

Chapter 9

MADISON

My footsteps echoed on stone. A white dress trailed behind me, heavy and unwieldy, as though someone had tied bricks to the hem. My family and friends crowded the pews. Accusatory whispers drifted to my ears.

"She's always been impulsive."

"It's never going to last."

Dad's expression filled with disappointment, but he held out an elbow. "Are you sure about this, Maddie?"

I rolled my shoulders back. A foul stench hit my nose. The bouquet in my hands suddenly weighed as heavy as a sack of rocks. The flowers rotted before my eyes. Flies buzzed around brown, leathery roses. I tossed it away in disgust. Bryce stood at the end of the aisle. He had a red napkin shoved into the collar of his tuxedo. A spaghetti carbonara sat on a small table in front of him. He didn't even look up as I started walking.

My eyes flashed open. Gasping, I sat up. Where the heck was I? I reached for the bedside table and grabbed my phone. Its blue light pierced my eyes. It was morning, but still early. I opened Instagram and stared at Bryce's photos. There hadn't been an update since the carbonara. I'd had this dream so many times. I always woke with this grinding weight in my solar plexus, smooth and round like a Magic 8 Ball full of vague, mystifying answers.

How could he do it to me?

Reply hazy, try again.

What am I supposed to do with my life now?

Concentrate and ask again.

How am I supposed to bear this humiliation?

Outlook not so good.

The floor was cold under my bare feet as I slipped out of bed and moved to the French doors. I pushed my nose against the icy glass. White flakes choked the air in a flurrying whirlwind. The weather looked even worse than yesterday. Barely visible in the distance, the lofty peak of Snowdon sat still and unmoved by my plight. It didn't care that my heart was shattered and I was stuck out here in the middle of nowhere, alone for Christmas.

Inconsiderate much, Mount Snowdon?

My mind drifted to last night, and warmth rose in my cheeks. I'd felt guilty about picking at Geraint's food, but my stomach always turned to lead when I tried to eat. The food actually hadn't been too bad. It was the first time in a long while that I'd wanted to take another bite.

I showered and selected some clothes from my suitcase. My jeans hung loose I'd lost so much weight this past couple of months. I crossed to the mirror and ran a finger over the ridges of my gaunt cheekbones. No wonder my form had been lousy. I hardly had the energy to run around the pitch for ninety minutes. I sighed. I'd have to force myself to eat breakfast, despite the churning in my gut.

Now what? What was I supposed to do here? My only job was sorting out my car, and Geraint had done that for me. It was good of him. Maybe I'd try to relax today and catch up on some reading.

My to-be-read pile was out of control, and the girls on the team kept giving me more recommendations. I'd been getting back into reading romance. As long as you remembered it wasn't real life, it was fine. Real-life men were disappointing. Better to stick with men of the fictional and battery-operated varieties.

Chapter 10

Geraint

A crash rang out as a glass fell to the floor. Young Aled groaned and bent down.

I twisted to call down the bar. "Leave it. I'll deal with it."

"I've got it."

"Please. Let me." I took the dustpan and brush from Aled, then crouched to sweep up the broken glass.

The doors swung open from the kitchen. A burning smell blasted out. Ewan appeared with a cocky smirk. "Is the guest here yet? The one staying over for Christmas?"

"Yes."

The American hadn't left her room all morning. I'd gone up to ask her if she wanted breakfast, but she'd opened the door a crack and dismissed me. Wasn't she hungry? What was this woman doing here all alone at Christmas?

"Well?" Aled gave me an expectant glance. "What's she like?"

"She's American. She's . . ." I paused, searching for the right word. Angry? Intimidating? Dazzling?

Young Aled spoke before I could supply an answer. "An American?" His gaze drifted to the wooden love spoons that lined the walls. "She'll be wanting to know about the spoons. Did you tell her about the spoons?"

"No. I didn't tell her about the spoons."

"She'll be wanting to know. The tourists always want to know about the spoons. They like to hear about Welsh things. Aren't you proud of your heritage?"

I held in my sigh. Aled and these bloody spoons. "It didn't come up."

Aled frowned. "But you told her about the history of the inn? About how your dad found that original stone floor and we polished it all up? All the details? Have you told her about the ghost?"

I suppressed my eye roll. "No. I didn't tell her about the ghost, because there isn't a ghost."

Aled gave an exasperated sigh. "Of course there isn't a ghost, but the tourists like to hear things like that. Are you looking after her well? We don't want another one of those reviews. What has she eaten? Did you highlight the Welsh specialties on the menu? Did she try the Glamorgan sausage? The tourists always like the Glamorgan sausage."

Ewan gave me a sly smile and spoke under his breath. "That's right, Big G. That's what we all want to know. Did you slip the American your Glamorgan sausage?"

This time I couldn't suppress my eye roll. "You both need to calm down. We've had Americans stay before. It will be fine."

Young Aled shook his head earnestly. "No, we haven't. We had that Canadian, and those Australians once. Did Daffyd ever tell you about the time he went to California? Oh, he had a ball. They have free refills over there. You have a soft drink, you drink it, and you get a free refill. You don't even have to pay. Isn't that something? And the food! You wouldn't believe the size of the portions. Daffyd had a lasagna that was so big, he had it again for lunch three days in a row."

As if on cue, the American glided into the bar. Her dark curls tumbled carelessly down her back. It had been so long since we'd had a woman under sixty stay here. My traitorous eyes couldn't help drink her in like an art collector discovering a new Van Gogh. She was absolutely divine. Pity she seemed to hate my guts, and my pub, and everything she came into contact with. At least she didn't seem to mind my cooking. I had that to hang on to.

Aled's drone about Daffyd's tedious California road trip faded to a murmur. I'd heard the story a hundred times before, and it never reached a conclusion. It was essentially a story about a man eating a lasagna for an extended period of time. The American perched on a barstool and drummed her fingers on the bar. Her T-shirt hinted at her strong, athletic frame beneath. My pulse quickened.

Aled smoothed his fine white hair over his shining bald patch. "I'd better see about getting her some breakfast." He shot down the bar as fast as a ferret to talk to her.

Ewan rested his chin on his elbow and gazed at Madison. His voice was low and dreamy. "Look at her teeth. They're so white."

"I know."

"Do all Americans have teeth that white?"

"I don't know."

"And her hair is so shiny."

"I know."

"Do all Americans have hair that—?"

I held up a hand to stop his waffle. "I don't know any other Americans."

His lips drew into a thoughtful smile. "I wonder if she's a Swiftie."

I rolled my eyes. If I wasn't listening to Aled's underwhelming anecdotes, I was listening to Ewan talking in raptures about Taylor Swift.

The door swung open. A blonde woman stepped into the pub. She brushed snow from her knee-length padded coat. Jill. I worked to keep the grimace from my face.

Ewan frowned. "She's back already?"

I'd told Aled and Ewan about my conversation with her. I'd had to. It wasn't fair to lie to them. I'd do everything I could to fight for this place, but I had to make sure they were prepared for the worst. Ewan had just bought a new place with his boyfriend, and Aled was paying for his grandson to go to university. I didn't want to be the one to make them unemployed.

"Don't worry. I'll handle it."

Ewan regarded me with open amusement. "Looks like you've got one taker on the Glamorgan sausage, at least."

Hopefully, she'd keep her hands to herself this time. "There won't be any sausages of any kind under discussion."

Ewan flashed me a sympathetic smile and patted me on the shoulder. "Good luck, mate."

"Hello, Geraint." Jill reached the bar and flashed a coy smile. "Can we talk?"

My heart sank. "Of course."

Chapter 11

MADISON

I watched Geraint pull out a chair for a smartly dressed older woman with silver-blonde hair. Who was that? His mom? She tossed her hair back and flashed a flirtatious smile. Definitely not his mom. I couldn't stop my gaze from roving over his impressive, rugged profile. Everything about him spoke of strength and power, but there was so much warmth and geniality about him too. A gentle sexy giant. My heart thumped uncomfortably.

Nope. You're done with all men, remember?

The elderly barman put a mug of tea in front of me. I snapped my gaze away from Geraint and frowned. "I didn't order tea."

"It's complimentary. I'm Aled. You must be Madison, our visitor from across the pond. Sorry I didn't get to be here for check-in. I hope Geraint made you feel welcome."

I examined the smartly dressed, white-haired barman. Age was carved in lines around his mouth and twinkling eyes. He carried himself with the distinguished air you'd expect from a butler in a stately home. At last, I'd found the first British person who actually looked like they could be in *Downton Abbey*.

"Geraint found me on the side of the road. He even gave me a lift to the door." I blew the steam from my mug and took a sip. "So tell me, are the Welsh as obsessed with tea as the English?"

The elderly barman held his head high. "Tea is a necessity."

A younger barman with straight curtains of dark hair framing his face sidled in next to Aled. His profile was sharp and confident under the gleaming lights of the bar. "It's true. Tea cures every problem. Sometimes you think your whole world is falling apart, but really you need to sit down and have a cup of tea." He held out his hand. "I'm Ewan."

I shook the younger man's hand, and his gaze roamed over my hair. I smoothed a palm over it self-consciously. Maybe it was sticking up or looking weird today.

Aled gave a somber nod. "True enough. A hot tea is a cwtch."

"A cwtch?"

"A hug." The older barman gave a significant lift of his eyebrows. "A Welsh hug."

A shadow of amusement went through me. "A hug is a hug in any language, isn't it?"

Aled shook his head. "A Welsh hug is different. There's no direct translation into English. A cwtch is a hug that's also a cubbyhole. A place to hide and feel safe."

Ewan's gaze continued to roam over my hair, inspecting it. "A hug that feels like home."

A pang pulled at my heart, but I pushed it down. "How quaint."

Aled wiped the bar in slow, methodical circles with his dishcloth. "Has Geraint told you about the Welsh spoons yet?"

I must have missed that treat. "No."

Aled's face lit with a reverent expression. "You'll have to ask him to tell you about the spoons."

"Yes. Ask him about the spoons." Ewan raised a sardonic eyebrow and covered his mouth as though stifling a yawn. "It's riveting."

Aled tutted. "Don't mock the spoons. Our traditions are important."

Ewan held his hands up in surrender, but his eyes were full of teasing laughter. "God forbid you mock the spoons."

Another flicker of amusement went through me. Their gentle sparring reminded me of the girls on the squad. It was one of the things I'd always loved about being part of a team, but I hadn't been able to get into the spirit of it here. For the most part, I'd kept my own company in the locker room. Nobody had pushed me too hard to join in. I was part of the team on the pitch, but away from it, I'd hardly bothered with anyone. I'd run away rather than go to the Christmas party. I could have made more of an effort. Everybody had been trying so hard with me. They'd been welcoming, and I'd scarcely given my new teammates a chance. They seemed like a great bunch. I owed them better. Great. A little dose of guilt to heap onto my misery.

My gaze drifted back to Geraint at the other side of the bar. Sunlight struck his dark hair and made it gleam like polished jet. One lock fell a little forward onto his forehead. Had he styled it to look that sexy, or was it natural? The woman was leaning so far across the table, she looked about ready to climb across it and into his lap.

Nope. None of my business.

Still, I couldn't help myself. "Who is that? Geraint's wife?"

"No. It's Jill from the brewery. Poor Geraint." Ewan gave Aled a questioning look. "Maybe we should go and rescue him?"

Aled's frown deepened. "No. He won't appreciate the interference."

My curiosity overtook me. "Rescue him?"

Ewan kept his eyes on the two of them and lowered his voice. "Jill's the rep from the brewery that owns this place. The brewery is thinking of selling. Geraint said she's very . . . handsy." Ewan sighed and raised a wry eyebrow. "He's not had a lot of luck with women. His ex-wife took him for everything he had, and I mean everything. She even took the light bulbs out of the fridge. He didn't fight her on any of it."

"Why not?"

Ewan shrugged. "That's Geraint." His chin set in a stubborn line. "This won't do. She's going to eat him alive. I'm going in. I'll say there's an emergency in the kitchen or something."

Aled stopped Ewan with a hand on his arm. "He wants us to look professional. Don't go shouting your mouth off about an emergency."

An idea slipped into my head. Geraint had helped me out. He'd rescued me from the side of the road. I owed him. If I helped him with this, we'd be even. "I'll do it."

Ewan's eyes grew wide with bemusement. "You?"

"Yes, me. I'll think of something."

"Wait!" Ewan's urgent whisper held me in place. "I have to ask you one question. Do you like Taylor Swift?"

I gave him a look as if the answer was obvious. I mean, it was obvious. I had ears. "I would defend her to the ends of the earth."

"Favorite song?"

I answered immediately. "'I Knew You Were Trouble.'"

He studied my face with an intense expression before a grin overtook his features. "Good. We've just fast-tracked to BFFs."

Chapter 12

GERAINT

I pulled out a chair for Jill by the fire. Better to sit opposite each other like this rather than in a booth. This way, I could see her hands the whole time so she wouldn't grope me under the table. My eyes drifted to the bar, where Aled and Ewan were chatting with Madison. She lightly fingered a loose tendril of hair. Her expression was somber. What were they talking about? Was Aled telling her about Daffyd and the lasagna? Hopefully, Ewan would get me out of hot water and get us a glowing review. Ewan was a walking sunbeam. Nobody could ever give him a bad review. If anyone could thaw our American ice queen, it would be him.

What was Madison doing here alone? Hiding from something? I knew the urge to disappear and pull away from everyone. After the injury and the divorce, I'd wanted to be alone to lick my wounds too.

Jill smoothed her skirt over her nylon tights. "I've had a word with the board, and they are willing to give you some time. You've leased this pub for a long time. Mr. Cartwright remembers your father and was fond of him. If you can put together a solid plan of how you're going to turn this place around, we will take it under consideration."

Relief spread through my body. "That's good."

Jill smiled. "I had to pull a lot of strings, obviously."

I swallowed. "Obviously."

Her eyes raked over me. "It would be easier for the board to evict you and take the offer on the table."

I was careful not to let my fingers touch hers as I pasted a smile onto my face. "Yes. I know. Thank you. I appreciate it."

She shot me another penetrating look. Her voice was soft but threatening. "I was hoping you'd call me about dinner."

If I agreed to dinner, then what? What was she expecting from me? What if I didn't do it? She had me over a barrel as long as I needed to keep the brewery happy. Was taking this woman out the only way to keep my pub? "Dinner. Right. I'm sorry. I've been busy."

Jill peered around the empty lounge. "Busy, huh?"

Even Simon the border collie wasn't here today. "It's not normally this quiet."

My gaze drifted back to Madison. Our eyes met for a moment. Warmth rushed through me. A pensive shimmer lurked around her eyes. She flicked her gaze back to Aled, who was talking in an animated fashion. Yesterday, she'd looked angry and irritated, but today she looked . . . sad. She'd had the same wounded, faraway look last night when she'd asked me about Christmas decorations. Maybe I could put the effort in this year. It wouldn't hurt to make the place look more festive. It might even put a smile on her face.

Jill raised her glass of wine, and her shrewd, flirtatious smile cemented back in place. "Anyway. Cheers. Here's to you and a favorable decision from the board."

My heart was as heavy as an ice block, but I clinked my glass of soda water against her wine. "Cheers."

Madison's eyes found mine from across the lounge again, but this time a spark lit them. She slid from the barstool and strode toward us. She moved like an athlete, sleek and powerful. What was she doing? Why was she coming this way?

Madison stopped at the armchair. Her arms encircled my neck from behind. My body jolted from the unexpected contact. My breath cut off in shock.

"Hello, sweetie." She pressed a light peck to my cheek and climbed into my lap. "Will you be much longer?"

Her sweet floral fragrance invaded my nose. Confusion made my senses reel. My body stiffened.

Her minty breath was hot against my cheek as she whispered into my ear. "Breathe. Go with it."

I worked to school my features into something vaguely neutral despite having a near-stranger sitting on my lap. An incredibly beautiful near-stranger. Madison pulled back slightly and crooked her neck to peer at me. Her lips curved into a dazzling smile. It was false. I knew it was false. She hadn't smiled like that once since she'd gotten here, but still it filled me with warmth. What was going on?

Her gaze drifted to Jill, and her smile stretched wider. "Aren't you going to introduce me to your friend?"

"Right." My voice came out a little awkward. "Madison, this is Jill. Jill, this is—"

"Madison." She lurched to thrust her hand in Jill's direction. "I'm Geraint's girlfriend."

"Nice to meet you, Madison. I'm Jill." Jill retained her affability, but there was a distinct hardening in her gaze when it landed on me. "I didn't realize you had a girlfriend."

Me neither.

58

I straightened in the chair. The heel of Madison's trainer pressed sharply into my shin. She shifted in my lap, and I felt an unwelcome stiffening in my trousers.

Madison's eyes were bright with mischief. "Of course he has a girlfriend. Didn't he tell you?"

Sunlight streamed through the window, glimmering over her face like beams of icy radiance. Was she enjoying this? How could she switch that smile on so easily, when she always looked so pissed off? I couldn't tear my eyes away from her. She looked beautiful. Then the realization hit me. Ewan must have put her up to this.

I cleared my throat. "Right. Yes. This is her. Madison. My girlfriend."

Madison put a hand over her heart. She spoke with a touch of boastfulness. "*Girlfriend*. I love how that sounds. So glad we made it official." She raked a hand through my hair, ruffling it through her fingers. My scalp tingled. "Before that, we were just friends with benefits." She lifted an amused brow. "Some seriously good benefits, but now I've locked him down."

Her fingers stroked up my bare arm sensuously, trailing over my T-shirt to stroke under my chin. My muscles tensed under the soft warmth of her touch. She leaned into me lightly, tilting her face toward mine. Her strong features were so attractive. How long had it been since a woman had looked at me like this? Desire spiraled through me. If only this wasn't an act. If only she was in my lap looking at me like this for real and this pub was empty.

"You're not from around here?" Jill's bitter voice raked through me. I'd almost forgotten she was here.

Madison's words were for Jill, but she kept her eager gaze on me. "I'm from the States, but I live in England. We have to do the long-distance thing. Isn't that right, sweetie?"

"That's right." I patted her hand on my shoulder, hardly daring to touch her. She was in control of this charade. Maybe she was an actress. It made sense. This was an Oscar-worthy performance. My body certainly believed in the endeavor wholeheartedly. The press of her ass in my lap was killing me. I couldn't let her feel how invested my body was in her little piece of improv. I shifted in the chair, nudging her away from my groin.

She studied me. Her eyes filled with longing. "It's hard, isn't it? Long distance? We miss each other so much."

"Yes. It's hard." *And getting harder.*

God. I had to get her off my lap and get a cushion there or something. This was too much.

I held my arms wide and open. "Well, thank you . . . darling. I'm sure you have things to be getting on with. Jill and I have a few more items to discuss."

"You don't have to go on my account. The two of you are so . . . sweet." The chill in her gaze rivaled the icicles outside the window. "You're lucky you found each other. How did you meet?"

Madison's smile widened. Such a glorious smile, even this false version. Her eyes were humorous and tender. Had this woman had this relaxed, easy countenance once, before whatever had chased her to a mountain in Wales? Even though this was fake, a growing flame warmed my insides at her attention.

Madison wrapped her arm tighter around my shoulder in a possessive gesture. Something mischievous sharpened in her gaze. "We met online. A . . . Dolly Parton fan group. G is a huge fan of Dolly. He knows all the lyrics to every song."

What the . . . ?

Surprise flickered across Jill's face. "I wouldn't have imagined that for you."

Me neither.

"Right? That's what I thought. Imagine my surprise when I found out 'Dolly Loving Dragon' was a big, strapping man from Wales. It's ridiculous how much he likes Dolly Parton. He insists on framed pictures all over the bedroom. I thought it was weird at first, but I've gotten used to it. He has his little ways . . ."

She stroked her finger lightly over my cheek. She was trolling me, and still my body sang at the contact. I had to fight the urge not to lean into her touch.

"When he came to visit me, I took him to Dollywood, and he was so moved he burst into tears. He's obsessed. It's just Dolly, Dolly, Dolly. Sometimes it feels like there are three of us in this relationship. He won't stop talking about her."

I should have eased her off my lap and ended this, but her eyes sparkled with delight. I couldn't tear my gaze from her. She looked so different from yesterday. So alive. From the cool edge to Jill's tone, it sounded like it was working, anyway. Maybe this would get Jill off my balls. Speaking of which, Madison was hovering dangerously near my groin again.

I straightened in the chair, shifting my hips to nudge her down my thighs into a safer zone. "That's right. I'm all about Dolly. Nine to five."

A chuckle escaped Madison's lips, and this time I could have sworn it was genuine. My eyes snapped to hers. Was she enjoying this? Even a little? She could laugh at me if she wanted, as long as she was laughing.

Madison's fingers brushed my cheek again. Heat blossomed under her touch. "Do you know what else is special about G?"

Jill raised a questioning eyebrow.

Madison's sweet floral scent filled my nose, and my breath caught. "He has an encyclopedic knowledge of the periodic table. It's his party trick. There is no end to the man's talent." She ticked off on her fingers. "He runs a pub, he cooks, he knows the lyrics to

61

every Dolly Parton song, and he can recite every chemical element. Isn't that amazing? Maybe he'll give you a demonstration . . ."

Jill's gaze flicked to me, and she wrinkled her nose in disbelief. My pulse pounded. Too far. We were going to get busted. This woman was an incredible actress. It was also possible she was completely insane.

I plastered a smile onto my face. "I'm sure Jill doesn't want to hear all that." Gently, I removed Madison's arm from around my neck. "Why don't you get a drink at the bar?"

Madison's smile faltered, the sparkle slipping from her eyes. She'd been having fun. I wanted to keep that smile on her lips. I wanted her to stay close to me. Maybe I could make her laugh again. I pulled her back down onto my lap. She gave a little yelp of surprise. I fitted her snugly in my arms.

"Really, I'm lucky I found such an understanding girlfriend. We indulge each other's hobbies. Madison is very into trains."

Madison arched a speculative eyebrow. "Trains?"

"Trains. Yes. Trainspotting. She has a little notepad and pen, and she goes out to the stations and makes a note of the train numbers. She gets so excited. Isn't that right, darling?"

The beginnings of a smile edged the corners of her mouth. "That's right. Big trains. Small trains. Fast trains. All the trains."

Jill's lips parted in surprise. "Trains. That's . . . unusual."

"It is, isn't it? So unusual, but so adorable." I lifted the back of Madison's hand to my mouth and pressed my lips to her smooth skin.

A shiver ran through her, and a rush of pink stained her cheeks. Did my touch affect her as much as hers affected me? Her gaze slipped away, and she shifted farther away from me. "If you'll excuse me, I'd better—"

"All the trains, and also model railways. You should have seen how excited she got when I bought her a new signaling box. It's one thing I find so endearing about her."

I trailed my finger lightly down her temple and across her jaw. She opened her mouth and closed it again. The flush that shadowed her cheekbones was the most beautiful shade of pink. Was I making her flustered?

Two can play that game.

She twisted in my arms, peering into my face. Her hand wrapped around my sleeve, stilling me. Too much. I'd pushed it too far. I dropped my hand away.

"What else do you find endearing about me, sweetheart?" Something wicked flickered in her eyes. "Because I've got plenty more things about you. What about the time you—"

"Your eyes. They're beautiful. So is your mouth. I like your smile."

Her nose wrinkled with displeasure before she smoothed her expression. She shuffled her ass, rearranging herself in my lap. The friction almost drew a groan from me. Her eyes met mine and widened with surprise. If she hadn't known the effect this little role-play was having on me, she knew now.

Shit.

"That's enough." Madison drew a breath. Her voice was hoarse and distant. "I'm sure Jill doesn't want to hear all this."

"No. It's nice. I'm happy for you both. You're clearly very much in love. You look perfect together." Jill reached down to her side for her briefcase. "I'd better head off. I have another appointment." She transferred her gaze to me. "I'll be in touch."

A tense silence wrapped around us as we watched Jill strut to the door. Madison waited until Jill had disappeared before she leaped out of my lap as though it was covered in hot coals. My body still hummed from her soft touches. I traced my finger over my cheek where her lips had been.

I tilted my head in bemusement. "Dolly Parton?"

She shrugged. "It worked, didn't it?" She rubbed her arms, the pensive shimmer in her eyes returning. She walked away, calling back over her shoulder, "You're welcome."

Chapter 13

MADISON

I crossed to the window of my time capsule bedroom and stared out at the bleak white terrain. I had the urge to open the French doors wide and let the snow pelt my face, just to feel something different. Restless energy crawled over my skin. Heat bloomed between my thighs. It wasn't a big deal. Nothing deep. It was only lust. I loved Taylor Swift because I had ears, and sitting on Geraint's lap had turned me on because he was huge and manly. An ovarian crush. Not something to consider pursuing. Not after Bryce. You couldn't believe a word that came out of a man's mouth.

Maybe I would call my parents. I picked up my phone, and my fingers hovered over the Messenger app. It would be morning in Lexington. My parents would probably be in the kitchen having breakfast. I didn't want to talk to them. Their worry and sympathy made everything worse. They wanted to fix me, but nothing could get rid of this scratchy feeling inside. Better not to drag everyone else down with me.

I collapsed on the bed. Faint music drifted from the bar downstairs. My mind filled with the image of Geraint's powerful shoulders straining against his sweater. My cheek tingled from the rough brush of his beard. A delicious vibration made me clench my thighs. It had been forever since I'd had urges like this. My sex drive was so dead, I'd considered holding it a memorial service.

I couldn't stop my fingers from dropping low to soothe the aching pulse. No point grabbing my Kindle and finding a spicy scene. The memory of Geraint's scent and the sudden unexpected feel of that giant bulge pressed against me was enough. Clearly, everything with this man was in proportion. I moved my fingers in a gentle massage. A quiver surged through my veins, and heat flooded my body. I was so out of practice, I couldn't even remember what felt good.

My mind drifted to the tall, dark beast of a man who had rescued me from the side of the road. Only now, I played out an entirely different scene in my head.

Geraint gets out of his truck. A blizzard swirls around us, but it's not cold. A blanket of snow covers everything. The world is white, even the sky. Geraint's massive shoulders fill the coat he wears, but this time he doesn't take it off and offer it to me.

"Hi, I'm Madison. I'm stranded here. Can you help me?"

He towers over me. His voice is a husky growl. "What help do you need?"

"I need you."

He crushes me to him. The ravishment of his mouth makes my heart pound. I return his kiss with reckless abandon. I'm not really a damsel in distress—I'm the Thornado, the terror of the midfield—but it's my fantasy, so I can do whatever I want. Geraint fondles my breasts through my sweater before he tugs my jeans down.

I push him down my body. "Get on your knees for me, Geraint."

Without a word, he drops to his knees in the snow, his mouth covering me, hot and wet through my cotton panties. He hooks a finger into the material and pulls it to the side. The press of his tongue makes me cry out. He probes and licks in firm strokes, hungrily searching my body. I rake my hand through his thick, soft hair, directing him. It's not enough. The throb between my thighs is a desperate ache.

"Enough. Now you need to fuck me."

In a flash, he's on his feet. Effortlessly, he lifts me and lays me flat on the hood of the truck. The engine is running. The vibrations lick over my skin like lying on a giant clothes dryer. Geraint yanks down his jeans and boxers, and his erection presses at my wetness. Lowering himself over me, he sinks into my slick heat. He's too big for a single thrust. He claims me, inch by inch. I welcome him into my body. Desperate need fills me. The world is nothing but his sharp thrusts as he grips my hips and pounds me on the vibrating hood. It's a raw act of domination, like nothing I've experienced outside of a fantasy.

He towers over me, planting an elbow next to my head, his eyes smoldering with fire. "You pronounce my name perfectly. It's such a turn-on."

"I know. I'm so good at it. Speak to me in Welsh."

A stream of words in a beautiful, melodic accent pours out of his generous lips. It's enough to push me close to the edge. The vibrations from the engine buzz up my spine, and my whole body shakes. Electricity sings through my veins, a sizzling, crackling charge that sparks with every one of Geraint's hot thrusts. Snow hits my body, but it melts the instant each frozen flake touches my feverish skin. I am fire and ice. I'm grasping for something just beyond my reach. A desperate need for release. A scream trapped. Glass that needs to shatter. I need this so bad. I want to feel something different. Something good.

Geraint lifts me, spreading me wider, opening me to him as he fills me over and over, thrust after thrust. His alien words, somehow both lyrical and growling, roll over my skin, leaving trails of goose bumps. Everything in me is tight, but I need to soften like snow melting and dripping in the sun. God. I want to soften. Believe me, I want to. I'm a spark caught inside flesh and bone. My body is a cage, and I need to be free. Gasping release hits me. A sudden avalanche of ecstasy. Pure and explosive, rocking me in intense shudders. I can't help my cry. It's a cry of relief but also surprise. The fantasy and the real world careen on their axes. Geraint disappears. The white, wintery land turns back into my strange time capsule bedroom.

My sharp gasps filled the air, and my body vibrated—trembling fingers, fluttering heart, tingling feet. A euphoric peace spread through my veins. Music and tinkling glass drifted from downstairs, a reminder of the world outside the physical confines of my body. I hadn't had an orgasm like that since . . . forever. Amusement flowed through me. It was better than anything I'd ever had with Bryce.

No man? No problem.

I couldn't stop a laugh from bubbling out. Time to call off the memorial service. My sex drive was back with a bang.

Chapter 14

Madison

The next morning, I went downstairs in search of breakfast. The bar and dimly lit pub lounge stood empty and cold. Strange. When I'd come down around the same time yesterday, a fire had blazed in the hearth. Where were the staff? The *Downton Abbey* guy and the guy with the nineties haircut? I followed the rich smell of coffee to the rooms at the back of the bar. The combination sitting room/kitchen was as shabby as the rest of the place, but at least it was homey and spacious. A wooden bookcase teeming with books and jigsaw puzzles sat in the corner. Cushions and wool throws were scattered over an inviting couch. Maybe I could curl up here later with a book.

Sunlight streamed through the enormous window over the sink. A patchwork of snow-covered fields divided by stone walls stretched in an endless spectacular panorama. I brushed the coffee pot lightly with my fingers. Still piping hot. Food covered the table—flaky croissants, cute glass jars of preserves tied with ribbons, every kind of cereal, a fresh fruit salad piled high in a white bowl. A note scrawled in blue ink sat under the coffee pot: *Help yourself to breakfast, Kentucky.*

I snorted. Kentucky? Did he even remember my name? A flash of movement drew my attention to the window. Geraint battled the snow to drag a gigantic pine tree toward the pub. His thick winter coat strained against his shoulders, and the trapper hat with ear flaps partially hid his handsome, grizzled face. He trudged methodically in heavy boots, bearing the massive tree over his shoulder. Heat flooded my body. This man was so strong and wild, like a bear.

This was the kind of man my dad had wanted for me, not a smooth-talking charmer like Bryce. Dad had been a farmer all his life. He valued hard work above anything else. Geraint was definitely a worker. He'd have to be, to keep a pub running. It couldn't be an easy life, running this place alone. I poured myself a coffee and nibbled a buttery croissant.

The back door swung open, and cold air rushed into the kitchen. Snow clung to Geraint's eyelashes, and his cheeks glowed with a rosy flush. He dumped the tree heavily onto the stone floor. His dark eyes fell on me. Memories of my fantasy pushed into my mind.

Get on your knees for me, Geraint.

Heat climbed the back of my neck.

Geraint pulled off his hat and raked a hand through his thick, unruly hair. "Bore da."

I tried my best to smile, despite my embarrassment. "Bore da?"

"Good morning."

"Good morning. Thanks for the breakfast."

He scanned the table, and for an instant his gaze sharpened. "Are you finished already?"

I patted my belly. "Yes. I'm full. Thanks."

He moved to the counter. His voice was a little awkward. "It's just the two of us today. None of the staff can get here with the roads blocked. If you want anything, you can ask me."

"Don't worry. I'll keep out of your way."

70

"I wasn't worried, but whatever your plans are, you'll have to cancel them. You're not going anywhere. The snow is worse than yesterday. No sign of it stopping. It's blocked every road around here."

This wasn't good. What was I supposed to do? Sit in my orange-and-brown room for the day, trying not to get a migraine from the wallpaper?

"Is there anything I can do within walking distance?"

Muscles bulged under his coat as he scraped a hand over his beard. Humor edged his melodic tone. "There are farms. Do you enjoy looking at snow-covered fields?"

"Not really."

"You could build a snowman."

"I'm not ten years old."

He shrugged. "Then there's nothing to do in walking distance."

Fine. Reading it would have to be.

I ran a hand over a spiky frond on the tree. "You're getting around to Christmas?"

He inclined his head. "May as well."

He dragged the tree across the stone kitchen floor into the hallway. It didn't seem as easy now he was indoors. His limp was more pronounced than yesterday. Maybe it troubled him more on some days.

He hesitated, measuring me for a moment. "Do you want to help?"

"Help?"

A faint light twinkled in his dark eyes. "Decorate the tree."

The scent of pine needles filled my nose, strong enough to outdo the malty smell of beer that clung to the pub. A pang pulled at my heart. That smell was bittersweet. I'd always loved Christmas with my family. They'd already put the tree up. My sister had sent me the pictures.

Awkwardly, Geraint cleared his throat. "It's fine. You don't have to, but if you're bored—"

"I'll help."

He rubbed the back of his neck. "Thanks."

"No problem, but only because it's a slightly better option than the snowman."

Chapter 15

Geraint

I dropped the huge crate of old Christmas decorations in the pub lounge. Madison put her hands on her hips and gazed up at the towering pine tree. She was an enigma. What was she doing here all alone over Christmas? Didn't she have any friends or family? She wasn't happy. That much was obvious. If she wasn't snapping at me, she was staring off blankly into the distance. It wasn't any of my business, but I couldn't help but be curious.

Her gaze fixed behind the tree on the decoratively carved wooden love spoons that Dad had mounted on the wall. She traced a finger over the intricate Celtic knots and hearts engraved into the wood. "Are these the infamous spoons? Aled said I should ask you about them."

I moved to stand next to her. The faint scent of her perfume filled my nose, fresh and cool like cucumbers. Aled had a well-rehearsed spiel about the love spoons. He was proud of our heritage, and the tourists lapped this kind of thing up. We'd even sold love spoons for a while. I'd enjoyed carving them. But then we'd had fewer and fewer guests, and it had seemed a waste.

I cleared my throat. "It's a Welsh custom."

"Go on. You can't leave it at that. My interest is piqued. What custom?"

Unease washed over me. Aled was the one who talked about the spoons. I could never remember the right things to say about them.

"It's just a tradition. You can look it up online."

"No, I can't. I'm sick of your Wi-Fi. Do you know the one thing that's worse than no Wi-Fi? Patchy Wi-Fi. Come on. I'm interested. You must know what they're for."

I tried to remember what Aled would say. "The spoons were a way for a young suitor to showcase his woodworking skills to a future father-in-law. It proved he could provide for his woman. The different symbols you see here have meaning. A horseshoe for luck, a lock for security, bells for marriage. They're a gesture of love."

A melancholy frown flittered across her strong features. Her lips thinned. "How romantic."

She hugged herself before she turned around to delve into the crates. She pulled out a long glittering string of tiny golden bells tangled in purple tinsel. "I used to love tree-trimming parties back home."

"Trimming? What is that?"

"You don't have those? My parents' tree-trimming parties are legendary. The whole neighborhood comes by. We have Christmas songs, cranberry cocktails, a cheese board. Last year I made Brussels sprouts wrapped in bacon. My sister and I take turns to decide the theme for the tree." She shot me a speculative glance. "Do you have a theme in mind for the tree?"

A theme? "Christmas. The theme of the Christmas tree is Christmas."

She rolled her eyes, but an indulgent smile lit her face. "Not just Christmas. An aesthetic?"

I didn't have an aesthetic. I had Dad's old crate of decorations that he'd brought out year after year. Jess had taken anything good in the divorce. Not that it mattered. A box of Christmas decorations was a box of memories. I'd been happy to see the last of it.

Madison pulled out another glittery string of tinsel. "Fine. I can work with this. This is giving off 'cozy traditional Welsh inn' vibes." Lines of concentration deepened around her pretty eyes. "I'm loving this aesthetic, actually. For my parents' tree last year, we did Scandinavian farmhouse chic. I found these to-die-for little glass ice skates and reindeer. The year before, Brooke went with mixed metallic eleganza, silver and gold, some white ribbons for texture. You know the kind of thing. I usually start planning in October. It's become competitive over the years."

"You plan your Christmas tree in October?"

"You have to give yourself plenty of time. My sister kept it simple this year with red and gold. She sent me the pictures. It looked amazing . . ." A shadow crossed her face as she stared at the fairy lights in her hand. Her voice took on a dull edge. "It's my first Christmas away from home."

I couldn't stop myself from asking the question that had needled me since the moment I saw her. "What are you doing in Wales?"

She lifted her gaze to give me a dark, cynical look. A chill edged her words. "It's not something I want to talk about."

I'd got it wrong by asking, and she'd shut me down. That was the one thing I'd always been good at with Jess. Putting my foot in it and pissing her off. My ex-wife's angry voice played in my head.

Use your bloody brain before you speak, Geraint.

A tight silence stretched between us. Madison turned her face away and pulled out a battered plastic snowman. A memory drifted to mind. Years ago—before my busted knee, before the divorce, before I'd lost Dad—we'd had one big family Christmas here together. It had been a happy one. Dad had burned the roast potatoes, and we'd ended up having turkey and chips. Still, it had been fun. If only Dad was here. He'd know how to look after this woman and make her feel welcome. He'd always been able to put people at ease. It was his gift. This pub had been full of laughter and life years ago, and it was all Dad's doing.

Madison rifled through the box, pulling out faded baubles and scraggly tangles of tinsel. Any traces of animation had vanished from her face, to be replaced by a scowl. Maybe I could make this better. It didn't have to be miserable. What would Dad do?

I moved to the bar and pulled out Dad's ancient CD player from underneath. I selected his favorite Christmas CD and held it up. "Music?"

Madison stood on tiptoe to wrap a string of tinsel around the tree. "No, thanks."

"Not even Tom Jones? Everybody loves Tom Jones."

She raised an unimpressed eyebrow. "I don't even know who that is."

"Please tell me you're joking."

She let the tinsel dangle in her hands. "Am I supposed to know?"

"Are you supposed to know who Sir Thomas Jones OBE is?" I blew out a breath and shook my head. "Yes, you're supposed to know. Thankfully, you're in Wales. The birthplace of the great man."

She watched me before she gave a dismissive flap of her hands. "Let's hear him then."

I slipped the CD into Dad's old device and hit play. Tom Jones's distinctive baritone poured out of the speakers. Madison opened her mouth to speak, but I held up a hand to stop her. "Wait. It hasn't got to the good bit yet."

She tapped her foot impatiently.

I held my arms open. "See?"

She wrinkled her nose. "See what?"

"That voice. The man is a legend."

Madison returned her attention to the tree. "He's fine."

Fine? The greatest singer that Wales had ever produced was *fine*? "I give up. There is no accounting for taste. A woman who is tired of Tom Jones is tired of life. There's no helping you, Kentucky."

She snorted. I moved to the vast inglenook hearth and stacked the logs to build a fire. In no time, the sooty odor of burning wood filled my nose. Amber flames crackled and built to a roaring fire.

I moved behind the bar. "Now for a drink."

She watched me with an uncertain expression before she folded her arms. "No, thanks."

"You don't fancy a beer or a wine?"

"I don't really drink alcohol."

"Isn't the trimming thing supposed to be a party? We're in a pub."

"Tree trimming is an activity best done sober."

"Why? Are you worried you might accidentally have some fun?"

Her lips twisted in a cynical smile. "I know how to have fun."

"Of course. No music. No alcohol. No whistling. I can see you're all about the good times."

Her eyes flashed dangerously, and she threw her hair over her shoulder. "Actually, you know what? Why not? It's the holidays. I used to drink any girl on my team under the table."

"Team? What team?"

She dropped the tinsel and strode to the bar. "It doesn't matter. I'll have something to drink." She hammered a fist on the bar, and her face lit with a wry smile. "Bring me your finest ale."

Was that a thawing in her tone? And a smile? Who would have thought? An idea slid into my mind. "If the theme is cozy Welsh inn, we'd better make a drink to match. We'll have some wassail."

Her smile turned into a chuckle. "Wassail? I didn't realize that was Welsh?"

"It's a traditional Welsh Christmas drink. Mulled ale with spices. We'll need to heat the ale. You're going to love it, but first, we need the finishing touch on the tree."

I moved to plug in the fairy lights and flick the switch. They blinked to life in a sparkling array of color that reflected in Madison's eyes. She gazed up at the tree and flashed a weak smile. "I think we've done a good job."

She pulled her phone from the back pocket of her jeans. "Do you mind if I take a picture? I'll send it to my nieces."

I held out my hand for the phone. "I can take it. Stand in front of the tree."

A thoughtful wrinkle appeared between her eyebrows. "Okay."

She smoothed her hair but offered no smile. Her expression was full of irritation, but there was something beyond that—a tired sadness around her eyes. I had the sudden urge to pull her into my arms and hold her. I'd never seen anyone more in need of a hug. A pang pulled at my heart. What was this woman doing out here all alone, looking so sad? It was easier to see her snarky and angry than looking like this. I snapped the picture and passed the phone back.

"Thanks." She chewed her lip before she slid me a glance. "Can we get a photo together?"

"Together?" I didn't do a good job of keeping the surprise from my voice. Why did she want one with me? Most of the time, she seemed irritated by me.

"It might be nice for my parents to see that I'm not all alone here." Her face clouded with uneasiness. "They worry. You don't have to, if you don't want to—"

"No. Of course. It's fine."

I stood next to her. She shuffled closer to get us both in the selfie. Her scent filled my nose. The shock of her closeness ran through my body, as disturbing as it was exciting. I longed to take her in my arms and kiss her. To do whatever it took to put a smile on her lips. To unwrap her under this tree, like a present just for me, peeling back her layers and undoing all the ribbons wound so tight.

She was only here for a short time. I'd had so many one-night stands after the divorce. My heart had been aching after losing both Dad and Jess, and lots of tourists had passed through back then. All those transient tumbles did was leave me feeling emptier than before. I'd vowed to stop. No matter if this woman stirred me up inside, I'd keep my distance. Besides, she acted like she hated my guts, and she didn't appreciate Tom Jones. You couldn't find two bigger red flags.

"Thanks." She took the photo and stepped away to examine it. Cold air raced in around me at the loss of her. The moment was gone. Good. Better to get through the next few days with no broken hearts and no bad reviews.

"No problem." I coughed to cover my awkward feeling. "Time for some wassail?"

Chapter 16

GERAINT

"Have you always worked here?" Madison peered over my shoulder at the ale heating on the stove.

"No. I used to play rugby."

"Professionally?"

I nodded.

Her guilty eyes roamed over me and lingered on my arms. "I wondered if you played sports. I don't know much about rugby. Is it like football?"

I stirred the dark mixture on the stove. A delicious smell of cinnamon and ginger hit my nose. "It depends which football you're talking about. The physicality is like American football, but we play at the pace of soccer. Rugby is our national sport—a part of Welsh culture that brings everyone together. It's all-out war for eighty minutes on the pitch, but we have strong values and respect for each other. That's what I love about it. Still, it's a completely different game to football. Different rules. Different scoring. No helmets. No pads. Just balls. It's a sport for real men."

She snorted. "Just balls, huh? You know women play rugby, too."

The more I opened my mouth with this woman, the more I put my foot in it. It wasn't as though I'd had much practice with my conversation skills of late. "I'm sorry. I don't meet that many women interested in rugby."

"Women play rugby and soccer. In fact, I play soccer professionally for one of the best teams in England. No helmets. No pads. Just balls."

A smile lifted her lips. It dripped with smug superiority, but I'd take it over anger or sadness. I couldn't take my eyes off her. That smile was so compelling. She had an air of calm self-confidence. The scowl she often wore slipped away like a mask she'd borrowed that didn't fit well. Right now, she looked beyond intimidating. Dignified. Strong. Beautiful. Was this the real Madison behind whatever made her defensive all the time?

I nodded. "That's very impressive."

It was, and it made sense. It explained why she moved like an athlete. I couldn't stop my gaze from roving over her toned, hard body and drinking in her sensuality.

"So you know how it is to be part of a team. It doesn't matter what's on the scoreboard—as long as you have each other's backs, you're winning every time you step out together. That's the part I loved—the community, and the camaraderie. You can't beat it. It's such a buzz."

Her eyes slipped away. "Right. It's a buzz."

"Who do you play for?"

"Calverdale."

"They're big. You've got that celebrity as a director, right? What's his name? Something Rivers?"

"Gabe Rivers."

"Didn't he push his own father down the stairs?"

She picked up an empty beer bottle and examined it before putting it back on the counter. "Opinion is divided on the matter. I didn't like him at first, but he's a slow burner."

81

"Some people are like that." I moved closer. Some invisible force compelled me into her orbit. She gave me a curious glance. Her guilty gaze found my lips, then darted back to my eyes. "Do you like working in a pub?"

I opened my mouth and closed it again. The question caught me off guard. At the start, I hadn't. I'd wanted to play rugby, not limp around here. Jess had wanted me to find a way to stay in the spotlight even after the injury, but I couldn't. Rugby had been my world. It was too painful to talk about it all the time when I knew I'd always only ever be on the sidelines. I'd come here after the divorce. Inheriting the pub had been the final straw for Jess. She didn't want anything to do with it. To Jess, this was all a mistake. When Dad passed, I couldn't leave. It had been his dream to run a pub, not mine. Sometimes, it felt like I was out here just treading water. Sometimes, I wondered if Jess had been right. It had been a mistake to take this place on. It's not as though I'd made a success of it. Now, it was about to be taken away from me.

"I like it well enough."

"You don't find it isolated? Is it just you here, alone?"

I poured some of the steaming wassail into a tankard and handed it to her. "Aled and Ewan are here too. Simon's also here a lot. He's my most loyal customer."

Her fingers brushed mine as she took the hot drink from me. "Simon? I haven't met him yet."

"He's a great guy. Not the best conversationalist, but he's yours for a belly rub."

She cast a puzzled glance. "Excuse me?"

"Simon is a border collie. Ewan's dog."

The briefest of smiles pulled at her lips. "Oh."

Her eyes were wide and inquisitive, as though she wanted to probe further but didn't dare. She turned her face to the window to watch the sheets of snow purifying the ground and making everything new. Strange to be in this kitchen with such an impressive woman. Talking to a woman hadn't felt so good or easy in years. There weren't many options around here. Not that Madison was an option. She'd be gone soon.

She blew steam from the tankard and took a sip. "This is good."

"Yeah?"

She nodded and took another sip. A small smile lifted her lips. Another windfall.

Warmth lit me. "So this is how I put a smile on your face? Alcohol?"

The smallest hint of amusement flickered in her eyes as they met mine. "Sounds about right."

Chapter 17

MADISON

Geraint moved confidently around the kitchen. He looked as comfortable here as he had out in the woods dragging that gigantic tree. How could a man who looked so big and wild be so domesticated? He tightened his white apron around his powerful body. I couldn't help my shiver of excitement from being here with him. Standing so close to him to take the photo had made my heart flutter wildly. His solid presence was potent and magnetizing. Every cell in my body had been aware of his strength and warmth.

I pulled out my phone and uploaded the photos of the tree to my Instagram feed. My finger hovered over the one of me and Geraint. It was a nice shot. The tree glittered, and the snow-capped mountains were visible behind the window. I hadn't bothered with my social media for so long. The Calverdale PR team encouraged us to do it, but I didn't have the will for it. I'd uploaded a couple shots of the stadium. That was about it.

I paused. My thumb hovered over the phone. People might talk if I uploaded a picture of myself with a man. I wasn't as high profile as some girls on the team, but I had a decent number of followers. I took a breath. Screw it. Let people talk. What did it matter up here?

"Do you mind if I put this photo on my social media? PR likes it if I keep it up to date."

"Fine with me. I don't do any of that social media stuff."

"Not even Facebook?"

"No. I don't have Facebook."

"You must have. How do you get guests? Don't you need it to advertise?"

He shrugged. "We have a website. I haven't really done much of the other stuff."

I pulled my phone out and searched online for the inn. I'd made my reservation through a booking website because it was the only one to offer accommodation at short notice. I clicked through a ton of annoying pop-ups before I found anything useful on the Dragon Inn website. The home page looked like it had been made around the same time the internet had been invented. A young Geraint—clean-shaven and bright-eyed—stared back at me from the *About Us* section. A gray-haired man stood next to Geraint with a proud smile and an arm around his waist.

Geraint peered over my shoulder at the phone. "I've never been good with computers. Dad set this up. We lost him a couple of years ago. That's how I ended up with this place."

"I'm sorry."

He nodded, and turned away, busying himself wiping the countertops.

I scanned the screen. "It says you played for Wales."

He rubbed the back of his neck. "I did."

"Wow. You must have been good?"

He shrugged. "I was okay."

I typed his name into a search engine, and it returned a page of hits: sports reports, news stories, and YouTube videos. There was even an Instagram account called *Mad about Madoc*, which took me to a grid of photos of a rugged-looking Geraint playing rugby.

The images were all similar—sweat plastered Geraint's hair to his forehead, a red jersey clung to his powerful body, and a rugby ball was tucked under his arm. Even with the mouth guard and head-gear, he looked insanely attractive. The fans seemed to agree. The comments section was mostly flame emojis.

A surprised chuckle escaped me. "You're downplaying it. You have a Wikipedia page. You appear to be particularly popular with the female fans. You should have told me I was hanging out with a celebrity."

He kept his eyes on his task, but pink tinged his cheekbones. Funny to see him looking so sheepish. It only made me want to tease him more, like when we'd been putting on a show for Jill. Making such a giant of a man blush was addictive.

His eyes met mine. "I could say the same about you."

"I don't have my own fan club. Look at this. This account has so many followers. There are so many comments."

And a few of them were even about his rugby prowess and not just his thighs.

I held the phone under his nose. "This is just a fan page. Imagine if you had an official account."

He lowered my hand with the phone away from his face. "Why? I'm retired. Nobody would care about what I'm doing now."

"Are you kidding? You could still have a presence online. It would be great publicity for the pub. People would come just to see you. Who wouldn't want a delicious meal cooked by a rugby legend?"

He smiled, politely. "I'm not a legend."

"But you were in the spotlight, playing for your country. Haven't you seen any of this stuff before?"

"I'm not interested." He stopped wiping the counter and held still with his back to me. "That's all in the past."

Something about his firm tone made me snap my mouth shut. He usually sounded so jovial. Maybe he wasn't enamored with the celebrity side of things. I got it. I'd seen a handful of stories about me and Bryce online. The British press hadn't been particularly complimentary about my performances for Calverdale Ladies. I tried to stay away from all that.

"Sounds like you're missing an opportunity. Every business needs a proper social media strategy." I kept my voice gentle. If his dad had made the website, the last thing I wanted to do was criticize, but it was in serious need of updating. No wonder the place was empty. "I'm not keen on the social media stuff, but it does have benefits for marketing. It's something to look into. You could use your celebrity to your advantage."

He cleared his throat. "It was all a long time ago."

"Not according to *Mad about Madoc*. Some of these posts are recent."

"I can assure you my rugby days are in the past." He pressed his lips together thoughtfully. "But Ewan might be able to help with the website."

"You should start an Instagram for the pub. It's easy enough to share photos."

My phone flashed with a notification.

Bryce Muller has liked your photo.

My heart jolted. The scent of cinnamon and cloves in the kitchen overwhelmed me. Before I had a chance to recover from the shock, a WhatsApp message flashed on the screen.

Hi! How are you? Are you on vacation?

Bryce. A knot of rage rose in my throat, stealing my breath. Was this some kind of joke? How dare he message me? We'd had no contact for months. My heart pounded. I couldn't talk to him. I shoved the phone in my pocket and tried to slow my heartbeat.

Bryce never commented on my social media. He hadn't even when we were a couple. Why now?

Geraint twisted to watch me. "Everything okay?"

"Yes . . . No. I don't know . . . I think I need to sit down."

His face dropped. "The wassail? Did I make it too strong? You need to eat. You're drinking on an empty stomach. Sit in the lounge. I'll bring you food."

My legs trembled as I left the kitchen. I sank into an armchair by the fire and pulled out my phone again. A new message pinged.

Who is that man you're with?

A bitter laugh escaped my lips. Oh, so that was it. He'd seen a photo of me with another man, and it had made him curious. Why? He was the one that had left me. My pulse pounded. He had no right! How dare he be jealous? The pictures had crawled under Bryce's skin. A smug sense of satisfaction invaded my heart like a shard of ice. Bryce was jealous. Good. Let it eat him up, the way his betrayal had messed me up.

Baubles twirled on thin threads, the reflection of flames dancing in the gleaming metal. I let my eyes blur the way I'd done as a kid, so the colors fused in a metallic kaleidoscope. Christmas had been magical on the farm. I'd loved watching my little nieces get excited. Being an aunt was fun, but it made me yearn for my own kids even more. Christmas was great if you were happy, but if you were miserable, it made you feel worse. A bitter feeling seized me.

I took another sip of the too-sweet spiced ale concoction. The ginger and alcohol heated my throat on the way down. I'd partied a long time ago at the start of my career. Not now. I didn't drink alcohol under normal circumstances and never during the season. But what the hell. It was the holidays, and my life was a wreck. Normal rules didn't apply. A sour feeling made my jaw tight, and I downed the rest of the hot ale. A grim, woozy feeling settled over me like a shroud.

Geraint put down a plate of charcuterie with cheeses and olives next to me before drifting around the pub lounge, straightening the stools under the circular wooden tables. His limp was more pronounced tonight. The man never stopped. It must have been difficult running this place alone, even if he never seemed to have any guests.

"I can't eat all this alone. Will you join me?"

He dropped into the armchair opposite me. Flames danced over his rugged, masculine profile. Yes, this was the kind of man my parents would have loved me to bring home. I should have paid attention to the fact that my parents disliked Bryce. Mom was right. I'd rushed into things with the wedding. I hadn't wanted to keep putting off kids. After watching Brooke go through cycle after cycle of IVF, I knew how hard that was for her. I'd cried with her and held her after the miscarriages.

Brooke had warned me, too. My sister knew me better than anyone, and I'd got so mad with her every time she'd tried to reason with me. That was the worst part. I'd put everything into defending Bryce and convincing everyone—including myself—that he was this amazing guy, and I was happy. He'd proven me wrong. I'd been so foolish.

I held out my empty tankard to Geraint. At least I was in the right place to drown my sorrows. "Can I get myself a top-up?"

"Are you sure? It's strong."

"I'm on vacation. I thought you were giving me a lesson in fun."

His brow flickered, but he nodded. His skin brushed mine as he wrapped his fingers around the drinking vessel. I gripped it tighter. It wasn't right to keep sending him on errands when his leg seemed to be troubling him.

"I can do it," I said.

He smiled. "You're the guest. Just relax."

"It's no problem. Don't trouble yourself."

"It's no trouble."

We stared at each other, both gripping the tankard. "You should rest. You don't stop."

His smile dimmed. "It's fine."

"You look like you need to sit down."

A shadow crossed his face and hurt glittered in his eyes. "I'm not an invalid."

Guilt heated my cheeks. I relinquished the tankard. "I didn't say that."

His muttered words lingered in the air long after he'd disappeared into the kitchen. "You didn't need to."

He returned and presented me with another full tankard of hot ale. My hand sparked at the contact. The delicious ginger aroma filled my senses.

"Thanks. I'm sorry if I caused any offense."

He rubbed the back of his neck. "It's fine."

I let my gaze wander to the tree. "You're missing a topper. Don't you have an angel or a star?"

The fire's glow smoldered in his dark, compelling eyes. "There must be another box somewhere."

He stood and moved slowly toward the tree. I resisted the urge to tell him not to do it right away. I finished my drink and let my head drop back. Snow swirled outside the window, as thick and persistent as ever. A pleasant warmth filled me, and the heat of the flames licked over my face. I could almost forget how twisted up that message from Bryce had made me. The fire and alcohol warmed and softened my body.

Who is that man you're with?

A wicked smile curved my lips. I closed my eyes and lost myself to the thick, woolly sensation in my head.

Wouldn't you like to know?

Chapter 18

Madison

Shadows bathed an aisle that stretched to nowhere, long and ominous. Silence cloaked the church. I took a faltering step forward. Every guest that stuffed the pews turned to look at me at the same moment. Their faces were blank and staring. I looked down to see that I was completely naked. Humiliation seeped into my bones. Something primal and full of anguish rose inside me. How could he do this? How could I ever go home?

"Madison."

A melodic voice drifted from the rafters. An enormous, grizzled beast of a man sat at the organ, his huge fingers spread across the keys. Light from the stained-glass window spilled over his hulking frame, painting him in luminescent rainbows. Geraint's dark eyes met mine. Then he was kissing me. Touching me. His lips hot and persuasive. I pressed my body against his, desperate to feel every hard inch of him. His hands locked at the base of my spine, and his lips traced a path down my neck to my breasts. Heat pooled between my thighs. A warming shiver jolted my spine. A moan escaped me.

"Madison?"

I woke with a start and sat up. An array of sparkling baubles twisted in the flames. My mouth felt dry and dusty, like old parchments. Geraint sat opposite me with a book in his lap. I wiped drool from my chin. "What time is it?"

He licked a finger and turned the page. "Nine p.m."

A pain blazed in my neck, and I rolled my shoulders. It had been so long since I'd had any decent sleep. Every night was the same horrible dream.

Thanks, brain! Great job. This whole jilted-at-the-altar nightmare is the gift that keeps on giving.

I looked up to find Geraint watching me with a curious expression. Heat still thrummed through my veins at the feel of his lips on mine. It had been so real. My face felt wet. Had I been crying? Worse than that, had I been moaning? I swiped my knuckles across my cheeks, brushing away the tears.

My throat felt thick. "I didn't say anything, did I?"

Geraint studied my face. "Like what?"

"I don't know. Sometimes I talk in my sleep."

Nervously, he moistened his lips. His eyes slid away. "You didn't say anything."

I'd never seen anyone look so shifty. I could have almost laughed. This guy had the worst poker face. "You're not a good liar."

His brow dipped into an even deeper frown. "Right. I never have been good at that. You said 'Bryce'."

Tired sadness washed over me. I watched the flames leaping and crackling in the hearth, but I hardly felt the fire's warmth. "Oh."

Geraint watched me, waiting for me to elaborate. Maybe it was the alcohol, but I didn't have the energy to bat the question away. What did it matter? It wasn't as if I'd have to see this guy again after next week.

"Bryce is my ex. I posted some photos, and he messaged for the first time in months. It must have made him jealous seeing me with a man." A strange, bitter laugh escaped me. "He has no right to be jealous after what he did. It serves him right."

"What did he do?"

My pulse quickened at his question. I opened my mouth and closed it. This wasn't the time. I'd come here to escape, not to be treated like an unexploded bomb again. "He let me down."

A wrinkle formed above Geraint's nose. "Is that why you wanted to take a picture with me? To make your ex jealous?"

"No."

He ran his thumb over his lips but didn't speak. His dark, steady gaze bored into me, but he looked unconvinced. "Right." Geraint leaned down and picked up a decoration at his feet. "I found a topper for the tree."

He passed me a small plastic angel. She wore a crumpled white dress. A tiny halo of glass buttons circled on a wire above her blonde curls. The sign in her hands read "Nadolig Llawen".

I traced a finger over the unfamiliar words. "What does this mean?"

"Nadolig Llawen. Merry Christmas." The words in his low musical voice sounded like a lullaby.

"Say it again."

Another tender murmur escaped his lips. "Nadolig Llawen."

I let the soothing sound wash over me. The little angel looked battered and disheveled. Once, she'd probably been beautiful. I brushed my finger over the soft blonde curls and white lace. A sudden ache speared my heart. What was I doing here? My whole family was back home getting ready for my favorite time of year, and I was here alone with a man I hardly knew in a country that wasn't mine. We spoke the same language, but everything in the UK was so different. Bryce had pulled the rug out from under my feet. He'd humiliated me in front of everyone. He'd taken the future I had planned and crushed it as though it meant nothing.

Heat gathered behind my eyes. I gulped hard, the sobs I wouldn't allow to break free choking me. A wave of fatigue hit me. I'd felt angry for so long. When I wasn't angry, I just wanted to sleep.

"I'd better go to bed."

I didn't give Geraint time to reply. I'd already given him more than I wanted to. On unsteady legs, I moved to the door. Geraint's hand wrapped around my wrist, stilling me. His grip was loose, but warmth prickled up my arm. He watched me with a heated gaze.

Despite the hard lump in my throat, a strange wave of excitement coursed through me at his nearness. He'd kissed me in my dreams. Those full lips had been all over my body, and that beard had rasped over my bare skin. It had felt incredible. A heavy silence crackled around us.

He dropped my wrist and passed me the angel. His voice was smooth but insistent. "Don't you think she belongs on the tree?"

The angel's battered porcelain face stared back at me. He was right. I drifted to the tree. It looked beautiful, but without the topper it was incomplete.

"I'm going to need a chair to stand on."

He moved behind me, so close I could feel the heat of his hard, tense body against my back. "I can help you."

My heart lurched to have him so close. His manly scent enveloped me. Before I could even think to protest, his huge hands wrapped around my waist. He lifted me into the air effortlessly, and for a moment I was weightless. Excitement, but no fear, buzzed through my veins at being held aloft. Geraint wouldn't drop me. I didn't know how I knew that, but I did.

He raised me higher. "Can you reach?"

"I think so." With a stretch, I positioned the angel on the very top. Geraint planted me carefully back on my feet. I twisted in his arms. My nose was level with his solid, muscular chest. I peered up at him. My hands rested on his broad shoulders. His muscles tensed under my fingertips.

His throat bobbed as he swallowed. "You can put more photos of us online if you want."

"What?"

A disheveled black halo of hair encircled his head like the angel's crown of buttons. "If you want to make your ex jealous. I don't mind."

His muttered words, lilting and soft, made my heart pound. "You don't?"

"No. You did me a favor when you pretended to be my girlfriend."

My hands still rested on his shoulders. I should have moved them, but I couldn't. It felt too good to be touching him, to have a warm body under my fingers after so long alone.

"You rescued me from a blizzard. We're already even."

His gaze dropped to my lips. "Still. I don't mind . . ."

What was I doing? I should have moved my hands. Now moving them would turn into a big thing. Awkward excitement wove a thread around us. I found myself tilting my face toward him. My pulse skittered alarmingly. Our lips were almost touching. His breath was warm against my face. I hadn't kissed anyone in so long. With Geraint's face so close to mine, I could barely think. I could barely remember to breathe.

His dark eyes were tender as they searched my face, seeking permission. I bit down on my lip, pretending not to be affected by his nearness or the way my body still tingled from when he'd lifted me. His rough finger traced my cheek and jaw before curling under my chin. A pulse thrummed in my temple. He brushed his finger softly against my other cheek. A shiver of nerves and anticipation raced through me. He lowered his face to mine. This was too soon. I hadn't come here for this. I wasn't over Bryce. In a couple of days, I'd be leaving. This wasn't me. Why couldn't I move away?

Screw it.

I pressed my mouth to his. He held perfectly still. The brush of his firm lips sent a hot shiver through me. With his large hand at my waist, he drew me roughly to him, closing the gap between us. His mouth moved over mine tenderly. His kiss was so different to any kiss I'd had before. Gentle but intense, like a whisper in the dark. It sent currents of desire racing through me.

I longed for him to pull me into his powerful arms, but he made no move to deepen the kiss. The sweet sensation was too much, yet nowhere near enough. He was being respectful, but that wasn't what I wanted from him. I put my arms around his thick neck and pressed myself to his hard body. My mouth moved with more urgency against his. He tasted of cinnamon and cloves, of warmth, of Christmas.

Desire pooled in my lower belly. Then we were moving. My back hit the wall. My gasp was lost under his punishing kiss. His lips left my mouth and scorched a path down my neck. I felt his hardness pressing against my belly. A pang of anxiety went through me. What was I doing? I hardly knew this man. This was so different to how it had been with Bryce. Bryce had never left me panting and trembling with desire like this. This felt dangerous and wild and way too fast.

My heart hammered against my ribs. His lips trailed down my temple and along my jaw. For such a gigantic man, his touch was gentle. The soft brush of his fingers around my throat made my knees weak. Every sense filled with him. He smelled like my dad's workshop, of wood shavings and honest work. My heart hammered wildly in my ribs. I wanted him to lift me against this wall and do all manner of things to me. I couldn't get attached to anyone new, but that's not what this was. This was a way to feel good, something to do while I was stuck in the middle of nowhere. It was either this or build a snowman.

His touch made me clench my thighs. I raked my hands through his soft hair and returned his passionate kiss. He groaned so low, it sounded like a feral growl. I wasn't over Bryce, but so what? What better way to get over him? Bryce didn't want me. This man did. Didn't I deserve to be desired for one night?

My lips found Geraint's ear. "Shall we go upstairs?"

He froze. With a sigh, he drew away and dragged a hand over his beard. His expression was tight with strain. "You've been drinking."

"I'm sober now. Look." I held my arms out and did my best to plant one wobbly foot in front of the other. "Would I be able to walk in a straight line if I was drunk?"

His mouth curved with tenderness. "Only drunk people feel the need to prove they can walk in a straight line."

Why were we talking when we could have been kissing more? "What's the problem? Are you worried I'll leave you a bad review?" I leaned up and whispered into his neck, since I had no chance of reaching his ear even on tiptoe. "That kiss doesn't get a bad review."

Humor flashed across his face, and he laughed, a rich, deep, masculine sound. "Now I know you're drunk. You're being nice to me."

Guilt prickled my shoulder blades. He didn't think I was nice? I supposed I wasn't great company most of the time. I didn't want to be such a dark cloud. Maybe this could be the start of something better.

I laced my fingers through his. "Come upstairs and let me show you how nice I can be."

His smile flickered, and he stroked my cheek. A deep frown set into his features. "Nos da, Kentucky."

"Nos da?"

He kissed the tip of my nose. "Goodnight."

He was turning me down? Of course. Why would he want me? The disappointment quickly shifted to anger. He didn't get to do this to me. I'd let Bryce leave me standing like a fool. Never again.

"I get the message." My voice came out sharper than I'd intended, but it was too late to take it back. I stormed off.

Geraint caught my hand and pulled me back to face him. His eyes searched mine, and he frowned. "What message?"

I shrugged out of his grip. "You don't want me. It's fine. Whatever."

His hands slipped up my arms, bringing me closer. There was a slight tinge of wonder in his voice. "You think I don't want you?"

"What am I supposed to think?"

His hands locked against my spine, and he whispered into my hair. "I want you, Kentucky. You don't have to worry about that."

He showered slow kisses around my lips and along my jaw. The rough scrape of his beard against my throat made me shiver with need. Despite my agitation, I couldn't help but relax into his embrace.

His breath fanned hot against my ear. "But if I take you to my bed, you're going to remember every minute. I won't have you waking up and regretting it. If you want me tomorrow when the booze has worn off, we'll do this properly. I'll make you breakfast, and then I'll make love to you."

Heat flooded my body. He planted a gentle kiss on my forehead. Our eyes met, and his look was so galvanizing it sent a tremor through me.

I couldn't help the smile that touched my lips. "Does it have to be in that order?"

"Yes. I enjoy feeding you, and breakfast is the most important meal of the day. Besides, you're going to need your energy for what I have in mind."

He stroked a line across my cheekbone, and his caress was a command. "Come and find me in the morning." A flash of humor crossed his face. "If you still feel like being nice to me."

He turned on his heel and walked in his unhurried way to the door.

Chapter 19

GERAINT

Ceri's face filled my tiny phone screen on video call. I propped up the phone on the kitchen island, and put her on speakerphone.

I tried to keep desperation from my voice. "There's really nothing you can do?"

Her lips pulled into a thin, tight smile. "I'm afraid not. I'm sorry, G."

I drummed my fingers on the kitchen island. Ceri was one of my old friends from school who managed the bank in the village. I'd hoped she could get me out of this mess. I'd thought about a loan to buy the pub in the past, but there hadn't been a point as long as I could lease it. The brewery was forcing my hand. If I could buy the pub outright, the brewery couldn't put me in this position again. It would secure our future.

"There must be something. I can't lose this pub. You know what it means to the village."

A low hum of conversation from the bank drifted down the phone. I kept an eye on the door. Madison could be down at any minute. I had to wrap this up. I didn't much fancy her overhearing.

Ceri fingered the collar of her smart blouse. "I wish I could help you. It's just not possible."

"I can pay money back on a loan. You know me. You knew my father."

She spoke softly but with authority. "This isn't personal, G. With your credit history . . ."

The skin at the back of my neck itched. There had been a time when I'd made good money playing professionally. The cash had slipped through my fingers so quickly. The divorce and medical bills had ruined me.

"I don't know what to do. The brewery wants me to write a business plan. I don't know how to come up with what I need to keep this place. The Dragon is a piece of history. It gives people a sense of community. My staff will be out of work, and what for? Yoga and bloody gong baths? What does that even mean?"

"Yoga is profitable," Ceri said matter-of-factly. "I can't speak to gong baths. I don't know what they are."

"Come on, Ceri. You're not going to help me?"

"If it was up to me, of course I would." She gave me a sad smile. "Unfortunately, it's not up to me. This is business, not personal."

I sighed. Jill had said the same.

I kept my smile polite. "Fine. Thanks for your time."

"Good luck. Take care, G."

I hung up and moved to the fridge to get things ready for breakfast. My mind drifted to last night. The kiss had taken me by surprise. It hadn't been a good idea, but the moment Madison's lips had touched mine, I was gone. Even though I'd sworn off one-night stands, I couldn't deny I wanted her. I hoped it wouldn't be awkward when she came down.

My phone buzzed on the island. Aled's name flashed. I'd already told him and Ewan not to come in until the snow cleared.

I answered the phone. "Aled? Is everything okay?"

"Everything is wonderful."

I could hear the grin in his voice. No doubt he was enjoying being snowed in with Mrs. Ackwright. I'd have to tell Ewan.

"I'm calling because some of the old folk are struggling to get out and about. The roads are a mess. The meals on wheels service can't get to the more isolated farms."

I moved the curtain aside to look at the thick blanket of snow. Maybe I could do something. A lot of these guys were Dad's old friends. "Can you send me a list of who needs help? The kitchens are well stocked. I'll get the truck through."

"You're a good lad, Geraint. I knew you'd help. How are you getting on up there with the American? You're on your best behavior? We don't want any more of those reviews."

"I'm on my best behavior, and I'm confident she won't give us a bad review."

That kiss doesn't get a bad review.

A wave of warmth washed over me. The kissing at least was five stars. The rest remained to be seen.

Chapter 20

MADISON

I pressed my nose to the cold windowpane. Sun glanced off the pristine white world outside, dazzling my eyes. Birdsong and the *drip, drip* of thawing ice filled the silence. Everything was so smooth and perfect, like the surface of a wedding cake. Bitterness radiated within. Bryce hadn't liked any of the cakes we'd tested. It was the only part of the wedding he'd bothered with, and it had just been to criticize. He hadn't cared about the planning. Maybe I should have paid more attention to his lack of interest.

How many red flags had I ignored?

The press had nicknamed me the "Thornado" because I took no prisoners on the pitch. Off the pitch, Bryce had taken me for a fool. Water dripped from the icy stalactites hanging from the fence outside. Everything was softening and melting. I rubbed my temples with my fingertips to ease the throbbing ache of my hangover.

Memories of Geraint's kiss pushed into my mind. My skin still prickled from the rough scrape of his beard. Warmth flushed the back of my neck. What had I been thinking, kissing him like that? It was going to be awkward to see him this morning. How was I supposed to act? This wasn't a good idea. Starting anything with him was pointless. What would it hurt, though? A few nights enjoying myself with a man like this couldn't do any harm if that was what he wanted too. He'd seemed to want it last night.

I'm going to make breakfast, and then I'm going to make love to you.

My skin prickled with excitement. I rolled my shoulders. They felt looser than they had in a long time. It was hard not to relax in such beautiful surroundings. I was stuck here for the time being, whether I liked it or not. Honestly, it was a relief. No pressure to perform on the pitch. Nothing to do and nowhere to go. Nobody who knew me. The company wasn't bad, either.

I'm going to make breakfast, and then I'm going to make love to you.

A small smile touched my lips. Neither sounded unappealing.

Downstairs, music drifted to my ears. The gravelly voice grew louder. I stuck my head around the corner to the kitchen. A delicious aroma hit my nose. Geraint had his broad back to me at the stove, stirring something steaming. He was singing. His voice was low, beautiful, and melodic. Who could have expected such a giant man to have such a beautiful voice? A floorboard cracked under my feet. I paused in the doorway. Geraint froze, then swiveled to look at me. He snapped his mouth shut.

"Don't stop on my account."

His laugh was rich and warm. "How long were you standing there?"

"Long enough. How did you learn to sing like that? Sunday school? Let me guess. You were an altar boy."

"My dad ran the choir, but I was no altar boy." His grin overtook his features. "How are you?"

I raised a rueful eyebrow. "Hungover."

He nodded sagely. "The wassail. There's a reason we only drink it at Christmas."

I moved closer, compelled by some invisible thread that tugged me into his orbit. This didn't feel awkward. It never did with him.

His mouth lifted in invitation, and a hopeful glint flickered in his eyes. "Do you want to talk about last night?"

I had the strangest urge to cup his face and stroke his beard. Bryce had always been clean-shaven. I'd never been with a man with facial hair. Geraint's beard had felt divine scraping against my skin when he'd kissed me . . . or when I'd kissed him. It had been me, hadn't it? The memories were fuzzy, but I knew I'd wanted him last night. I still wanted him, but in the cold light of day, my recklessness was easily swept aside. We couldn't do this, could we?

Geraint's huge, hulking presence made it impossible to think straight. Neither of us was drunk. If we kissed again, this would head one direction. The crush of his embrace had made me lose my head. His touch had triggered a shockwave of passion through my body. He'd seemed eager too, which had only been more of a turn-on. This was a physical attraction. No big deal. This man probably spent his life bedding tourists. His moves were no doubt polished to perfection. Who would be able to resist that boyish smile when those dimples appeared above his beard? It didn't mean I had to get carried away.

His eyes on me were gentle and contemplative. Silence swirled between us. A jolt went through me, and it could have been excitement or panic. Maybe both. I'd come here to escape, to lie low and lick my wounds. Not to get into something with another man. This was so unexpected. Could I go to bed with a man and never see him again? It wasn't something I'd ever done before. How could this possibly be a good idea? My heart was already a puddle on the floor.

I took a breath and stepped away. "We were both drinking. It was a moment of madness. Best forgotten about."

The animation left his face before he smoothed his expression. "Right. Of course."

Heat stroked my cheeks. Why hadn't I hidden in my room for the day? I scanned the kitchen, looking for a change of subject. Tupperware boxes littered the huge central island.

"What are you doing with all this food?"

Geraint cleared his throat and turned back to the stove. His low voice was a little dull. "I'm making deliveries. Some of the older people are in remote locations. They can't get to the shops, and the meals on wheels people can't get through."

"You're going to help?"

It shouldn't have surprised me. It was the decent thing to do. I'd grown up in a small community too. Everybody was all up in everybody's business, but in times of crisis, we rallied together. It was wonderful, except when I'd been the focus of everyone's sympathy and attention. Then it had been too much. Would I ever be able to go home again and feel normal?

"I'll be gone for the morning. I'll make you some breakfast before I go."

Just breakfast.

A sudden longing wrapped around my heart. If he went, I'd be here all alone with my thoughts. Just because I'd chosen not to go to bed with him didn't mean I wanted to spend time without him. I was so tired of my thoughts and all these raw, painful feelings that wouldn't budge. I liked his company. Maybe he'd let me come. Even if it was a little strained between us now, awkwardness was preferable to this permanent sorrow that weighed me down.

"Do you need help?"

His expression brightened. "You want to come?"

I did my best to smile, despite the lump that always lingered in my throat. "It's either that or look at fields."

Chapter 21

MADISON

I sat in the passenger seat of Geraint's beat-up 4x4. Outside, rugged countryside flashed by—a world blanketed in white, as though someone had used correction fluid to erase all their mistakes and start over. Snow-tipped mountains loomed large, and icy lakes sparkled. We could have been in a different era. This landscape must have looked the same for centuries, wild and unspoiled.

I sighed and slumped in the passenger seat. Ever since the wedding, it had been like my insides were caught in a Chinese finger trap. Everything inside me felt tight and stuck. The more I pulled against that feeling, the worse it became. Maybe this was what I needed. To relax in this wilderness. To stop struggling against this horrible scratchy feeling that kept me awake all night. If only I could let go, even a little. If only this hard ball inside could soften.

The food aroma filled the entire truck. We drove in silence as the enormous vehicle trundled through the snow. From time to time, Geraint glanced at me, but he held his tongue. We'd hardly spoken since I'd offered to come with him. It wasn't awkward. Something about his silence soothed me. Sitting in this truck and gazing at glacial lakes and pristine beauty was as close to peaceful as I'd felt in months.

The wheels skidded and revved over snow toward a ramshackle farmhouse. We pulled up next to a stone wall topped with a layer of snow at least as high as the wall itself. A field stretched between us and the house.

"I can't get the truck through there. We'll have to walk the rest of the way."

I pushed the truck door past a mountain of snow and stepped outside. Freezing air blasted me. Geraint loaded his arms with Tupperware boxes.

"This is Daffyd's place."

I grabbed some boxes of food and picked my way through the snow, then hopped over the fence. I twisted to see Geraint still on the other side. His dark brows slanted into a frown, and his mouth clamped thin. Perhaps this wouldn't be easy for him with his limp. Shame made my insides cold. I hadn't even thought to ask if he needed a hand. I didn't dare. He might take offense again. What had happened to his leg? Some kind of injury? I was curious, but it wasn't my place to pry.

He scanned the fence and flashed a faint smile. "There's a gate down there. I'll meet you on the other side."

I waited while he plowed his way through the snow. On the other side, we continued our difficult trudge to the farmhouse. Before we'd made it halfway down the drive, the door to the house swung open. Three golden spaniels darted out and sprinted straight for us. They dashed around us in excited circles, jumping at Geraint. He laughed and held the Tupperware boxes high. His arms were too laden with food to pet the dogs, but I had a feeling that was what he would have been doing if he could have.

The man at the front door looked as crooked and old as the farmhouse. His face lit with a beaming smile when he saw us. He called out something in Welsh, and the two men conversed. The man's eyes flashed to mine and back to Geraint. He wore a teasing smile, and whatever he said made Geraint roll his eyes and grimace in good humor.

Daffyd's aged face crinkled into a welcoming smile. "Come in, both of you. I've got the kettle on." The man's eyes landed on me. "You need to introduce me to your new American girlfriend. I went to California once. I'll have to tell you about it."

Geraint toed at the ground. "This is Madison. She's my guest at the Dragon. I told you, she's not my girlfriend, and I'm sure Aled already told her about the lasagna."

"No. I'm his fake girlfriend to be drafted in in emergencies, and this is the first I've heard about a lasagna."

The old man's smile widened, and his eyes twinkled. "The two of you make a handsome pair. In you come. You won't believe how many lunches I got out of it."

Every delivery was the same. The farmers all insisted we come in for a cup of tea. After the first couple of houses, I'd thought Geraint might be more forceful with his polite declines, but he wasn't. He went through the motions every time. He seemed happy to sit at a kitchen table and be told about a lasagna for an hour. I'd never drunk so much tea in my life. My bladder hated me. After the fifth house and cup of tea, I slid into the passenger seat next to Geraint.

"These farmers can really talk."

He smiled. "True."

I cast an eye up at the sky. The sun went down early in winter. We'd be doing this all day and night at this rate.

"We're not going to get to everyone if we keep stopping to chat."

"We'll get round to everyone."

"Right, but maybe we can wrap the next one up quicker. We don't need tea every time."

Geraint scraped a hand over his beard and wrapped his fingers around the steering wheel. "Daffyd's wife died a couple of years back. He lives out here alone. This is probably the only conversation he's had all week. It's the same with most of these old folk. They're alone. Every cup of tea is important."

Guilt heated my cheeks. Geraint turned the key in the ignition, and the engine revved to life. I couldn't help but glance at him. His massive shoulders filled the coat he wore, and his profile was rugged and strong against the weak sunlight. He'd given out enough food today to cater an entire restaurant for a month.

I settled back in the seat. "It's nice that the community looks out for each other."

"That's what Dad loved about the Dragon. He didn't want anybody to feel alone."

"He sounds like he was a kind man. My dad is the same. He'd do anything for anyone."

Geraint inclined his head in a nod. "It's a good way to be."

A memory drifted back to me. Bryce had taken me for a fancy meal once, and he'd spent the whole time moaning about how much the food had cost. He'd been so rude to the waitress that I'd apologized to her when he'd left to go to the bathroom. I'd always overlooked his behavior and written it off with excuses. Now I saw it in a whole new light. No wonder my parents hadn't liked him. Helping people in need was the kind of thing that came naturally to my dad. He was always the guy raising money when people needed it. Bryce wasn't that guy. Why hadn't that bothered me? How had I been so blind? These were the things that mattered most.

Geraint flashed a jovial smile. "It's what anyone would do."

My parents had brought me up right. They'd taught me to do my best to help people, but the thing was, not everyone was like that. Some people were selfish. Some people didn't care that they hurt others, as long as they were happy. Bryce had hurt me, and he hadn't apologized. I was breaking my heart over a man who could do something so horrible without remorse. My hands bunched into fists in my lap.

"No. They wouldn't."

Geraint gave me a questioning glance.

"You said anybody would do this. They wouldn't. Not everybody." I sat taller in my seat. "This village is lucky to have you."

He rubbed the back of his neck and mumbled, "The pub is important to this community. We only have a handful of regulars, but it matters to them. I can't stand to see it vanish."

"Why would it vanish?"

"My lease is up, so the brewery wants to sell. If I can't put together a decent plan, I'll have to leave. I'll have to let Aled and Ewan go. My dad loved the pub. I have to hold on to it for him."

"What will you do if you can't?"

His affability slipped for a moment, to be replaced by a look of tired sadness. "I don't know."

"You can't buy it yourself?"

"It's too much. The bank won't lend me that much."

It would be awful for him to lose the place that clearly meant so much to him. There had to be a way I could help. I was in a fortunate position financially. I'd played professionally for a long time, and I'd made some good sponsorship deals and investments. My parents had grown up poor, and they'd made sure I understood the value of money. I'd been prudent over the years.

"I could loan you the money."

Geraint's jaw clenched. "It's too much."

"It's only money."

He glanced at me incredulously. "Only money?" He shook his head. "It's a huge amount of money."

"I can afford it."

His brows drew downward in a frown. "I'd never be able to take that from you."

"But if the bank offered you a loan, you'd take it, wouldn't you? What's the big deal? If you really want to save your pub, there's no place for pride—"

"I would never feel comfortable with that." His forehead creased with worry. "Please don't ask me again." A flash of gray stone caught my eye. An old chapel sat in a shallow valley in the center of the snow-covered fields. Memories crashed into my head. My breath caught in my lungs. I'd seen this place so many times in photos.

"Wait," I cried. "Stop the truck. That's the church. This is where my parents got married."

Chapter 22

Madison

Ice-capped mountains surrounded us as we powered through fresh powder to the tiny stone chapel. The church sat amid an endless white panorama. It didn't look like much—a heap of cracked stained glass and crumbling stone piled at ramshackle angles, as though it was sinking into the snow. The drip of melting ice greeted us at the arched wooden door.

Geraint pushed the door open with a huge creak, and we stepped into the cool, echoing stillness. Strange that they didn't keep it locked. I supposed it was so remote, it was unlikely to fall foul of trespassers. Wooden beams creaked overhead, and weak sunlight streamed through the ancient stained-glass windows. A faint musty smell like the pages of old Bibles hit my nose.

I ran my hands over a worn wooden pew. "Have you been inside here before?"

Geraint stared at the faded lectern with a critical squint. "Yes."

My boots squeaked on the stone floor as I walked up the aisle alone, trailing slush. My parents had stood on this spot all those years ago and exchanged their vows. They'd been so young. No kids or house. No responsibilities to tie them down. Just a young couple in love. Pain speared my heart. It was masochistic to come here. My parents' love story had always filled me with such hope. I'd wanted so badly to find a love like that.

Everlasting love was for other people.

Geraint stood next to me, both of us facing the altar. His solid presence made my breath hitch. My heart pounded at his nearness. The silence thickened, and I spoke to break it.

"I grew up hearing so much about this church."

He glanced at me. "My parents married here, too."

"They did?"

He swallowed and kept his gaze fixed on the font. "So did I."

I waited for him to say more, but the echoing silence pulsed around us.

"How long were you married?"

He rubbed the back of his neck, and his boot squeaked as he dragged it over the stone floor. "Two years."

I peered at the stained-glass window, which depicted a woman in a white dress with flowing red hair and a crown of flowers. Saint Dwynwen. This was her church. The Welsh patron saint of lovers. A heavy weight settled over me. My parents must have been so excited and joyous all those years ago. That was how I'd felt before the rug was pulled from underneath me.

I swallowed past the fiery ache in my throat. "Mom used to tell me the story of Saint Dwynwen. She drank a potion to forget about a man she was betrothed to, but it turned him into a block of ice. Do you know it?"

Geraint inclined his head. "It's a well-known story here. We have Saint Dwynwen's Day. It's a day for lovers, like Valentine's Day. Dwynwen begged God for three wishes." He counted them on his fingers. "To thaw her lover, to help lovers be together, and to never marry. She lived the rest of her days as a hermit."

I couldn't help my bitter laugh. "Good for her."

The silence stretched tighter until Geraint cleared his throat. "This man that makes you cry in your sleep. What did he do to you?"

He crushed my dreams for the future. He made me into this person I don't want to be.

I couldn't bear to tell him. It had been nice to be treated normally for once. Easier to give the abridged version. "He broke my heart."

Geraint's voice was as low and melodic as a hymn. "Then he didn't deserve it."

The truth wrapped around me, as crushing and life-sucking as a boa constrictor. No. He didn't. I'd been impulsive. My biological clock had been a drum marching me toward a firing squad. I'd been desperate to quit soccer and start a family. I'd leaped into an engagement like jumping into the deep end of the pool, eyes shut, holding my breath, feet first. Bryce was the wrong man. He'd always been the wrong man. I'd ignored every red flag, despite how violently they'd flapped in my face.

I'd thought that moving halfway across the world would help, but I couldn't get away from my own thoughts and feelings. It didn't matter how far I went, I couldn't get away from this grim ball that weighed heavy inside. I longed to go back to normal.

Geraint rubbed the back of his neck with one hand and slipped off his heavy hat with the other. He scuffed his boot on the stone floor. "My wife left me after I knackered my knee and couldn't play rugby anymore."

An injury. I'd suspected as much. Why else would a rugby player so young end up in a kitchen? I kept my voice low and soft. "What happened to your knee?"

"An ACL tear. I landed funny after a dive. I heard it pop before I even felt it."

My heart sank. An anterior cruciate ligament tear was one injury that I'd always feared. It was common in soccer, too. Even more common in women than men.

"They couldn't repair it?"

He sighed. "Two surgeries and then nine months of rehab. I spent every penny I had on experts, and my first week back it tore again. Another two surgeries. Another year of rehab. I gave up after the third tear. It wasn't meant to be. Sometimes your body just won't let you do the things you want to do."

"I'm sorry."

"It is what it is. It caused me a lot of trouble at the start. Rugby was my life. I didn't know who I was without it. I'm sure you know what I'm talking about."

Guilt rushed over me. I couldn't remember when my interest in soccer had faded. The training schedules, the early mornings, and the stress of match days had all become too much. In my lowest moments, I'd secretly hoped for an injury. Nothing terrible, but enough so I could take a break and reassess my life. It was all a grind. Bryce had been my way out.

Geraint raised a wry eyebrow. "We stood in this very spot and made the vows. Jess liked the *in health* and *for richer* parts. Just not the other bits."

How could he be so jovial about it? It must have been an awful time. "Aren't you angry?"

He frowned. "Angry? No. Not anymore. I was for a long time. Furious. I wasn't fun to be around, but I don't blame Jess for wanting out. She'd married an athlete at the top of his game, and she got stuck with an invalid. She didn't want to be a nurse, and I couldn't stand to be fussed over when my life was falling apart."

He glanced at me. "The thing about anger is that it doesn't help anything. It's like pushing a rugby ball under water. The harder you push, the harder it comes back to smack you in the face. With time, I realized I wasn't angry anyway. I'd lost my career, my wife—everything. Then I had to move back here with my dad. I was angry because it was harder to admit the truth."

"What truth?"

He rubbed his beard thoughtfully. "Anger is easy. It makes you feel powerful. You don't get to feel powerful when you're sad. But that was the truth. I was sad." He rolled his huge shoulders. "It's in the past. I wish Jess all the best. I don't miss her. People come and go through this place. It used to be easy enough to find a woman to share a bed with. It's difficult to meet someone to build something with."

Amusement passed through me. "Easy, huh?"

He pressed his lips together and shrugged. Is that how he spent his summers? Bedding tourists? No doubt women threw themselves at him. I couldn't blame them. What was it with this man? I couldn't decide if I wanted him to give me an orgasm, a hug, or cuss me out for being such a grump all the time. Maybe all three.

I knew one thing. Something about his affable demeanor made me want to bait him. He was a mountain—solid and strong—and I wanted to crash against him and make a dent. If only I could be a mountain too, instead of always being the storm. It wasn't fair to him. That was the worst part of being angry all the time, the way it hurt everyone around me.

Maybe I was sad too. I still hated Bryce for what he'd done to me, but I missed being with someone. I missed the feeling of being wrapped in strong arms. It had been so long since I'd been held, or touched, or cared about. I missed the feeling of being with a lover. How could I trust another man? Bryce hadn't just betrayed me, he'd humiliated me in front of all my family and friends. I'd never put myself into such a vulnerable position again. Even being in this church gave me palpitations. Maybe I didn't always have to be angry. If Geraint had moved on, did that mean there was hope for me?

Geraint's hand brushed mine. My breath caught in my throat. His kiss last night had been sweet but persuasive. How would today have gone if I'd been brave enough to admit I wanted him? I wanted to kiss him again. Would he have me? A rush of nerves made my heart race. I'd only ever slept with Bryce and my high-school boyfriend. We were standing in a church, and I was having feelings about this man that were decidedly unholy.

"So, you've slept with a lot of women?"

His eyebrow arched in surprise. "I don't think you're supposed to ask people about their body count in church."

Amusement ran through me at his prim, serious expression. "Their body count?"

"Yes. It's completely inappropriate." He raised a playful eyebrow. "Shame on you, Kentucky."

A small laugh bubbled up and escaped. It echoed in the church, loud and strange. A long-forgotten sound.

His brow lifted higher. "It's not funny. I came to Sunday school in this church."

I laughed harder. It wasn't funny, but for some reason, I couldn't stop. A wave of warmth passed through me. The more I tried to suppress my giggles, the more laughter rocked my body. My laugh filled the echoing chapel, until I had no idea why I was laughing. I just knew it felt good. It had been so long.

Geraint's face was full of amused wonder. "You're laughing."

My stomach hurt with laughter, and I gripped it. "It's your face."

He frowned. "What about my face?"

"You look so serious. I didn't take you for a prude."

"I'm not a prude, but we're in a church." He dropped his voice to a whisper. "I don't think it's the decent thing to be talking about in a church."

A sudden rush of recklessness made a smile pull at my lips. I wanted this man. To heck with the consequences.

His smile contained a sensuous flame. "Can we at least go outside and have this conversation?"

I laced my fingers through his, feeling his rough, calloused palm. "Come on, then."

Chapter 23

MADISON

The graves were white lumps in the snow outside the church. I still hadn't let go of Geraint's hand. Excitement sparked through my veins. I held still, forcing him to stop.

"We're outside. Are you going to kiss me?"

He cupped my cheek, his face serious. All traces of laughter had disappeared. His fingers were cool as they curled into my chin. "Are you sure that's what you want?"

The words took me back to my dad's tractor and his worried face on the way to the church.

Are you sure about this?

I wasn't sure about anything, only that it had been good to laugh, and I wanted to hold on to some goodness. A swath of dark hair fell over Geraint's forehead, and my fingers itched to brush it back. Geraint was good. He was hardworking, fun, and gentle. I could have pushed him away with something snarky, but he looked too sincere. Every part of my body burned with need.

"I'm sure."

Geraint pulled me into his arms. The warmth of his body was so hard and bracing. Wet flakes flurried around us, but I hardly felt them. He clasped me tightly, his mouth capturing mine. His kisses were surprisingly restrained. The sweet tenderness of his lips on mine made me tremble. I wanted something fiery and devouring. I wanted to forget myself, but Geraint's kisses were the dreamy, intimate kind that left you weak and confused. He showered slow, shivery kisses around my lips and along my jaw. He kissed the tip of my nose and whispered against my cheek, "You're going to get cold. Let's go."

I didn't want to. I could have stood outside the church and kissed him like this until we turned to ice, but he didn't give me time to protest. His hand wrapped around mine, and he led me to his 4x4. He opened the passenger door and helped me inside before he sank into the driver's seat.

He flashed me a tender glance. "Seat belt."

I held my hands up. "I think my hands might be too cold again. You'll have to help me."

The look on his face mingled eagerness and tenderness. "Oh, I see."

He leaned across me and took the belt from my fingers. My heart hammered to have him so close. I wanted something wild and reckless like my fantasy. I wanted him to make me forget about Bryce and the sorrow that had weighed me down in the church. My lips touched his. I wound my arms inside his heavy coat and around his back. The feel of his mouth on mine sent a giddy pleasure through my veins. Sliding my hands down his body, I worked the button of his jeans. His hands gripped mine, stilling me.

I froze. "What is it?"

His broad shoulders heaved as he breathed. His voice was low and hoarse. "There's no room."

"Make some."

He fumbled around by the side of his seat. My body jerked as he found the lever to push the seat back. I pushed him lightly back into the seat and climbed onto his lap, straddling him. My thighs wrapped around his hips. He was so huge, I had to crane my neck to stop my head hitting the roof of the cab. The steering wheel pressed against my backside, and one knee drove against the gear lever. My lips found their way instinctively to his.

He returned my kiss before he groaned. "Someone could see us."

I buried my face in his neck. The masculine scent of his cologne filled my nose, cool and fresh. His beard rasped my lips as I planted kisses on his throat. "There's no one around."

He held perfectly still. Unease crept over me. Why wasn't he kissing me back?

"I thought you wanted this." I shifted in his lap and peered up into his face. The hard press of him between my thighs electrified me. It felt like he wanted it.

"I told you. I want you." He tilted his brow, looking at me uncertainly.

"Then what's the problem?"

His dark eyes shimmered with light from the window. "Not like this. Not in the truck."

"Why not?"

"Because we're going to do this properly. This isn't what you need."

Impatience surged through me. I didn't even try to keep the sarcasm from my voice. "What I need? There's nothing I love more than being mansplained what I need."

With a rough finger, he traced the line of my cheekbone and jaw. His expression stilled and grew serious. His voice was tender. "I'm going to give you what you need. I'm going to make you dinner, and then I'm going to make love to you."

My body flooded with heat at the same time as a twinge of discomfort went through me. That wasn't what I wanted from this man, or any man. Nothing deep.

What a way to kill the mood. "Oh, really? And here I was thinking I just need an orgasm."

Laughter flickered in his eyes as they met mine. My irritation only seemed to amuse him. "Don't worry, Kentucky. There'll be plenty of those."

Chapter 24

Madison

Silence wrapped around us as we drove over one treacherous mountain road after the next. The energy between us had shifted into something charged and wild. My heart pounded with anticipation at what would happen when we stepped inside the pub. His soft words kept repeating in my head.

I'm going to give you what you need.

No. Ridiculous. I needed to get off. I needed to feel something different. That's all this was.

Geraint stopped the Ford outside the pub and walked around to open my door. I slid out of the truck. Cold air wrapped around me. I shivered and pulled my coat tighter. Geraint looked down at me intensely. Concern lit his dark eyes.

"You're freezing. Let me get the fire on and warm you up."

He unlocked the front door and turned back to me. With one huge hand at my waist, he drew me to him. I brushed my lips against his. This couldn't last, but so what? I couldn't live my life with the regret of never being with this man. His kiss was tender and sweet, but I wanted more. My mouth moved with more urgency against his. He groaned a low, wild growl of desire. Then I was weightless. He swept me into the cradle of his powerful arms, and I wrapped my thighs around his middle. His kiss grew hungry, leaving my mouth burning with fire. His lips didn't leave mine as he carried me through the dark hallway to the pub lounge.

I whispered into his ear. "You can put me down if it's hurting your knee."

His mouth found a path along my jaw and neck. "I don't want to put you down now that I have you."

My skin smoldered where his huge hands cupped my ass. He deposited me gently in front of the giant hearth. I helped him throw the logs in and watched as he lit the fire. I held my palms to the growing flames. The heat soothed me.

"I'll make you something to eat."

I flashed him a glance. "Don't you dare disappear into that kitchen. I'm not hungry. Not for food."

"You need to eat. It's been a long day."

I pulled him to me. "I'll eat. Just not yet. I have other needs first. I thought you wanted to give me what I need?"

He studied my face for a moment before his dark eyebrows arched mischievously. "Then you'd better lie down."

"Here?"

He inclined his head in a nod. "Here."

I lay down on the soft sheepskin rug in front of the fire. He lowered his heavy body over mine. The delicious weight of him drew a moan from me. His eyes met mine, and I had the strangest feeling, like I was scaling a mountain. The summit was unknowable, but once I got there, I wouldn't be able to go back the way I'd come. There was only forward. I hardly knew this man, but I had no desire to back out of his embrace. His solid, affable presence was safe and peaceful. I wanted him, even if it was just for today. I couldn't leave here without knowing what it was like to be with him.

I broke away from his kiss and propped myself on my elbows. I took a breath, pulled my sweater and T-shirt over my head, and dropped them to the side. His gaze dropped over my breasts nestled in my bra. I wished I'd worn something sexier, but I hadn't expected to be laid out like this on a rug in front of a fire. He caressed the planes of my back and slipped his hands slowly up my arms. I lay back down, the warm rug soft and delicious under my bare back. The searing heat from the fire and his touch made me moan with anticipation. With deft hands, he unhooked my bra and tossed it away.

"That seemed well practiced."

He smiled, and his gaze dropped over me. "Maybe, but I don't think I've ever had a view I've enjoyed quite like this."

My nipples swelled to hard peaks under his heated gaze. I moaned when his cool hands smoothed over my breasts. "Look at you. So perfect."

The contrast between the warmth of the flames licking over my skin and his icy palms was divine. He bowed his head, caressing my sensitive, swollen nipples with his tongue. One hand slid across my waist to the swell of my hips. A thunderous noise snatched my attention to the window. The soft snow had given way to huge hailstones that battered the glass. My heart hammered along with the frenzied noise.

Slowly, Geraint peeled off his cable-knit sweater and T-shirt to reveal his colossal muscular torso. The fire cast its flickering orange glow over a bloom of intricate Celtic tattoos that painted his left shoulder and disappeared beneath the thick, dark covering of hair on his chest. He was a beast of a man, all ink and hard muscle. Illuminated by flames, he looked savage and brutal, a caveman ready to hunt his prey, but his touch was tender and his voice soothing and melodic. Heat pooled between my thighs. Bryce was a twig compared to this goliath. Was I really about to do this? How had my life led me here? Half-naked in front of a man I hardly knew, desperate for him to claim me.

He hooked his finger into the waistband of my panties, and I lifted my hips to let him pull them off. His rough hands smoothed all over my body. Heat rushed to every place his calloused palms grazed. I couldn't help my sighs of pleasure. No man had ever touched me like this. Bryce had never taken the time. Heat climbed my neck as Geraint's intense gaze drilled into me.

Just as I was starting to worry something was wrong, he bowed his head between my legs and planted hot, open-mouthed kisses all over my inner thighs. It was so leisurely that the anticipation was driving me mad. His tongue traced a line up my delicate folds and rested on my clit. The intense sensation sent a shockwave through my body. A moan escaped my lips. His tongue flicked in deliberate strokes where I needed him to relieve the aching pulse of need. He gripped my ass, lifting me, spreading and opening me wider. Pleasure radiated from where he devoured my hot flesh as though he had no intention of ever coming up for air.

I combed my fingers through his mass of soft hair while my brain whirled and skidded. No one who knew me would ever imagine I'd be spread on this rug like this, with this man drawing these moans from me. Low growls escaped Geraint's lips. He feasted as though I was the most delicious meal in the whole pub. His fierce probing and sucking made my bones turn to jelly. While one hand reached up to tantalize my nipples, the other hand slid up and down my ribs. Then he stopped licking and hummed.

My head dropped back. An unintelligible stream of words left my lips. If I hadn't been able to pronounce his name before, I definitely couldn't now. Everything in me tightened, hurtling toward release. Even the feeling I'd had in my fantasy couldn't come close to the real Geraint between my thighs. A series of gasps left my lips.

Release tore through me. I ground against him, raking my hands through his hair and digging my nails into his huge shoulders.

He spoke in his soft, melodic way, but I couldn't understand a word of it. I managed to grind out some words. My back arched, and he gripped my hips. He planted hot kisses up to my collarbones.

"I have condoms upstairs." His breath was a hot whisper against my throat. "Will you come to my room?"

"No."

He froze. His face was still and serious. "No? You don't want to? It's okay if you've changed your mind or—"

"I'm on birth control. It helps my skin . . . long story . . . don't stop."

His intense eyes locked with mine. He pulled down his boxers, and my eyes dropped to follow the movement. His erection sprang out, huge and impressive, like every other inch of him. I swallowed past the nervous lump in my throat.

He lowered his weight over me again. "Are you sure you want this?"

"Yes."

He wrapped a hand around the base of his shaft, and then his hardness pushed against me. I squirmed, the muscles inside of me bearing down, desperate to be full. He swirled the tip of his shaft up through my folds and in firm circles around my clit, spreading the wetness. A moan escaped me at the teasing motion. I was so ready for him. Every cell in my body screamed for him to press me into the rug.

He slipped inside. Just the tip. The sudden stretch and burn made me gasp.

He pressed his forehead against mine, breathing hard. "Okay?"

"Don't stop."

He pushed inside a little further. An electric shock scorched through my body. As much as it felt good, he was huge, and it was a struggle to adjust to the size. I wrapped my fingers around his back, bracing myself. He pushed forward, claiming another inch of me. I gritted my teeth. With a snap of his hips, he sheathed himself to the hilt. The sudden fullness burned, but in the best way possible. Another moan slipped from me.

He pressed my palms high over my head as he worked inside of me. I buried my face in his shoulder, yielding to the movement that pinned me to the rug and to the excruciating need where our bodies joined. His tantalizing manly scent wrapped around me.

His breath was hot against my ear, his words a tender murmur. "That's it, baby. Let it out."

His fingers found where I ached for his touch, and he strummed in smooth strokes in time with his thrusts. Everything inside of me tightened. I wasn't climbing a mountain anymore but losing my grip, hurtling down, not knowing if I'd be saved or smashed to pieces. Nothing existed beyond tight, agonizing need. Nothing but the summit of a mountain I was desperate to reach.

My breath came in surrendering gasps. The intense sensations overwhelmed me. Heat caressed my skin where our bodies molded together. The heavy pelt of hailstones thundered in my ears. The relentless sharp pounding inside me made me cry out and grip his broad back.

His voice was a low growl. "Look at me, baby. Don't close your eyes."

I did as he commanded. Flames smoldered in his dark eyes. This was supposed to be physical, nothing more. I shouldn't have been gazing into his eyes. I shouldn't have noticed the rawness and vulnerability flickering in their depths. Without a single word, everything was spoken in our deep, lingering eye contact. It was an intertwining beyond skin on skin and tangling limbs. An indefinable moment of understanding between us that sent a shockwave through me.

A rush of emotion overwhelmed me and pushed me over the edge. Release tore through me, a hot, sharp explosion of pleasure that made me shudder and gasp. Pleasure radiated in waves from my core. He worked me through every quiver with long, slow strokes until my body went limp. He groaned, and his face contorted as he found his own release. We lay together on the rug, panting and trembling as we came back to earth. A sudden wave of emotion surged through me like a door unlocked. Heat pressed behind my eyes.

Geraint twisted me in his arms. His face was full of concern. "Are you okay? What is it? Did I do something wrong?"

A tear slipped down my cheek. "No."

The animation left his face. "You're crying. What is it? I went too rough?"

He looked so worried that I moved to cup his cheeks. His rough beard scraped my palms. "No, you didn't. It's not you."

A faint thread of panic edged his voice. "Then what?"

I wiped my cheeks with the back of my hands. What was wrong with me? This was supposed to be a physical thing, and here I was weeping. "It's not you. I just feel . . . I don't know . . . overwhelmed."

The harder I tried to hold back my tears, the stronger my sobs grew. "I'm sorry."

His voice was a husky whisper. "Never say sorry for how you feel. You don't need to apologize to me, cariad."

"Cariad?"

"Darling." Geraint sat up and opened his enormous arms. "Here."

I moved forward, and he wrapped me in the warmth of his powerful embrace. He stroked my back gently, and I sagged against him, naked and spent. The strength and safety of his arms soothed me.

I wiped my tears and tried to come back to myself. My heart ached, but Geraint's arms felt like a hiding place. Somewhere to feel safe. His breath was hot against my cheek as he whispered his comforting words in a language I didn't understand. I'd cried for weeks after the wedding day, before the numbness and anger took root. I hadn't expected to cry again. Not here. Not now. In Geraint's powerful arms, I cried for the little girl who had always dreamed of a perfect wedding day, and for the teenager with Pinterest boards full of white dresses and bouquets. I cried because I was so far from home and so lost. The warmth and strength of him gave me a refuge. A cubbyhole. I cried until there was nothing left.

My stomach growled, then clenched in a sudden, unaccustomed pain. Another rumbling sound escaped my belly, and it churned hollowly. My cheeks warmed, and I slipped my hands to my middle.

Geraint stroked my hair back from my face. "Are you okay?"

I took a breath. I hadn't had an appetite in so long, I hardly recognized the feeling of hunger. Surprise lifted my eyebrows. "Maybe we *should* have started with the dinner."

His rich laughter was a full-hearted sound. "I can help you with that."

Chapter 25

MADISON

Geraint passed me his T-shirt. It was far too big, falling past my knees, but the manly scent that enveloped me was divine. He laid out a tartan picnic blanket in front of the fire and brought me plate after plate of delicious food: soup, cold meats, stew, buttered leeks, freshly baked bread. The rich aroma filled the entire pub. I ate with relish, each bite interspersed with a groan of pleasure. I raised my eyes to find Geraint watching me.

A glint of humor flickered in his eyes. "Good?"

I didn't want to stop eating to talk. I gave him a thumbs-up until I'd finished my delicious mouthful. "So good. My compliments to the chef."

He raised a bemused brow. "And how is the Glamorgan sausage?"

It was perfection. Crisp golden breadcrumbs coated mild, fresh Caerphilly cheese that melted in my mouth. "You already know I'm a fan. I could get used to Glamorgan sausage."

His eyes grew openly amused. "I'm starting to worry. You seem to be enjoying this part more than what happened on the rug."

I smothered a warm bread roll in rich butter. "My compliments are to the chef in both respects."

His laugh was rich and warm. After all these months, my appetite had returned with a vengeance. It was as though I'd been wandering lost in the desert, and I'd finally found a place to eat. Outside, fresh snow fell in soft flakes that floated silently past the windows. The spiraling flurries gave no indication they might slow, but this time they melted as they hit the wet ground. A pain speared my heart. When the snow vanished, we wouldn't be alone here anymore. I couldn't think of that now. In this moment, we were a scene in a snow globe, caught under a glass dome in perfect isolation. We'd made our own world on this rug, and no one could disturb us.

Orange flames curled and flickered in the hearth. Weariness made my body heavy and relaxed. I couldn't stop my guilty gaze from roving over Geraint's impressive muscular frame. I was drooling over the sight of him, as much as the delicious feast. I could get used to a man who cooked like this.

"I'm going to be dragging myself around the pitch after all this food. The Calverdale nutritionist is not going to be impressed with you. As divine as they are, Welsh cakes are not part of my dietary regimen."

He waved a dismissive hand. "You're on vacation. No regimens, no training. I remember what that was all like. You need a break from it sometimes. As long as you bring your A game when you need to, you're fine."

Right, except I'd left my A game at customs before I got on the flight to the UK. I sighed, and pulled myself up into the armchair by the fire.

"What is it?" Geraint gave me a concerned look from where he lounged at the foot of the armchair.

I shrugged. "Gabe Rivers brought me here because he wants his team to go up the league. He's probably regretting that decision now."

"Oh?"

I kept my gaze fixed on the fire. The words got caught in my throat.

Geraint rested his chin on my knee and gazed at me. "You're part of a team. You all work together. Whatever the problem, it's never all on one person."

"Believe me, this is on me. Ever since I left the US, it feels like . . ."

The words got stuck again. Geraint's curious gaze made the back of my neck hot. It shamed me to think how readily I'd been willing to let soccer go when I'd met Bryce. Soccer was my greatest passion, and I would have thrown it aside for him, as if it meant nothing. I'd lost myself so completely. Everything had been about Bryce, but I'd pretended to myself, and everyone around me, that I liked it that way. We ate in the restaurants he favored, we went on daytrips to the places he wanted to visit. I stopped seeing my friends, and hardly called my family from LA. Somewhere along the way, I lost myself. Maybe that was why I hadn't known better about Bryce. I'd overridden my own intuition so many times. My family had seen the problem, and I'd ignored them whenever they'd tried to talk to me about it. Worse than that, I'd been so stubborn, I'd doubled down on them and defended Bryce so vehemently.

When I'd first stepped on the pitch, wearing the Calverdale jersey, my heart had raced with excitement. I still had the spark, but I hadn't performed anywhere near my normal level. I'd abandoned soccer for Bryce, and now soccer had abandoned me. Gabe was wasting his time if he thought I could help his team. All I could do was let everyone down. My eyes filled with sudden tears. The fire roared in my ears.

Geraint's voice was gentle. "Feels like what?"

"It doesn't matter." I pulled my knees up close to my body and hugged them. "I don't want to talk about it."

Silence wrapped around us. Flames flickered over Geraint's rugged features as he watched me, but he didn't push it. When I went back to work, we'd be playing one of our most important matches, a local derby with one of our biggest rivals, and our first to be televised. If we won, there was a chance we could go to the top of the league table. It would be a battle to stay there, and one we probably wouldn't win, but for a team that had earned promotion so recently, even a couple of days at the top would be incredible. This was why Gabe had brought me here.

My form had been terrible so far, but it hadn't cost us too much. This game would matter. The team would be expecting big things from me. Worse than that, everyone would be watching on TV back home. I'd have another chance to humiliate myself in front of everyone who had been sitting in that church. A wave of tiredness engulfed me. I smothered my yawn.

Geraint flashed a faint smile. "Room for more dessert?"

I patted my middle. "Not unless I want to burst."

"Come on, then."

He rose to his feet and swept me out of the chair into his huge arms. He carried me out of the lounge and to the staircase. I moved to return to my room, but he grabbed my hand and pulled me down the landing.

His expression was intense and serious. "No. You're in my bed tonight."

I should have protested, but thinking about returning to play football had stoked up so many horrible feelings. I just needed to forget it all, and being wrapped in Geraint's arms helped to block everything out. We collapsed into bed together, exhausted and satisfied. He held me, stroked my hair, and planted gentle kisses on my forehead and along my jaw. For the first time in as long as I could remember, I fell asleep with something approaching a smile.

Chapter 26

Geraint

Madison stirred in my arms. I stilled so as not to wake her. The sheet slipped from her body, and I couldn't keep my gaze from drifting down her athletic legs. An unwelcome tension made my shoulders tight. I'd promised myself I wouldn't do this again. These flings only ever made me feel used and hollow. Still, I couldn't resist her. Not after hearing her laughter echoing in that church.

My fingers itched to stroke her soft, shiny hair, but I wouldn't disturb her. She looked peaceful like this, without whatever was haunting her gathered in the shadows under her eyes. Would she regret it? She'd leave me soon, the way women who passed through here always did. I'd had so many fleeting attachments, but none like this. Yesterday, in the church and when we'd feasted in front of the fire, she'd laughed and made jokes. I wanted to keep making her laugh. I could care for her. I could put the color back in her cheeks and more meat on her bones.

Her eyes flashed open and held mine. For a moment, she looked confused. Then the beginnings of a smile tipped the corners of her mouth. "Bore da."

I kept my voice deadpan. "I didn't realize you spoke Welsh."

She smiled. A beautiful smile. A genuine smile. "Did I get it right?"

"It was perfect."

She cocked her head to the side with bemused suspicion. "Really?"

"No. Absolutely terrible."

She stared at me, then burst out laughing. Sometimes it was awkward waking up after a night like that, but she seemed relaxed. My fingers itched to touch her again, but I had to get a sense of how she felt about what had happened between us. Maybe she regretted it. I hoped not.

"Did you sleep well?"

Her brows flickered a little. "I closed my eyes and now it's morning. I didn't have a single dream." Her face took on a relieved expression. "That's good. Really good. I've been having a lot of nightmares."

"I'm sorry."

She stretched her arms above her head. The covers slipped low, revealing her beautiful breasts. A blush like a shadow ran across her cheeks, and she covered herself. That wouldn't do. I couldn't have her going away from our time together feeling embarrassed. I had to fight my overwhelming need to pull her toward me and bury myself in her. As much as I needed to feel myself moving inside her again, it wasn't for the best. She'd leave soon. I'd have to let her go.

Her eyelashes fluttered against her cheeks, and she edged closer. "It was nice yesterday, wasn't it?"

I kept my voice casual. "Very nice." I pressed a kiss to the soft hollow of her neck.

She frowned and moved away. "I haven't showered."

Good. I'd loved the taste and smell of her on my tongue last night. I whispered low in her ear. "It doesn't matter."

Her eyes searched my face. If she wanted to kiss me, I'd let her come to me. Her lips were so close to mine. Her hand slipped lower. A groan left my lips, unbidden. I'd woken up so hard this morning. My whole body ached with longing. She moved her hand up and down my erection in a slow, torturous movement. My head fell back on the pillow.

A sigh of pleasure escaped me. She increased her pace, working me. She nibbled my earlobe before moving her lips to my neck. Then she disappeared under the covers, planting soft kisses down my torso to my belly button. Her lips left a tingling trail of fire.

"You don't have to do that," I said.

"I know." Her playful words came muffled from under the cover.

She licked and kissed a line up the base of my shaft, teasing me. Pleasure radiated through my body, and my muscles softened and released like thawing ice. This woman was wicked. Her hot mouth closed around me. A sigh of pleasure escaped my lips. I'd take care of her today and put a smile on her face. Whatever it took. I stroked her soft hair and whispered my praise as she took me deep. Then I closed my eyes and let myself melt.

Chapter 27

MADISON

We hardly left Geraint's bed for five days. We made love and ate, with little in between. It was the longest break I'd ever taken from training, and my body felt sluggish and out of condition. I had to do something, even if it meant going for a run in the snow. I found Geraint in the kitchen. He cast a dubious eye over my running gear. "You're not thinking of going out in this weather?"

"I have to. I needed a break, but not for too long. I can't keep lounging around here. I'll go straight into training when I get back. It will be brutal."

Geraint rested his knife on the chopping board. "Come with me. I have something to show you." He beckoned me from the kitchen toward a set of stairs that led down into darkness.

I couldn't help my laugh. "The basement? Do I want to go down there with you?"

"You'll like it."

He folded his body in half, and I followed him down the creaking steps. He opened a door at the end and flicked on another light. Inside, a host of dusty gym equipment lined a neat open space.

"I would have told you about it earlier, but I'd forgotten I had all this old stuff."

This had been here the whole time? I'd been working out in my room. It couldn't have come at a better time. I couldn't afford to take any more time off from training. There had been plenty of cardio last night—and twice this morning—but it probably wasn't the kind the coaches had in mind.

I gave him a teasing smile. "I thought you might be taking me to some kind of Christian Grey Red Room. This is disappointing."

He smiled in confusion. "What?"

I couldn't help my laugh at his puzzled expression. "It doesn't matter."

He toed the rowing machine. "It's all yours. I used the equipment at the start when I thought I had a chance at rehab."

My heart ached for him. Had he thought he could go back to rugby? How crushing it must have been to let it go when he clearly loved it so much.

"I was hoping I'd be able to keep up my running program out here, but it's too hard in the snow."

He folded his arms. "The snow is clearing."

That meant the roads would open. We wouldn't be on our own here anymore. Soon, I'd have to go. A sour feeling sat in my throat.

I kept my voice light. "It would be nice if things were different, wouldn't it? Maybe if we lived closer . . ."

His thumb smoothed over his lips. His dark eyes were inscrutable. "That would be nice."

A pang pulled at my heart. What did I expect him to say? This was just a fling. A rebound. It was a distraction to make myself feel better. It was important to be clear about that up front. None of this was part of the plan.

"But you have this place, and I have my job. I have to go where the team is." A sudden ache gripped my heart. I couldn't get attached to this man. "You live here. I live there. There's no way we could be together. We can't get too deep with any of this. You know that, don't you?"

His eyes slipped to the rowing machine. He raked both his hands through his hair. "I know."

My heart ached. This was supposed to be making me feel better, but it was only making me feel worse. "Do you?"

"Yes. I can see you've been hurt. I don't need to know the details if you don't want to tell me. You don't want to get hurt again. I promise I won't hurt you."

"Maybe you wouldn't hurt me on purpose, but it doesn't mean you won't hurt me. You can't make that promise."

He frowned but stayed silent. My reflection stared back at me from every angle in the mirrored walls. I ran a finger over my cheekbone. I didn't look as gaunt in the face anymore. All this food must be doing me good. Still, a heavy feeling weighed me down. "Well, I'm sure you have things to do."

I moved to the door, but Geraint blocked my way. His lips crashed down onto mine in a hot, desperate claiming.

Somehow, I broke away from his persuasive mouth. "Did you hear anything I said?"

"Yes. Every word. I'm not asking you to fall for me. I'm not asking anything from you." His lips brushed mine when he spoke. "Just let me be with you until you leave me. We still have time. Be mine until it's time to go. Then it's done."

I cupped his cheeks. "It's going to make it harder to leave you. It's easier to stop now."

"Yes. It's easier. I don't need easy." He pressed his forehead to mine, his warm breath fanning my face. "Let me feed you. Let me put a smile on your face and make love to you. When it's time to say goodbye, I promise we'll say goodbye with no regrets."

"No regrets?"

My heart thrummed. I didn't want to live with regrets either. If I let this slip through my fingers, I'd regret it. It had never felt this exciting with Bryce. What if it never felt this way again? I'd been so unhappy for so long. Was it terrible to want something to feel good? As long as I kept my heart out of it.

"I'm taking you out, Kentucky. I know a place . . ."

"I told you. You don't have to do that. I like indoor fun. We're not dating. We keep things casual. You can keep calling it making love if you want, but I don't need anyone to make love to me. That's not what we're doing here. This is physical. We keep emotion out of it."

He raised a brow. "If that's what you want, but 'let me make you smile and have casual sex with you' doesn't sound as poetic."

"Good. I don't want poetry, or flowers, or expensive dinners. It's all meaningless."

A line formed between his brows. "What do you want?"

"Orgasms."

He laughed, and I pulled him back to my mouth. His tongue forced my lips open, and I succumbed to him, melting into his hard embrace. We stumbled back together, pulling off each other's clothes and discarding them as we went until he lifted me into his arms. I wrapped my legs around his huge waist, and his lips branded a path over my neck. Soon, I'd have to let him go, but treacherous words resounded in my head.

Hold tighter.

Chapter 28

GERAINT

Madison's eyes lit with delight as we ambled through the stalls of the Christmas market. Winter sun sparkled diamonds on the narrow river that wove its path through the tiny village. Mountains surrounded us, ice-capped and stoic. A delicious scent of mulled wine and roasted chestnuts hung in the air. I knew Madison would love it here. I had to take her to do at least one touristy thing while she was here, and a Christmas Eve market was the perfect opportunity. As much as I wanted to keep her in the Dragon with me, she needed to have fun.

Madison's warm hand slipped into mine. "This is like a fairy tale."

A blast of Christmas carols hit us as we passed the local choir. Madison wrapped her arms around my middle and pressed close. It almost felt like we were a normal couple.

A secret smile pulled at her lips as she stopped to watch some children playing hook-a-duck. I pulled her closer. My heart lit with warmth. She'd looked so angry when I'd found her at the side of the road, like something wild and cornered. She was smiling now. In this short time, she'd transformed. I wanted to keep her like this. To hold the world on my shoulders, so it couldn't crush her anymore and she'd never again weep the way she had in front of the fire. I didn't want this woman to ever feel that burden of sadness.

But how can you stop it?

My phone buzzed in my pocket. Ewan. If it was anyone else, I would have ignored it and concentrated on Madison, but I'd left him in charge for the day. For all I knew, the kitchen was going down in flames.

"I have to take this call."

Madison smiled and drifted closer to the laughing children.

I answered the phone. "Which finger have you chopped off now?"

"Hilarious." Ewan's voice dripped with sarcasm. "Jill's here. I thought you might want to know."

Not Jill. That was all I needed. "What does she want?"

"She said she wants a catch-up on your progress with the business plan."

I hadn't done a damn thing on the business plan. I'd been too busy with Madison.

A pause. Ewan's voice was soft. "How *are* things going with your progress?"

I swallowed. "Fine. Tell her I'm creating a social media strategy. Every business needs a social media strategy."

"Are you creating a social media strategy?" His voice was full of teasing.

My neck itched at the lie. "Yes."

"How's it going?"

I'd made the error of asking Ewan to help me make an Instagram account. Predictably, he found it hilarious that I was finally stepping into the twenty-first century, although at least he seemed to know what he was doing. He'd also shown me how to create a Facebook page, although I drew the line at updating the website myself. We'd have to pay someone to do that.

"It's . . . going great."

"Right." He didn't sound convinced.

Ewan might be a terrible chef, but he was too sharp to fall for lies. I blew out a breath and flashed a glance at Madison as she admired a row of nutcracker dolls. I'd buy her one as soon as I got off the phone. If I had the money, I'd buy her the lot. But I didn't have the money. I didn't have the money for anything.

She picked up a toy soldier and smiled. My heart felt as though it was being squeezed in the nutcracker's little wooden vice. As amazing as it felt to be with her, it could never get too deep. She had a life in England. An amazing career. I'd been a professional athlete once. I knew the commitment and effort it took to stay on top. If I kept hold of this pub, I couldn't leave it, but I couldn't ask her to move here and leave everything behind. Besides, she didn't want to catch feelings either. She'd been hurt, bad. Maybe she'd feel safe enough to tell me about it at some point. What had made her build walls so high? My hand clenched around the phone. For her, this was a rebound. A quick holiday fling. It had to be the same for me.

"Are you with Madison?" Ewan's amused voice brought me out of my reverie.

"Why would you think that?"

"Because she's not here and neither are you, and I couldn't help but notice how good she was at pretending to be your girlfriend. There didn't seem to be much acting on either of your parts."

I couldn't help my laugh. Always so damn nosy. "It's none of your business. Get back to work. Don't burn down my kitchen."

Ewan's chuckle filtered down the line. "Wait. Aled wants to speak to you. He said you need to tell her about the spoons."

"I'm not talking to him now. I'm busy. Tell him I've told her about the bloody spoons."

"Was that before or after you served her the Glamorgan sausage?"

I snorted. "Goodbye, Ewan."

"Good luck with your TikToks, G."

Madison smiled and linked her arm through mine. We meandered through the market, stopping at stalls to browse or eat. The divine smell of cloves and hot sugar donuts hit my nose. The songs from the choir wrapped me in their warm glow. Madison admired a snow globe in her hands, turning it upside down and watching with a wistful expression as the white flakes settled.

Soon she'd be gone. How would I let her go? "Let me get that for you. You can take it back with you. A souvenir."

She replaced the snow globe on the stall and wrapped her arms around herself. Her breath came in white puffs. "I haven't bothered with Christmas this year. I haven't been in the mood."

"Just one thing." I perused the table and picked up a red candle with a gold ribbon. "To remember me by."

She grabbed my arm. Her eyes were earnest and shining. "I don't need anything to remember you by. I'll never forget you."

People bustled around us, but we held still, looking at each other. There was so much I wanted to say, but I'd never been good with words.

She pulled her phone out. "Can I take a picture?"

"To make your ex jealous?"

She tensed. "I don't need to do that anymore. I won't even put it on social media. Just to send to my parents." She bit her lip. "And for me."

She angled the camera and got us both in the selfie. She pressed herself to me, and a smile lit her lips.

"Won't your parents ask awkward questions?"

148

"They can ask whatever they want. I think my dad would die of joy if he knew I was here with a man who can chop down a tree. He'd have you working on the farm before you realized what happened."

I smiled, though I felt a sharp twinge of sadness at the same time. It didn't matter what her parents thought of me. I'd never meet them. We carried on walking in silence, meandering through the bustling Christmas market. Madison popped a chestnut in her mouth and passed me the hot paper bag. A look of uneasiness crossed her face. "I have the last match of the season when I get back."

She didn't look happy about it. Didn't she want to play anymore? She'd shut me down the one time she'd started to open up about playing. "Oh?"

"This is the first televised match for this team. Everybody back home will be watching."

She munched her chestnut. The haunted look I'd thought long chased away reappeared in her eyes. It hurt to hear the tired edge return to her voice. She'd been smiling all morning.

I stopped and cupped her cheeks with my gloved hands. "Are you nervous? I get it. My games were on TV. It's extra pressure. You can only do your best. Don't worry about the cameras."

She nodded woodenly. The hardest part was that she'd been going through it alone. "Do your parents ever visit?"

"I tell them not to."

"Why?"

Her eyes slipped away. "It's better for everyone."

The words burned in my throat.

I'll come. Ask me and I'll come.

I'd told her I'd let her go. I'd stand by it. No matter how much I wanted to keep her, I'd have to let her walk away.

"Maybe your parents would come watch your game if you asked them?"

Her eyes were icy and unresponsive. "It doesn't matter. I won't be asking."

"What about your team? Have you spoken to them? I bet they're nervous too. You don't have to go through these feelings on your own."

She chewed her lip. "It's not that easy."

"Why not?"

Her eyes slipped away, and she hugged herself. "Shall we go back? It's getting colder."

I stopped and wrapped my arms around her. "Whatever is bothering you about this game, you should reach out to someone in the team. Talk it through."

She kept her sad gaze on her boots as she toed at the snow. "I don't want to mess this up in front of everyone, and I don't want to let the team down."

My heart contracted at the vulnerability in her voice. "These are just normal human emotions. You're allowed to feel however you feel about this match. You're not letting anyone down by being honest. You're in it together. That's the point."

She nodded, and her eyes slipped away. "I don't want to talk about any of this. I'm here on vacation."

"Okay, but if you do want to talk, then I'll listen."

A faint smile touched her lips. "I know. Thank you."

Later that evening, I left Madison alone so I could make dinner. The chicken breasts sizzled in the pan, and I rifled the cupboards looking for a notepad and pen. I'd make her last days here memorable. I still had the old sled in the shed. We'd go out and have fun in the snow. Madison needed to laugh, whether she could admit it or not.

Maybe she didn't want me to buy her anything to remember me by, but I needed to give her something. The notepad wasn't particularly pretty, but it would do the job. I set to work, keeping my handwriting as neat as I could. A warm glow of satisfaction enveloped me. Even if I couldn't be there for her anymore, hopefully I could still put a smile on her face.

Chapter 29

GERAINT

"You don't mind me watching you cook, do you?" Madison sat on a tall stool at the kitchen island while I worked on breakfast.

She shifted on the stool, and the T-shirt of mine she'd thrown on this morning rode up her bare thighs. Nothing had ever looked better on her. "No. I like the company."

She peered at the mushy black seaweed mixture in the bowl. "What are you making?"

"Laverbread."

Her eyes widened with a puzzled look. "Bread? Nothing about this looks like bread."

"Laver is a seaweed that grows along the coast here. You boil it to make a paste and spread it on bread or mix with oats into patties and fry. It makes a lovely breakfast with bacon and eggs."

She wrinkled her nose and gave the mixture another suspicious glance.

I couldn't help my laugh. "It's good. I promise. This is Welsh caviar. You'll like it. Haven't you ever eaten nori? It's not that different."

She rested an elbow on the island and propped up her chin. "Fine. I'm going in with an open mind."

We fell into companionable silence while I worked. With the mixture cooking gently on the hob, the kitchen filled with the pleasant briny aroma of the sea.

"I could watch you cooking all day." Her eyes lit up and her brow furrowed with focus. "Actually, I just had an idea."

She slipped down from the stool and rapped her knuckle against the wall that partitioned the kitchen and the bar. A hollow thud rang out. "Is this wall load bearing?"

"No. Why?"

"The bar is behind this wall, isn't it? Imagine if you took it out. You could open this place up so customers can see you cooking in here."

I felt my brow draw downward in confusion. "Why would I do that?"

Her nose wrinkled as though the answer was obvious. "People love that kind of thing. I've been to so many fancy places in LA where you can see what's going on in the kitchen. The customers come for the experience. They want to see Geraint Madoc in action."

I came to the pub to get away from the spotlight, not focus it on me like an exhibit in a zoo. "I doubt it. Besides, I don't want people gawking at me while I'm trying to concentrate."

She frowned. "It's not about people gawking at you. It's about showcasing your skills. You don't need to do it like that if you're not comfortable. You could just do it online." She picked up her phone from the island. "Let's do an experiment. I'm going to film you cooking. I'll show you how easy this could be."

An alarm bell rang in my head. "You want to film me?"

"Ewan set up some social media accounts for the pub. This is the content you need."

Ewan had gone ahead with it, then? That had to be why I'd seen the two of them messing about on Ewan's phone and giggling behind the bar the other day.

"I suggested you should cook without a shirt, but Ewan said you wouldn't go for it."

She shot me a flirtatious smile that gave me half a mind to stop cooking immediately and whisk her straight back to the bedroom. I enjoyed making her moan with my cooking, but I preferred making her moan beneath the covers.

"Ewan's right. I'm not going for it."

She raised a suggestive eyebrow. "What about just wearing the apron? Nothing underneath."

"Nothing underneath?" I tapped my lips as though considering, then flattened my expression. "Nope."

Her eyes twinkled with laughter. "Spoilsport."

She angled the phone to capture me in the shot. "Can you explain what you're doing as you make it?"

I tried to keep my face natural despite my unease. Jess had wanted me to pursue work in the media after the injury. I'd been in the wrong headspace for anything like that back then. The last thing I'd wanted was to be the center of attention.

I grabbed a handful of oats and added them to the seaweed paste. "I'll look like an idiot. What am I supposed to say?"

"Just be yourself. That's all you need to do."

I shook my head. "I'm not really into this kind of thing."

Her smile was encouraging. "But you could try?"

The back of my neck heated. "No. Sorry. I don't think it's going to work."

She chewed her lip and lowered the phone. "You're going to have to do something, Geraint. You don't want to lose this place, do you?"

The mixture started to boil over, and I pulled it off the hob. Just talking about doing this was making me lose focus. It had been so long since I'd performed or done anything to put myself out there.

She pursed her lips. "You do want to keep the pub, don't you?"

"Of course." My voice sounded unenthusiastic even to me.

She studied my face with a strange intensity. "You told me before this place was your dad's dream. What about you? Is it your dream?"

My dream? No. My dream had been to play rugby, but that had been taken from me. I'd been running this place out of obligation, coasting along, trying to keep it going. If the brewery took the pub away, it freed me from the pressure to keep it on. Maybe it was even for the best. If I'd done a good job then we wouldn't be in this position.

She chewed her lip, her voice tentative. "Maybe you feel like you're . . . trapped here, but you're not. You can leave if you want to. You can do anything you want."

"Like what?"

She wrapped her arms around my waist and tilted her chin to peer at my face. "What do you want to do?"

That was a question I didn't ask myself. The answer was irrelevant. I'd wanted rugby, and I'd lost it. I'd wanted to hold on to Jess, but she'd left me. No matter how I'd tried, I couldn't save my career or my marriage. I'd been living like this ever since Dad passed. Somewhere along the line, I'd stopped trying to improve things.

"You can't do all this just for everyone else. This has to be what you want, too." Madison's gaze traveled over my face. "There must be some parts of being here you like?"

"I like it when you're here." The words slipped out before I could think about it.

Her brows knitted, and she cupped my face with her smooth hands. "You need to figure out your plan for when I'm gone. Even if you're too stubborn to accept money from me, there are plenty of ways that you can bring business here. You can sort out your marketing. You can diversify: hold trivia nights, let Aled do a ghost tour and talk about the spoons, cater weddings or events, run cookery courses or retreats. If people are so keen on yoga, hire out the space to community groups in the evening." She lifted her chin in determination. "There is a way through, but you have to decide if it's what you want, and commit to a plan."

I sighed. Maddie was right. I hadn't put my mind to this. There was so much about the pub that I liked, but it had become a millstone around my neck. Maybe things would be different if I could make a success of it. If I had the will to step up and make it into a hub for the community again. I had to believe that it was worthwhile, and I had to shift my mindset to at least try.

I pressed my forehead to hers so that our breath intermingled. "Those are some good ideas."

"Right?" She flashed a triumphant smile. "Maybe I should come and run this place for you."

I swallowed. "Maybe you should."

It was a joke, but the words lingered in the air and took on too much significance. Maddie cleared her throat and stepped away. "Write a serious plan if you want to keep this place, and if you don't, you need to think about your next steps."

I put the mixture back on the hob and returned to my task. I spoke, more to clear the awkward tension than anything else. "Come on, then. Let's try this video."

Her eyes darted to mine. "Are you sure?"

"I'm sure. Maybe educating the world about seaweed is my true calling."

She clapped her hands together. "You'll be great. You could do tutorials focusing on Welsh specialties. If people like it, you could think about cookery classes, or retreats."

I chuckled at her enthusiasm. Once it had been hard to coax the smallest smile from her, and now she was practically jumping up and down at the prospect of a video about seaweed. It was worth making a fool of myself, just for that. "One step at a time. You haven't seen me on camera."

"You're going to be great. Just talk about this bread thing that's actually seaweed, and people will love it. If it doesn't sound good, we'll try it shirtless. Then it doesn't matter what you're talking about." Her expression brightened with amusement, and the suggestive smile returned to her lips. "No one will be listening."

Chapter 30

MADISON

"Merry Christmas, Kentucky." Geraint wrapped his powerful arms around my midriff from behind.

I settled back against his solid frame, like a wall of muscle, enjoying the feel of his warmth. "I'm not in your way, am I?"

"You're fine. I'm not expecting anyone. We stay open Christmas Day, just in case."

I sliced a loaf of bread, and he grunted. "Why won't you let me do it? I can make you a toasted sandwich if you want."

"This is my culture. You're not the only ones who like your fancy grilled cheese. A Hot Brown is a Kentucky version of a Welsh rarebit. I don't want a Christmas dinner today. I want to do things differently."

"Christmas dinner is tradition."

I stopped chopping to kiss the tip of his nose. "The best thing about traditions is you can make new ones. Get on board. This is happening."

A delicious smell of turkey roasting in the oven wrapped around us. His mouth trailed against my neck. Heat raced to every place his lips touched. "Fine. I'm on board. So, this is our shared heritage? We both know a lot about hot cheese on toasted bread."

Technically, I didn't know *that* much about hot cheese on toasted bread. I'd had to phone my mom and ask her how to make it. It was our first conversation that had felt relaxed and normal for so long. Neither of us was dancing around the topic of Bryce, and she wasn't commenting on how underweight and ill I looked. In fact, she'd told me I looked like I was glowing. Warmth crept up my neck. I suppose that's what a week of mind-blowing orgasms and the best food I'd ever eaten does to you.

Geraint's hands slipped up and down my arms, making me shiver with delight. "Tell me the recipe again."

"Bacon, ham, and turkey. Then there's a mornay sauce on top. This isn't the normal cheese I'd use, but I'm rolling with it."

"Please tell me you don't make this with American cheese?"

Playfully, I shrugged out of his arms and gave him an admonishing look. "What's wrong with American cheese?"

He snorted and wrapped his arms around me again, locking his hands behind my spine. "Let's not go down this road. We've been getting on so well."

I pushed him away lightly. "Get out of here. I'm cooking. Not you."

"I'm used to running the kitchen. You don't know how difficult this is for me."

"Well, I'm running the show. You're going to have to get used to it."

A smile pulled at his lips. His voice dropped low and hoarse. His eyes clung to my face. "I can get used to it, Kentucky."

His lips touched mine, and he kissed me slowly and deeply. My mouth moved with increasing urgency against his.

Reluctantly, I pulled back an inch. "I'm supposed to be cooking."

His hands slipped under my sweater, caressing the length of my back. He whispered low in my ear. "I know, but there's something else I want to eat."

His cool fingers traced the bumps of my spine, sending jolts of pleasure through me. Heat flowed through my veins like warm honey. "Stop distracting me. The mornay is going to burn."

"I don't care. Turn off the hob. Put it on hold."

His hands slipped up to ease the cup of my bra aside. His fingers traced the outline of my nipple. A moan escaped my lips. His touch was light and painfully teasing.

Yes, chef.

Screw it. The food would have to wait.

My elbows got stuck in my sweater in his eagerness to pull it over my head. His tongue tantalized my swollen nipples while his hands slipped down to pull my leggings off. He swept me into the strength and comfort of his strong arms and deposited me on the kitchen counter. A gasp escaped me as his hot lips tracked a path along my jaw and down my neck. He dropped to his knees. "I'm interested in the main course, but first I want my starter."

I looked down my body to watch him kneeling in front of me. "It can't wait?"

"No. You never keep a chef waiting in his own kitchen."

I laughed. "That's not a thing. You made that up."

He planted a hot, open-mouthed kiss over the thin fabric of my cotton panties. "Trust me. It's a thing."

With one huge hand, he caressed the length of my leg. "I've been waiting for this all morning. You're not going to keep me waiting, are you?"

He hooked his fingers into my panties, and I lifted my hips so he could pull them off. I groaned as his tongue probed the sensitive, swollen area between my thighs. I couldn't disguise my body's reaction to him. It had never been like this with Bryce. One kiss made me feel wild and out of control.

He pushed back to a standing position, and I couldn't help my moan at the loss of his tongue.

"Where are you going?"

He moved to the freezer. "Patience, Kentucky. I have plans for you."

A chinking sound drifted to my ears, as he collected ice in a glass. He planted himself in front of me. Gently, he took hold of my legs and spread me wider. A swift sense of embarrassment made me want to close my legs, but I fought the urge. He'd spent so much time down there over the past couple of days. What did it matter now?

"The most important thing in cooking is balance. Some flavors are complementary. They balance each other like hot and cold." He stared deeply into my eyes, and held up an ice cube between his fingers. "I want to try something that's going to make you feel good. Will you let me?"

"Try something?"

A wicked smile pulled at his lips, and his hungry gaze fixed between my legs. He licked his lips. "The ice could be an interesting sensation."

My mouth dried as I realized what he was suggesting. Despite my surprise, I managed to force words out. "With ice?"

"Not just ice." He pulled his tankard of wassail along the counter. "Don't worry, it's not too hot." His lips touched mine like a whisper. "Only if you want to. No pressure."

My heart pounded with anticipation. Why not? I'd always liked to try new things. "Okay."

His lips recaptured mine, more demanding this time. "Tell me if it gets too much."

He ran his free hand up my calf, then he pressed the ice cube between my thighs. The burning invasion on sensitive nerves nearly sent me flying off the counter. A shocked yelp escaped me.

"Okay?" He withdrew the ice cube. His voice was soothing as he kissed a line along my jaw to the corner of my mouth. "Only if it feels good . . . Can you trust me to make it feel good?"

"Yes."

Tingling sensations pulsed between my legs from that one graze of ice. Geraint's eyes didn't leave mine as he brushed the ice cube slowly through my folds. A shivering gasp escaped me. He pressed the ice to my clit. The burning, numbing sensation was as excruciating as it was delicious. My head fell back, and a whimper left my lips.

Geraint reached across the counter for his tankard of wassail. His eyes held a sensuous promise as he took a sip and held the liquid in his mouth before he swallowed. He bowed his head and planted a hot open-mouthed kiss where the ice cube had been. The sudden change in temperature made me cry out. His hot breath fanning my sensitive, swollen flesh drew another whimper from me. He licked and probed the pulsing ache between my thighs. My heartbeat skyrocketed. Waves of sensation throbbed with every swirl of his tongue. He replaced his mouth with another ice cube. An electric chill shot through me, making my toes curl.

My whole body jolted. "Fuck!"

Geraint planted gentle kisses along my jaw. "You're going to tell me if it's too much, aren't you? You're doing so well. Nothing turns me on as much as getting you off."

His intense gaze fixed on my face as he circled my clit with melting ice. Water dripped down through my folds, so cold it burned. My hands gripped the edge of the counter.

His rough palm caressed the length of my bare thigh. "Do you like it when I make you feel good?"

"Yes." The word was little more than a murmur.

He lifted the ice away and took another sip of his wassail, holding it in his mouth again before swallowing. Then he bowed his head and licked me in firm, fiery strokes. The hot, soothing close of his lips over my raw flesh was so exquisite, I couldn't stop my hips from bucking and rising to meet him.

"I love the noises you make." A low growl left his lips. "I love the way you taste. I love how well you're taking this."

He grabbed my backside, spreading me, and continued his lapping and probing. The urgent need between my thighs was overwhelming. My nails dug into his broad shoulders. He smoothed his palm over my stomach and up under my T-shirt to massage my breasts. The need for him to stop messing around with ice cubes and just take me left me gasping for breath.

I slipped my hand down to rub his hard length through his jeans. "Stop torturing me. I want you. I need it."

Gently, he peeled me away. "No. Not yet. We're not done." He held the ice cube to my clit again and his head slanted as he studied my face. "It's not too much, is it?"

Blood rushed to my clit in an aching, desperate surge. "I can take it."

"Good." Geraint's dark eyes didn't leave mine for a moment as he gently pushed the ice cube with his finger and held it inside of me.

A series of strange gasps left my lips. "Oh . . . Oh . . . Ah . . . Fuck!"

His tongue flicked in quick, sharp movements that were almost unbearable against my numb flesh. Just when I couldn't take another second, he began to hum. The intense vibrations sent a shuddering wave of pleasure through me. My release was so explosive, it was painful. Muscles clenched around the melting ice cube. With his tongue and skilled fingers, he nursed me through every shivering judder. Then he stood and his mouth covered mine, forcing me to taste myself. His kiss was slow and drugging as the ice inside my heat melted. He planted his lips against the hollow of my neck and whispered into my hair, "You can relax now, cariad. You did so well."

The need to feel full of him made me ache. I reached down to the button on his jeans. "Don't make me wait anymore."

His words were a hot whisper against my throat. "I won't. What do you need?"

"You know what I need."

He slid down his jeans and boxers. I guided him to me, feeling the hard press of his shaft. I never would have been able to have sex in this position with Bryce, but Geraint was so tall he made it work. He gripped my hip with one hand, and we both groaned as he slid into me. The marble counter was cool under my backside, but my limbs flooded with heat. His forehead pressed against mine, his ragged breath fanning warmth against my face. He worked in slow, deep thrusts that made us both moan. Pleasure built where our bodies joined, sending goose bumps racing over my skin. His hands explored the hollows of my back.

"You're so beautiful, cariad." His voice was a husky growl.

Shivers of delight coursed through me. I yielded to the searing need. Sweat prickled my body. His eyes searched my face. Gripping my legs, he spread me wider and thrust in swift, hard strokes. The sudden change in pace sent a wave of pleasure through me. I gripped his broad shoulders and surrendered to his intoxicating manly scent and the strength and beauty of this inked beast who had me at his mercy. Everything inside tightened unbearably. Coiling tension rippled under my skin. My breath came fast and sharp, escaping me in desperate gasps.

A stream of unintelligible words slid from Geraint's lips. His fingers slipped downward. The moment he touched my too-sensitive clit, release exploded. Waves of pleasure cascaded through me. I sagged against him, our bodies plastered together with sweat. Gradually, the outside world filtered back in. Hail tapped against the window. The kitchen's steam filled my nose. It took time before either of us had the will to speak.

Cupping my cheeks, he searched my upturned face. "Are you okay?"

It hit me that he was looking for tears. This time, there were none. I couldn't help my incredulous laugh. How long had he been cooking up this wicked plan to torture me? He was always so affable and sweet. "I'm good. I mean, that was my first ice-gasm, but I'm good."

A smile lit his face, and he kissed the tip of my nose. "Happy Christmas, Kentucky."

I ran a hand over his beard, and I couldn't help my smile. Passionate Christmas Day countertop sex was definitely a new one.

If only it could become a new tradition.

Later that evening, I sat in the armchair in front of the fire. Geraint emerged from the kitchen carrying a small, square parcel wrapped in green paper. He held it out to me.

"For me?" Guilt clawed at my shoulder blades. "I didn't know we were doing presents. I didn't get you anything."

His smile was bashful. "It's fine. It's nothing much."

I unwrapped the paper to reveal an A5 notebook full of neat blue handwriting. I scanned the first page and read aloud. "Glamorgan sausage. 25g butter, 155g leeks, 175g breadcrumbs." I looked up at him in surprise. "What is this? Recipes?"

"It's everything I've cooked that you seemed to like. You don't have to use it if you don't want to. I thought it might be nice . . ."

My lips parted in surprise. I hadn't expected him to go to so much trouble. "Thank you."

He pulled another spherical parcel from behind his back. "I also got you this."

I unwrapped the smooth ball to reveal a snow globe. A man and woman sat on a park bench beside a Christmas tree in a miniature village. I held it upside down and watched the flurries spiral. My throat tightened with realization. This was the one I'd been looking at in the market.

"You went back for this?"

"Yes."

"You didn't have to do that."

Fairy lights glimmered in his dark, earnest eyes. "I know. I wanted to."

Warmth spread through me, melting every trace of the ice piercing my heart. Nothing remained to protect me in its wake, to fight off the raw, painful ache that made my guts churn.

I have to leave him here.

How can I leave him?

Chapter 31

GERAINT

Christmas Day was always dead at the pub, but Boxing Day was turning out to be busier. We had two customers, not including Simon. I poked my head around the door to the kitchen, where Ewan stood peeling potatoes.

"Everything under control?"

He flicked a piece of paper above the stove. "I've got one cawl, and one egg and chips."

I grabbed my apron from the hook next to the door. "Do you need help?"

Ewan rolled his eyes. "I can manage egg and chips." He glanced at the door. "Where's the lovely Madison?"

Naked in my bed. It had been painful to leave her. My feet itched to get back upstairs, but it wasn't fair to leave Ewan to manage without at least checking in on him.

"She's . . . around."

Ewan reached for an egg, a secretive smile softening his lips. "The two of you have been getting on well. You've been keeping her all to yourself. It's not fair, you know. She likes Taylor Swift. We've got a lot to talk about."

Curiosity got the better of me. "I see you talking sometimes. Does she ever say anything to you about me?"

Ewan cracked the egg on the edge of the frying pan and turned to look at me. "Like what?"

The delicious steam from the cawl wrapped around me. Embarrassment that I'd even asked made my jaw tense. "I don't know. It doesn't matter."

Ewan gazed at me before chuckling softly. "You like this woman a lot, don't you?"

I busied myself unloading the hot pint glasses from the dishwasher. Yes. Too much. "We enjoy each other's company."

Ewan's gaze sharpened. "Don't tell me Big G has fallen in love. You old softie."

The back of my neck heated. "Of course not. It's only been two weeks."

"So? When it's the one, you know. It doesn't matter how long."

A sudden weariness enveloped me. Of course I knew. I'd known the moment she climbed into my lap and swore she'd met me in a Dolly Parton fan club. It had happened fast, but I'd fallen for this woman. Underneath the snark, she was full of spirit, humor, and warmth. I'd felt it. I'd basked in it. Her eyes were lively and sparkling in those moments when she put down whatever burden she carried. I wanted to be the one to take care of her. I wanted her to be mine.

Ewan waved his wooden spoon at me. "As long as all this is not putting you off writing the business plan."

Oh God. The business plan. I'd hardly done a damn thing on the wretched thing. I had a meeting set up with the board to present it. Madison would be gone by then anyway. I'd have time to work on it. How was I supposed to let her walk away? I could tell her how I felt, but it would trap us into an impossible choice. I couldn't leave this place, and I couldn't ask her to give up her life after two weeks together. Besides, I didn't have the right words to win this woman's heart. I'd never been good with romance. Jess hadn't liked it when I'd brought her flowers. She always said it made me look guilty.

Ewan put down his wooden spoon and picked up a metal spoon to sample the soup. He held the steaming concoction out to me. "Here. Come and taste this. More salt?"

I moved to take the spoon from him and sampled the steaming, meaty stew. The idea slid into my consciousness.

A smile pulled at my lips. "A spoon."

Ewan shot me a look as though I'd lost my mind. "A spoon?"

"A spoon is meaningful."

I didn't have the right words, but I could still show Madison what she meant to me.

Ewan chuckled. "What are you talking about?"

I put the spoon in the sink. "I'm going to be busy today. Can you manage?"

"Of course."

"Good." I headed for the door. "And yes, more salt."

That evening, after Madison had gone to sleep, I spent the night in Dad's old shed. It had been a while since I'd carved a love spoon. They'd always been for the tourists. I'd never made one that meant anything. While I carved, my thoughts lingered on all the young Welsh men in the past who had done the same, whittling wood to win the heart of a woman.

By the time I got to bed, the birds were singing. Madison stirred and pressed herself into my arms. I held her snugly. Her beautiful smooth breasts pressed against my chest. It was divine to hold her like this. She fit perfectly in my arms.

"Where have you been?" Her voice was thick with sleep.

I pressed a kiss to her forehead. "I had something to do." I kissed her eyebrows and the tip of her nose. "I'm here now. You can go back to sleep."

She murmured softly. The peaceful lines of her face relaxed, so different from when I'd watched her sleep in the armchair by the fire. She'd called out for her ex with tears streaming down her face. Awful to think that she'd been wounded like that. Whatever happened, I'd never hurt her.

She smothered a yawn and let out a long sigh. "I don't want to get up, but I have to. The real world is calling."

The real world could stay away. If she didn't return my affection, I'd have to let it go. I promised I wouldn't make it difficult.

If only it wasn't so damn difficult.

What would it be like if she didn't have to go? What if I could spend the rest of my days feeding her, ravishing her, making her smile? She sat up in bed. Her hair tumbled carelessly down her back. Every inch of her spoke of strength and power, but vulnerability lurked in the shadows under her eyes. Her cheeks were pink, and a sparkle glimmered in her eyes that hadn't been here when she'd checked in. The memory of how she'd cried after our first time forced its way into my mind. What life was she returning to that made her cry like that? How was I supposed to send her back to it? I wanted to keep her safe with me, where I could protect her.

She trailed tickling fingers up my arms. "It's our last day together. What shall we do?"

If this was all we had, we had to make the most of it. I kept my voice light. "You never did build that snowman."

She arched a questioning eyebrow. "I hope you're joking."

"I'm not joking. Come on, get dressed. We're going to have some fun."

She looked me over seductively. "But it's so cold out there. Can't we have some indoor fun first?"

Her hands slipped up my arms. She showered kisses along my jawline and neck. My heart turned over, and I drank in the comfort of her nearness. The past couple of days, I'd been trying to learn all her features by heart so I could keep her. She was slipping away from me like silk through my fingers. How could this ever work? We could try long distance, but could she fit me into her world?

She buried her face against my throat. Her voice was a rough whisper. "Do you know what I need, G?"

"What do you need?"

Her eyelashes fluttered against my cheek, and her breath was hot and uneven against my face. "I need you to make love to me."

Amusement bubbled up inside me. I'd thought she was so fierce and intimidating when she'd arrived here. She was both things, but not all the time. Sometimes she was vulnerable. Sometimes she wore this smile, and it felt as though it was only for me. "Not just an orgasm, then?"

She flashed a devilish grin, and her hand slipped below the covers. "I'll take both."

Chapter 32

MADISON

Gathering heavy lace and organza in my hands, I waded through the snow in my wedding dress. A tiny ramshackle stone church stood in front of me. I knew this place. The staccato trill of a cardinal filled my ears. The little red bird hopped onto the pristine snow. A cardinal in Wales? Anna dashed to meet me at the entrance to the church. I braced myself, waiting for her anxious expression, but she smiled and held the door to the chapel open for me. An echoing silence met me. Candles flickered in the darkness, lighting a path up the aisle like golden arrows. My footsteps rang out on stone as I approached the altar.

My heart pounded. No one had come to meet me.

The dark figure of a man stepped out of the shadows. The light from the stained-glass window danced over his gigantic frame. He was so big and imposing, but his gentle smile wrapped me in tenderness.

With a large hand, he pulled me toward him. I tilted my chin to look into his face. Confusion overwhelmed me. "You're not supposed to be here. Neither of us are—"

A low buzz pierced my consciousness. My eyes flew open. My phone vibrated on the nightstand. I reached for it to silence it. Then I saw the image flashing on the screen.

Bryce.

Panic flooded my system. I should have switched it off, but some strange instinct made me grab it and run out of the room. I couldn't have Bryce calling me while I was in bed with Geraint. I raced down the landing to my bedroom and darted inside. My finger hovered to decline it, but some stupid impulse made me answer instead.

Bryce's face appeared on the screen.

"Madison?"

A horrible sick feeling overwhelmed me. He raked a hand through his sandy hair, which was light in contrast to his deep tan. Bryce's well-groomed appearance had always impressed me. Wherever he went, he took a piece of LA sparkle with him.

He frowned. "Where are you?"

I found my voice to speak in a hushed whisper. "It's none of your business."

"What time is it there?"

I dropped onto my bed and held the phone up high, so only my face was in the shot. Bryce didn't need to know I was wearing a man's T-shirt. Not that it mattered. I could do whatever I wanted. Why now? How dare he call me?

"Why are you calling?" My voice came out as an odd hiss.

"I want to talk."

My mouth clenched tighter. "So you call me unannounced?"

"You don't answer your messages. How could I announce myself?"

There was no sarcasm to his tone. It was a statement of fact. Still, it gave me a hot snap of anger. Why should I answer my phone after what he'd done?

"I was hoping you'd give me a chance to explain."

"To make yourself feel better?"

"No." His voice was soothing, which made it all the more annoying. "To make you feel better."

My breath came in quick, shallow gasps. I didn't want to do this. Why hadn't I ignored the call? It wasn't too late. I could still hang up. I snorted. "Since when did my feelings matter to you?"

He blew out a breath. "Hear me out. You won't give me the chance to explain, but I'm sorry, Maddie. If I could turn back the clock I would. I messed up. It was all too much for me, and I panicked. I was getting ready in the morning, and my parents were arguing about something stupid on the breakfast menu, and something broke inside me. You know I was little when they got divorced. It messed with my head. I didn't think I'd ever get married, but then you came along and swept me off my feet."

He shot me a rueful smile. I glared back at him. This wasn't a cozy little trip down memory lane. Anger blazed so hot it burned my throat. Every feeling I'd tried to push away had been triggered the moment I'd laid eyes on his smug, narcissistic asshole face again. He was lucky an entire ocean was between us. I wanted to rip off his balls and shove them down his throat.

He shook his head. "That morning, I saw our lives laid out in front of us, and I realized I was making a mistake. We rushed into things. I wasn't ready to get married. It sounds crazy, but this voice in my head kept telling me to run." He spoke in a suffocated whisper. "I got on a bus. I didn't even know where I was going."

"And you didn't think of me once." A pang made my breath catch. "You didn't think how I would feel when I got to that church and you weren't there. Do you know how awful that was? How humiliating? Everybody we knew was there."

He gave a grudging nod. "I'm sorry. I don't know what else to say." He frowned. "Maybe I shouldn't have called. I just thought maybe we could talk about it." He bowed his head and murmured, "It wouldn't have been right, Maddie. Deep down, you know that.

174

We were good together, but it wasn't enough. Something was missing. You must have felt that too? It wasn't enough to build a life together."

I turned my face away. He was right, of course. It was only now I felt this way about Geraint that I understood he was right. I'd loved Bryce. I really had, but it wasn't the way I felt about Geraint. It wasn't the deep sense of peace and home I'd found in Geraint's arms. Bryce's hugs had never made me feel like I was somewhere safe. It had never been easy with him. In two weeks with Geraint, my feelings were stronger than after years with Bryce. Still, Bryce had screwed me over so badly.

Bryce sniffed and brushed his cheeks. "I've felt awful. The guilt has made me sick. My parents are furious at me. They all loved you, Maddie." He gave a sharp bark of laughter. "They loved you more than they love me. They won't forgive me. My sisters won't even talk to me. I don't have the right, but I'm asking you to forgive me. I'm sorry, I really am."

A couple of months ago, I would have gladly heard all the ways Bryce was suffering, but sitting here and watching the pain in his face brought me no pleasure. The truth was startlingly obvious. That day had hurt me more than anything, but he'd done me a favor. I didn't want a life with Bryce, a man so scared of commitment he had to run away instead of being honest. I wanted a man that was all for me. A man obsessed with me, who couldn't wait to spend the rest of his life with me and stand at the front of a chapel and tell everyone we knew he wanted me.

Bryce had never been that man.

Yet, still I couldn't forgive him. Still the anger clawed inside of me.

I want to be better than this.
Why can't I be better?

I took a breath. "You're right. We wouldn't have been good together. My snoring would have driven you mad. You would have left the toilet seat up one too many times, and I would have snapped. We'd have been lucky to make it a year until the divorce."

He didn't even smile. Bryce had no sense of humor. He'd never understood me, not the way Geraint did. Geraint faced my dark moods and anger and still wanted to dig to find the gold.

"When are you coming home? Maybe we could get dinner and talk this through properly."

I couldn't help my snort. I wasn't about to sit down with him over tapas. Besides, what did he mean by home? LA? That wasn't my home anymore. Lexington didn't feel like home either. It was a place I felt suffocated. Where did that leave me? Because England definitely wasn't my home.

"I don't know when I'm coming home."

Because I don't think I have one anymore.

Bryce glanced over his shoulder. "I have to go . . ." He chewed his lip. "What do you say? Can you forgive me, Maddie? Please. I need you to forgive me."

What did it matter to him? Since when did Bryce care about my forgiveness? "Why?"

"Because everyone is so mad at me. I need to make this right."

The horrible, heavy rage I'd carried inside me clawed at my throat. An indignant snort escaped me. Of course. This wasn't about me. Bryce hadn't suddenly developed a conscience. His family were giving him a hard time. Heaven forbid things got awkward on the annual Muller family skiing trip. Good for them. I'd always had a lot of appreciation for his sisters, Julie and Nicole. Bryce could deal with his own family drama. Not my problem. It was enough I'd even answered his call.

I'd defended Bryce to everyone so many times, and he'd betrayed me. Now he wanted me to do it again. He really expected me to get him off the hook, and tell his family what a great guy he was. Absolutely not. He'd taken me for a fool so many times. Never again.

His voice was pleading. "Can you forgive me, Maddie?"

My breath came sharp and hot in my lungs. Part of me wanted to say yes. I was tired of all this anger and pain, but how could I? He hadn't even apologized. I couldn't stand another second of his whining.

I took deep breaths until I was strong enough to give him an answer in a level voice. "You ruined my life, Bryce. Of course I can't forgive you. Never call me again."

I trudged through swirling snow. I needed to think. Talking to Bryce had made me nauseous. He was a reminder of my old life. I didn't want to go back to any of it, but I had to. I had a job and commitments. The next match for Calverdale was my first one to be televised. My family would be watching back home. They'd see my terrible form. Another humiliation.

If only I could stay here with Geraint. It had been a perfect escape from reality. His arms had been a refuge from my life. I felt safe here with him, but still it wasn't enough to quiet the Magic 8 Ball that swirled hot and heavy behind my ribcage, constantly grinding, making me ask questions I had no answers for.

How dare Bryce ask for my forgiveness?

Cannot predict now.

Why was I foolish enough to let myself get attached to a new man?

Reply hazy, try again.

Is there any way I can keep Geraint?

My sources say no.

Calverdale was great. They'd been so welcoming. Even Gabe Rivers wasn't the man the media painted him to be, but I couldn't give them what they needed from me. My head wasn't in the game. I was screwing everything up. Snow battered me. A white wilderness of fields sprawled around me. I'd have to go back. The blizzard was becoming too heavy.

A familiar sight caught my eye. A beautiful stone chapel stood in the distance, faint through the whirling snow. Saint Dwynwen's. Had I walked so far? I'd have a look while I was here. It was a chance to find some shelter and wait for the snow to ease. My heart ached as I clambered over a wall and landed in deep snow in the next field.

Only love could hurt this bad. I hadn't come here to fall in love. None of this had been part of my plan. But what if it could be? What if I moved here? I'd finally felt peaceful, until Bryce called and shattered it. Could I give up my life and come here? It didn't seem that big a sacrifice when the reward was Geraint. A bitter wind whipped around my neck, and I pulled my coat tight. First things first. I needed to not be freezing cold. With a shove, I pushed open the heavy door of the church.

Chapter 33

GERAINT

I poked my head around the door to the kitchen, where Ewan stood peeling potatoes. A sour taste filled my mouth. Madison wasn't here either. I'd woken up and reached to pull her into my arms as usual, but her side of the bed was cold.

Ewan frowned. "You look stressed. What's wrong?"

"Madison's gone."

Ewan waved the potato peeler dismissively. "She's fine. I just saw her. She went on a walk. She said she needed to clear her head."

Clear her head? I peered out the window at the swirling snow. "It's freezing. Why didn't you stop her?"

"How could I stop her? She's a grown woman. She had a coat on."

I grabbed my hat and pulled it down low. "I don't like the idea of her walking around alone in this weather. I'm going to bring her home."

Ewan arched a bemused eyebrow. "Home?"

My throat closed up. "Back here. You know what I mean."

Ewan reached for another potato, a secretive smile softening his lips. "Have you told her yet?"

"Told her what?"

He laughed. "Don't play innocent. Have you told her how you feel about her?"

I touched the long wooden spoon hidden inside my padded jacket. I'd been waiting to pull it out like an engagement ring. Maybe she wouldn't like it. She might think it was twee and quaint, something silly for tourists. Still, it was the best I had.

A rush of nerves went through me. Ewan moved in front of me. Despite being five years younger than me, he patted my shoulders like a proud father about to send his son off to prom. "God speed, Big G. Go and bring your woman home. You've got this."

My heart pounded as I drove through the epic glacial landscape in search of Madison. Where could she go? Snow swirled relentlessly, like the churning in my gut. This wasn't the weather to go for a hike. Snowdonia was beautiful, but wild and unforgiving. What was she thinking? What had made her rush out like this? Everything had been going so well. I'd fallen asleep, and she'd disappeared. Was it something I'd said? It had always been so easy to put my foot in it with Jess, and not even know why. Sometimes my ex-wife had stopped talking to me for days on end and would not even tell me what I'd done. I racked my brain trying to think of what I could have done to upset Madison. We'd been laughing, and she'd fallen asleep in my arms. It didn't make sense.

Snow fell in thick flakes, clogging the windshield. Another wave of panic gripped me.

Breathe.

She'll be okay. Ewan said she looked fine.

Why had she just walked out without saying goodbye? My heart ached. Pretty soon, she'd be doing this for real. If I couldn't convince her to stay, I'd have to watch her drive away from me.

Maybe she'd just needed some fresh air. We'd been cooped up together in the pub for so long. But where would she go? The village? It was walking distance at a stretch, and the only place worth visiting. The truck powered through the snow, and I scanned the endless sweep of white. Memories pushed into my mind. It had felt so barren and bleak here when I'd arrived from the city. I'd been a broken man back then. I'd thought my life was over. My career was done, and my wife had left me. Every morning, I woke up disappointed that I had to face another day.

Dad had been so gentle with me in those early months. It was a blur now. A busy pub had been too much for me. I'd stayed in the kitchen out of the way where it was quieter. Learning to cook had given me purpose again. Dad had encouraged me to apply for culinary school.

Everybody needs to feel like they're good at something, son.

For me, my meaning in life had always been rugby, but cooking had given me my confidence back. Maybe that was the key to holding on to this pub. That was the part I liked best about being here. It hadn't been so bad making the cooking video with Maddie. In fact, I'd enjoyed it when I'd loosened up. I didn't have any answers about my future, but I'd never been more certain about one thing: I wanted Madison so badly. I had little to give her, no stack of presents under the tree, but I could love her, if only she'd let me. If only there was a way for us to be together. Was it enough? How could I ask a woman with the world at her feet to give everything up to be with me here in the middle of nowhere?

I parked the truck in the little snow-blanketed village parking lot and climbed out. The narrow winding streets were empty. I went from shop to shop, asking if anyone had seen her. Everybody knew I had an American visitor at the pub. We were a hot topic of gossip. News traveled fast around here. With every dead end, my anxiety grew. Nobody had seen her. She wasn't here. Where else would she be?

I headed up the street past the village church. Bells rang out, piercing the air, and it hit me. There was only one other place Madison had shown any enthusiasm for, beside the Christmas market. Saint Dwynwen's hadn't even crossed my mind because it was such a long way to walk, but Madison was both physically fit and determined. If anyone could get there in this weather, it would be her. Would she remember the way? A shiver lashed my spine. It would be so easy to get lost. I breathed through my worry. I'd be no good to anyone in a state. If she wanted to do something, she'd do it. Back in the truck, I turned the key, and the engine roared to life. If she wasn't at the church, then I'd call in some favors and get a search party going.

For now, I crossed my fingers and said a silent prayer that she'd be at Saint Dwynwen's.

Chapter 34

Madison

Footsteps echoed on stone behind me. I turned to see Geraint ploughing up the aisle. He planted himself next to me and looked me over as if running an inventory of possible injury. Light from the stained-glass window danced on his flustered face. The cold rushed off him in waves and made me shiver.

His voice was hoarse with emotion. "Thank God you're here. Are you okay? Has something happened?"

I took a deep breath to calm the swirling agitation inside. "I'm fine. What are you doing here?"

"I woke up and you'd gone. I've been looking all over. I was so worried about you."

"Worried? Why?"

He scraped a hand over his beard. "I didn't know where you'd gone. I didn't know if I'd done something, or said something—"

"It's not you. I just needed . . . some air."

Running out hadn't worked. I couldn't shift the horrible feeling that Bryce's face had triggered. Being in a church didn't help. I'd just needed to get warm, but this place was making it worse. Geraint opened his mouth and closed it again. He rubbed the back of his neck with his hand, and I noticed his fingers were trembling. Had he really been all over, looking for me? He'd had to rescue me from the snow once before. I'd probably terrified him without meaning to. A rush of affection filled me. He'd come for me. Every day since I'd left the US, I'd felt so alone, but for the first time it felt as though I had someone on this side of the ocean who would notice if I went missing in a blizzard.

Silence stretched tight between us. I could just tell him about Bryce, but then I'd have to tell him what a fool I'd been. The right thing to do was to forgive and move on, but I couldn't risk opening myself up to being treated badly again. Geraint had forgiven his ex-wife and moved on. I couldn't forgive Bryce.

The floral displays arranged along the aisle overpowered me with their scent. The flowers looked fresh. Maybe somebody had married here recently, somebody who had actually made it through the ceremony. I spoke just to break the silence.

"It looks as though there was a wedding here recently."

"Right. Maybe."

Geraint gazed at the crosses and crucifixes on the walls. He scuffed the tip of his heavy boot on the stone floor. I took a breath. Maybe I couldn't talk about Bryce, but I could talk to him about us. We'd agreed this would be over and I'd have to walk away. Did he still want that?

I cleared my throat, trying to think of the right thing to say, but he beat me to it.

"My wedding day was an absolute disaster from start to finish. It should have clued me in. Everything that could go wrong went wrong. You'd never seen so much rain. Jess was mad all day about her mascara."

I wrapped my arms around myself. "That doesn't sound fun."

A thoughtful expression came over his face. "We were such different people, but I didn't see it."

"Oh."

I had a sinking sensation. Geraint and I were so different too: different countries, different backgrounds, different lifestyles. Geraint was laid-back and sweet, and I was always wound up and snarky. He was a golden retriever, and I was a black cat. How could it ever work? I'd ignored a hundred red flags with Bryce. Love made you ignorant. Really, it was a sickness of the heart. How could I trust my feelings? I'd got it so wrong. Everybody around me had known I'd got it wrong, and I'd been such a fool.

Geraint cleared his throat. His hand drifted to his jacket pocket. He gave his head a small shake, turned, and picked up a Bible. He leafed through the pages in an absent fashion, then made to return it to the pew but missed. The book fell to the stone floor with a heavy thud. Awkwardly, he scooped it up.

Bryce ran away because he didn't want to commit to me. My parents had known. They'd tried to warn me, but I'd been stubborn and naive. Here I was being naive again. I'd known Geraint for two weeks. Two weeks! How could I ever explain this to my parents?

Hey Mom and Dad, remember I wanted to marry that guy you all hated? Well, now I've met another guy, and I fell for this one after two weeks. You'll love him. He makes the most delicious seaweed.

This was all crazy. It had been this way with Bryce. I'd been swept up in a whirlwind, every scrap of common sense had left my body, and I'd lost myself. Geraint was nothing like Bryce. He was kind and gentle, and this had all been amazing. Even so, I couldn't risk repeating the same mistake.

"Jess had wanted to honeymoon in the Maldives, but I'd wanted to do a safari. We couldn't even agree on the fun parts."

Why was he still blathering on about his ex-wife? I'd wanted to talk about us. My heart pounded. What was I doing? How many women had been in his bed on a vacation and fallen for him like this? He'd admitted he spent his time bedding the women who passed through here. I was just another notch on his bedpost.

The chapel's coldness crept into my bones. Moments ago, I'd been considering giving up my life and moving here to be with him—a man I hardly knew. How could I trust my gut when it had let me down so badly? The only place I knew my own mind was on the pitch. Soccer was easy like that. These kinds of things were so difficult. I didn't trust my heart anymore. It had led me astray.

This thing between us was nothing but blind lust. A rebound. It could never work, could it? We were too different. He had a life here, and my life was in England. We were even more different on the surface than me and Bryce. At least Bryce and I spoke the same first language. Half the time, Geraint was mumbling something incomprehensible in Welsh. I couldn't even pronounce his name properly!

The memory of riding to the church with my dad pushed into my head.

Are you sure about this?

I wrapped my arms around myself. I'd wanted an escape from all the pressure and upset of my life, and it had worked for a while. Now it was making me feel worse. I needed to heal my broken heart, but instead I'd found another unsuitable man to destroy it all over again.

Geraint patted his jacket pocket and coughed. "There's something . . . I'm not good with words . . . Sometimes my brain is not connected to my mouth . . . I know you're probably going to think this is silly, but—"

"The guys in the bar told me there's something different about a Welsh hug."

He looked puzzled. "A Welsh hug?"

"You know. That word. I'm not even going to attempt to pronounce it. They said it's a hug and a cubbyhole. A safe place."

Geraint smiled. "A cwtch?"

My breath caught. That smile. So full of warmth. The realization settled in my gut like a sack of stones. He'd been so good to me, but this had to end. I couldn't make another mistake. My heart didn't get to make decisions. It had failed me. I had to think with my head.

"I didn't believe them. I thought it was some stupid spiel for tourists, like the spoons."

"The spoons?" Something flickered in his dark gaze. His arm fell from his jacket and pinned stiffly to his side. "Oh."

A ball of sadness ground in my gut.

Geraint studied my face. His thumb traced the outline of my jaw. His voice was a tender murmur. "What is it?"

The pain in my heart became sick and icy. "I believe them about the hug. When I'm in your arms, it's a place to hide. That's what this was for me. An escape. Now I need to go back to my real life."

He held perfectly still. A shadow crossed his face. "Do you have to?"

I swallowed past the lump in my throat. "Yes. I have the car now. I have to get back for training."

I kept my gaze fixed on the stained-glass window, on the woman in a white dress with flowing red hair and a crown of flowers. Saint Dwynwen. She'd drunk a potion to forget about her lover and forsaken all men. If a potion existed to get rid of this feeling of rage and betrayal, I would have gladly drunk it, but there wasn't. I had to be strong and never be stupid enough to make the same mistake again.

"They need me at the club. I can't miss training. I have a game coming up."

His eyes searched my face. "Is that what you want? To go back?"

I wanted nothing more than to fall into his arms and stay wrapped in this little bubble forever, but it couldn't last. It had been wonderful, but it was over. This wasn't a man I could have a future with.

"My life is in England."

Something dark flickered in his eyes. "You're not happy there though, are you?"

"I didn't say I was unhappy."

"You don't need to. Every time you talk about going back, you lose the sparkle in your eyes. What are you so worried about? You can tell me. I might be able to help you."

"It's just something I have to deal with. Please don't make this more difficult than it needs to be."

He held his hands up and stepped back as though I'd slapped him. "I don't want to make anything difficult for you. That's the last thing I want. I've been trying to help you. All I want is to help you."

"No. You're not helping. You're making this difficult. If you want to help me, you'll let me go. We were always clear about what this was, Geraint. I have been honest with you. This was a fling. It was fun while it lasted, and I'm grateful, but I have to go now. It's time."

"I'll honor my promise to let you walk away, but not with you thinking this means nothing to me. This isn't a fling for me. I won't look back on our time together like that. You told me I need to think about my future—well, I've figured it out. I want you. That's all I know, and I know it with absolute certainty. You can walk away, but not without me telling you how much I want you to stay. I've fallen in—"

"Don't. Please stop." I held up my hand to quiet him. A lump formed in my throat. "Please don't say it."

His face dropped, but I had to harden my heart. This was for the best, even though it hurt. Bryce hadn't just shattered my heart,

188

he'd ripped away the future I'd envisioned. He'd taken everything. This was what men did. If you gave a man your heart, you gave him too much power. I'd never let anyone pull the rug out from under my feet again. I cupped his rough cheek. "You can't say that to me. We both agreed that we'd keep this casual. This was always temporary. We both knew that. It's been two weeks."

"It doesn't matter how long. When you know, you know."

I thought I'd known with Bryce, too. I couldn't trust myself. "You promised you'd let me go, remember? No regrets."

He opened his mouth and closed it again. His voice was low and sad. "I remember, and I'll never bother you again, if that's what you want."

I gripped my determination, wrapping ice around the parts that were too soft. It was no use being soft in this world. Better to be realistic. No man would ever leave me standing at an altar again like a fool. This time, I'd be the one doing the walking. My boots squeaked on stone as I walked out of the chapel.

Chapter 35

GERAINT

Madison's suitcase wheels rumbled over the stone floor of the pub. My knee burned as I raced to help her. I reached for her case. "I've got it."

Her voice was impatient. "It's fine."

"Please. It's heavy."

She tightened her grip on the handle. "I can manage."

I spoke too loudly, the words strange on my tongue. "I know you don't need my help, but let me do at least one thing for you. Please."

Her brow lifted in surprise. Shame ground in my gut. I hadn't meant to sound desperate, but this hurt too much. She was leaving me.

This is just a fling. Don't make it difficult.

Her eyes roved over me, and she took a step back. She folded her arms defensively. "Be my guest."

"Thanks."

She followed me across the empty pub lounge and outside to the parking lot. I loaded her luggage into the trunk of her eggshell Mini Cooper. The spoon weighed heavy in my jacket, as though it was carved in stone. It made the back of my neck burn with shame. What had I been thinking? Madison didn't want me. A piece of wood wasn't going to change that. I'd lost so much in my life, but I still had my integrity. No matter how much it sickened me to watch her go, I wouldn't make this difficult for her.

Icy rain hammered us. It battered the roof of the car in a deafening sound. Madison moistened her lips. Her voice was distant and faraway. "Thank you."

Which part was she thanking me for? The stay? The food? The part where I fell in love with her, and she wouldn't even let me say the words out loud?

I tried to smile, despite my racing heart. "You're welcome."

She gripped the handle of the driver's door. Anger darkened her stern face. It was the way she'd looked when I picked her up at the side of the road.

She set her chin in a stubborn line. "When is your meeting with the brewery?"

"On Wednesday."

"The same day as my match." She nodded absently. "And you're sure you won't let me lend you the money?"

Embarrassment made a muscle quirk in my jaw. No way would I accept that kind of money from a woman. I was old-fashioned like that. It was a man's job to provide. I'd take care of my woman, not the other way around. If she'd have let me give her the spoon, I would have been able to explain that to her. "I'm sure."

She gave me a narrow, glinting glance and folded her arms. "I didn't realize you were so stubborn."

A sense of inadequacy swept over me. "Maybe you don't know me that well."

She chewed her lip, and her eyes slipped away. "Maybe."

The patter of raindrops filled the silence between us.

She peered at me, blinking rain from her eyes. Unspoken words wound tight between us. I wanted to pull her into my arms and kiss her until my lips burned, but who would it benefit? That wouldn't make it easier for her . . . or for me. My guts churned. We'd spent so many intimate moments together, and I'd never felt like a stranger. I had a horrible sense that I was floating, that none of this was really happening.

"Can I call you?"

A shadow darkened her eyes. "It's better if you don't."

My heart sank. I spoke to break the excruciating awkwardness between us. "Goodbye, Kentucky."

She gave me a grudging nod, but she wouldn't look at me. "Take care, Geraint."

Geraint. I tingled to hear her speak my name. For the first time, her pronunciation was perfect. "Well done. My name. You sounded like a local that time."

She sighed heavily and closed her eyes. Then she got in the car and drove out of my life.

Chapter 36

MADISON

A white sign loomed on the road ahead with "Welcome to England" emblazoned on it. My heart sank.

Screw England.

Rain pounded the roof of the car. The repetitive squeak of the windshield wipers grated on my nerves. Geraint drifted into my head. A stab of wild grief ripped through me, and I fought to push the feeling away. It was over. I had a job to do. A game to win.

I'd known the whole time it couldn't last, and still I'd let myself fall for him. I was smarter than this. I couldn't get involved with another man when my heart was so twisted up. The training schedule at the club left no time for a social life, and running a pub was a full-time job.

My heart was heavy with pain. The Magic 8 Ball was back.

Why hadn't I done a better job of protecting my heart?

Reply hazy, try again.

Did I do the right thing walking away?

My sources say no.

◆ ◆ ◆

I dragged my case along the sterile corridor to my fancy apartment. I opened the door and held in my sigh of relief. The club-sponsored cleaner had visited while I was away. The surfaces gleamed, and the cream carpet looked pristine. A lovely smell of floral furniture polish wrapped around me. It was a million miles from the cozy pub I'd been staying in. I wandered around the open-plan living area, feeling lost and empty.

For anybody in my position, England would be an adventure; but this modern monochrome apartment could never be homey like the Dragon, with its crackling fire and peaceful silence. The gray apartment building in the middle of the city was austere and soulless. No beautiful white blanket of snow or quiet mountains, just relentless traffic splashing through dirty slush. I brushed the feelings away. This was post-vacation blues. Who didn't feel like crap when they got home from a vacation?

My heart ached, but I'd done the right thing, hadn't I? The goodbye was inevitable. Men couldn't be trusted. Bryce had proven that. This was how they got you. They made you fall for them with kind words and masterful kisses, and then they stabbed you through the heart. Better to rip off the Band-Aid now. I stiffened my spine, fighting to get some control over my emotions. One thing was for certain: leaving Wales felt terrible. It wasn't just heartache that pained me. It was homesickness. I wanted a home, and the only thing I knew for certain was that it wasn't this sterile apartment or this gray city. It was anything but this.

Chapter 37

GERAINT

I propped Ewan's laptop on the bar. I had an entire business plan to write, and I hadn't done a thing. There was no way I'd be able to write this, not when Madison occupied my every thought. Women always left, but I'd had this strange hope in my heart that couldn't be extinguished. This time, I'd wanted it to be different. I loved her. I had no idea how to cope with this feeling, but it was because I loved her so much that I had to let her go. She didn't want to be here. She wanted to go back to her life, even if it made her unhappy.

A chilly breeze rushed in as Ewan entered the pub. He stomped the snow from his boots and hung his coat up.

"Bore da," he called cheerily.

It was too early to be so happy. I forced a smile. "Bore da."

He disappeared into the kitchen and returned ten minutes later with two mugs of tea.

"You look like you need this." He offered me the hot drink and surveyed the empty pub.

"Thanks."

"She's gone then?"

The churning in my guts started all over again. "She's gone."

Silence wrapped around us.

Ewan watched me over the rim of his mug. His eyes were teasing, but I didn't share the joke. "What on earth went wrong?"

You tell me. Something had changed in that church. I'd managed to put my foot in it without even knowing how.

Ewan watched me with a grim expression. "Are you okay, Big G?"

No. I'm not okay.

Ewan's eyes burned into me. "Did you tell Madison how you feel about her?"

"She didn't want to hear it."

It had been a mistake to even try. I'd stopped trying with everything else a long time ago, I should have known better than to try with Maddie.

I let out a sigh. "We have different lives and commitments. I have to keep this pub going. I promised Dad. A promise is a promise."

Ewan's shrewd gaze roved over me, and he bit his lip. "John was a good man and a good father. The atmosphere in this pub was electric whenever you played. John would sit in front of that TV so close he almost had his nose pressed to it." An unconscious smile curved Ewan's lips. "He'd throw a fit if anyone disturbed him. He was glued to that screen watching his boy. I think that's what he loved about this place. When you played, the whole community was in here with John, cheering his son on. He was so proud of you. He had the biggest smile on his face on match days."

A sudden sorrow made me ache. Dad had never been one to open up. It wasn't his way, but I'd found boxes of scrapbooks full of newspaper clippings down in the basement. He'd followed my career at every step.

"I miss him." My voice sounded hoarse.

"I know." Ewan twisted a coaster between his fingers. "We all do."

The refrigerators behind the bar hummed in the silence.

A thoughtful expression came over Ewan's face. "What do you think John would say if he was here now and he saw how much stress it was causing you to hold on to this place? If he thought you were only doing all this for him?"

"I try not to think about that kind of thing."

"You should, because John would want you to be happy. This pub was important to him, but it was important because it was filled with the community who came together here. It was never about the bricks and mortar. It was the people that he cared about gathering around that TV on match nights and celebrating his son's success. He wouldn't have wanted this place to be a burden on you. If you want to keep it, you have to do it for yourself because it's what *you* want. If you need to let it go, then let it go. John would have understood. He'd want the best for his only son. Your dad would only ever want you to be happy."

This wasn't just about me, though. The Dragon was important to everybody else. It was a local landmark. A piece of history. "What about you and Aled? What about the regulars? This pub is important to the community . . . the locals. I can't just up and leave on everyone and let this place become full of downward dogs and gong baths. I still don't know if gongs are being banged while people are in a bath. It makes no sense."

"It's not your responsibility. You can't fight progress. Gong baths are gonna gong. We might even like them." Ewan's face brightened, and he grinned mischievously. "Aled has been moaning about his back for so long. A few downward dogs might be just what he needs. The point is that you have to make a decision about your future. If you want this pub then you can find a way to keep it. If you put your mind to it, you can do anything, Big G. You've lifted the Six Nations trophy. You can turn this around, but only if it's the right thing for you."

Heaviness pressed me down. My gaze found the armchair in front of the dusty old TV on the wall, and I let myself imagine my dad sitting there watching me play. That TV didn't even work anymore. It had broken, and I hadn't bothered to replace it. It would hurt Dad to see what had become of it. This pub had thrummed with life and now it was dead. I'd let him down, but all my energy had gone into keeping up with repairs, and it had all been so costly.

"Dad would hate to see the Dragon looking so tatty."

"Don't be so hard on yourself. You did your best." Ewan's eyes flashed with sympathy, and he pulled out his phone. "I've got something that might cheer you up. Look who's become the latest TikTok sensation."

"If you're about to show me something about Taylor Swift, I swear to God, Ewan—"

He chuckled. "It's not as good as that, but it's pretty good. You've got over 500,000 views."

He clicked on a video that Maddie had made of me whipping up a batch of Welsh cakes on the griddle pan. "Is that good?"

"It's great." He scrolled through the comments section. "You've got a lot of engagement. You're reaching a whole new audience. I was thinking I could call the local newspaper and bring them here to talk about your new venture as a celebrity chef."

I laughed. "Celebrity chef? Steady on."

"Why not? We might even be able to get you on the local news channel. We've got to try everything, haven't we?" He shot me a speculative glance. "But only if that's what you want? If you need to let this place go, we'd all understand."

The clip looped, and I watched myself sprinkling sugar on top of the Welsh cakes. It didn't make me cringe half as much as I thought it would. In fact, it didn't look bad at all. I'd enjoyed it. It was a similar buzz to when I'd played rugby. I got to be creative and show what I could do, even if it was a totally different set of skills.

A warm feeling spread through me. Maybe Ewan was on to something. I'd been looking at this wrong. I'd only ever focused on the bricks and mortar, and everything going wrong with this place, but it wasn't all bad. I loved the people. The Dragon could be something exciting again, but it needed commitment and effort. I could turn the pub around, and put my own spin on it. I could do it for Dad, and all the people around here, but not if that was my only reason. I had to do it for myself, too.

I gave Ewan a nod. "You're right. I want to try and keep this place."

"*We* want to try. Aled has some ideas too. We're a team." He tilted his head downward and drew a circle on the bar with his finger. His voice was playful. "Maddie and I were discussing the possibility of you doing these videos shirtless—"

I snorted. "Absolutely not."

"Take it under consideration. Five hundred thousand is a good start, but we can do better."

"Nope." I rolled my eyes, but I couldn't help my laugh. "Get back to work. No time for chitchat. I've got a business plan to write."

Chapter 38

Madison

We gathered in the hotel conference room to finalize the game plan for the match the following day. The team sat shoulder to shoulder in Calverdale hoodies. Under normal circumstances this room would buzz with light-hearted banter and jokes, but everyone wore the same intense expression. Shit was about to get real. A local derby was always a big deal. Plenty would tune in to watch a match with such bitter rivalry. There were no televised soccer games tomorrow except ours. A win would position us at the top of the table—a significant feat for a team who had been in the professional league for such a short time. The press had predicted that tomorrow would be a world record crowd for Women's Super League. The team was thrilled. I, less so.

Claire's animated instructions washed over me, and I fought with everything I had to track her enthusiastic sketching on the whiteboard. The squeak of her marker pen gnawed at my brain and made my teeth grit. This was important, but all I could think about was how to get out of the pre-match bonding dinner. My appetite had gone back into retreat, and I didn't want to sit pushing broccoli around a plate and getting into intense discussions about the weather and TV shows I'd never heard of. I just had to come up with a decent excuse.

Sorry. I can't. I need to focus and get my head together for tomorrow.

I've always preferred my space before a match.

My heart feels like it's shattered beyond repair, and I can't face talking to any of you. Yes, it rains a lot. No, I don't watch EastEnders. Please leave me alone.

Maybe not the last one. I'd felt so much better in Wales, but now the empty, sick feeling had crept back into my bones and smothered me. I missed Geraint terribly. No matter how I tried to block him out of my mind, I couldn't. The sorrow etched into his face when I'd driven away wouldn't leave me. What if I'd let him say the damn words? Sweat dripped down the back of my neck. This room was too hot with us all in here. No. I'd done the right thing. A two-week casual fling. That's all it had been. We'd made an agreement. It wasn't my fault Geraint had tried to change the rules.

Claire went through the patterns of play we'd been trying to perfect in training. I hadn't managed to get any of them correct even once. None of us had any reason to think tomorrow would be different, except tomorrow my failure would be in front of a packed stadium and broadcast to all my friends and family back home. Maybe Bryce would be watching. He'd missed out on witnessing my humiliation first-hand by not turning up at church. He could watch me die inside again tomorrow instead.

I looked up to see that Claire had stepped aside, and now Gabe was talking. Guilt made my shoulders tight. This man had brought me here because he thought I could help his team win this match tomorrow. I'd wasted his money, and his time. He'd wise up soon and get rid of me. Then what would I do?

Gabe stood tall and confident at the front of the room. He dusted his hands together. His emerald eyes blazed with purpose.

"I don't need to tell you how important this match is. The supporters want this win above all. This is why we play, for the community who come together to support us. There will be a few nerves tomorrow, and that's okay. Above all, we're here to make memories. This is our chance to make the fans proud. To pay them back for their support, and to show everyone what Calverdale Ladies are made of.

"You've all had your own personal journeys to get here. You know mine, and you know what this means to me. I promised my wife if she stuck with me, I'd take us both to the top." His dazzling smile lingered on our striker, Miri. "And she was crazy enough to join me on this ride."

Miri gave him an indulgent smile, but her eyes sparkled with pride. "It's been a pleasure, Rivers."

His grin widened, and he put a hand over his heart. "I'm a lucky man. I get to witness my wonderful wife do the thing she was born to do, and I get to see my team perform. I have no doubt every one of you will leave everything out there on the pitch tomorrow. When it's tough, let the fans give you the energy you need to keep pushing. In my eyes, you're all champions. Remember the sacrifices you've made to get here. Remember that togetherness is our strength. We fight for each other, and we support each other."

Heads bobbed in agreement, and a couple of girls whooped. A flutter of excitement stirred inside.

Gabe paced back and forth in front of the whiteboard. "A win takes us to the top of the table. I don't care if we're there for a day, a month, or if we're there at the end of the season. I just want us to have our moment at the top." His voice was firm and commanding. "We're going to show everyone what it means to be Calverdale. We've built something here together that is unstoppable. We're not just a team, we're a family."

Applause broke out around the room. Despite my misgivings, my heart raced. The nerves and excitement were palpable. This was going to be one hell of a match. I wanted more than anything to believe I could do this. I wanted to go out onto the pitch and play the way I had before. If I could play at my normal level, I could score goals for this team. The trouble was, I hadn't had a single good match since I came to England. I had no reason to believe tomorrow would be different.

The team rose and filed out of the conference room. Lana was to my left. I tried to dodge past her and get to the foyer so I could dash to the elevator before anyone questioned me. Lana's friendly voice stopped me in my task. "The dining room is this way, Maddie."

I spun. "Oh, is it?" I pasted a casual smile onto my face. "I thought I'd give dinner a miss, actually."

She raised a brow and ran a hand over her red ponytail. "You're not coming for dinner?"

"I like my own space to focus before a big match."

"If you're sure? I can make a plate for you and bring it up?"

"No need. I'm good. Thanks."

I turned so quickly to get away that I collided with Skylar. Damn it. I'd successfully avoided my captain all day.

"Maddie? Are you okay?" Skylar stepped away and gave me a tentative smile. "We've had no chance to catch up. I need to hear all about Christmas in Wales. I tried to ring a few times, but I couldn't get through."

Guilt washed over me. "I'm sorry. The phone reception was terrible."

Not entirely a lie. The reception wasn't great, like the Wi-Fi, but I could have called back if I'd wanted to.

Skylar nodded. "How was it in Wales? Did you have a good time?"

I shrugged, but my heart felt heavy. "It was okay. No big thing. Just a few sheep, and a lot of snow."

And a Welsh giant I can't stop thinking about.

"Have a good night." I dashed to the lift before I'd have to come up with more excuses. "See you tomorrow."

Chapter 39

MADISON

I examined my face in the mirror in the hotel bathroom. My troubled reflection stared back at me. The hollows of my cheekbones had filled out a little, but my face was still gaunt and pale. The hotel room gave me a panorama of towering skyscrapers and city lights twinkling in the night. It was ugly and bleak compared to the wild wintery scenes I'd driven away from. I missed sunlight sparkling on snow, beautifying everything, and the crunch under my boots every time I stepped out. I missed the cozy lounge with its roaring fire and comfy armchairs. Most of all, I missed Geraint's giant arms around me, and his hugs that were a cubbyhole, which had made me understand why the Welsh had their own word for that wonderful feeling.

A knock sounded at the door. I grabbed a robe and pulled it over my pajamas.

"One second."

I opened the door to find Skylar holding an enormous wicker hamper wrapped in layers of cellophane and covered in red bows. She shot me an apologetic glance. "Sorry to disturb you. I've been meaning to give you this. This is your Christmas present from the team."

She passed me the heavy basket, and my arms buckled under the weight. What had they bought me? A ton of bricks? A wave of guilt washed over me. I'd been so set on escaping this place, I hadn't even thought about exchanging gifts.

"It's just a few bits and bobs. When I was in LA, I craved proper tea bags and Jaffa Cakes. This is some American snacks we thought you might be missing. Personally, I'm a big fan of Milk Duds."

I peered through the cellophane at the packets of Cheetos and cans of Mountain Dew. There was even a bottle of Woodford Reserve bourbon. The hamper was huge. It must have taken so much effort to gather all these things. I couldn't keep the surprise from my voice. "Where did you find all this stuff?"

She flashed a jovial smile. "It was a team effort."

I'd thought no one would care about me being away, but they'd put together this thoughtful hamper. This was so nice and unexpected. "Thank you so much."

"Of course. We missed you at the Christmas party. I've been worried you'd be feeling homesick. I remember how it was when I played in the States. It's tough playing away from home. Anyway, I'll let you get on. I know you said you wanted to be left alone."

She flashed a smile and turned on her heel.

"Wait." I set the hamper down. Skylar had made so much effort with this. The least I could do was be polite. "How long did you play in LA?"

She paused in the corridor. "Six months."

Weird that we'd never really talked about it. We'd both played for the Halos, although I hadn't been there at the same time as Skylar. We probably knew all the same people. It shamed me to realize that I hardly knew anything about my captain, or any of the other women on the team.

"Did you like playing with the Halos?"

Skylar drifted back to the door. "I loved the team. I learned a lot, although it was tough out there. My form wasn't great at the start."

"Probably better than mine at the moment."

She fiddled with the silver ring in her nose. "Remember, we all have our ups and downs. A player's form peaks and troughs." She glanced down the corridor and kept her voice low. "It takes time to settle at a new club. Everybody understands. It took me time in LA, and believe me, my form has dipped in the past. Before we got into the WSL, I wasn't playing well at all. I had a breakup that threw me. These things happen. It's life."

"Gabe brought me here to create and score goals, and I feel like I've done nothing."

Her eyes filled with empathy. "Gabe brought you here to join us as a *team*. No team is about a single player. You'll find your feet again. In the meantime, we're all here to support you. We all know how good you are. When the women see the 'Thornado' in the locker room, everyone raises their game."

I cringed. "Don't call me that."

"Why not? You're a force of nature."

My heart contracted. "Maybe, in the past. Not anymore."

"You're Calverdale. That's enough. If things don't go our way tomorrow, that's something we get through as a team. I thought I'd never get back to playing at my best, but I did. Form comes and goes, but quality is permanent." She put a hand on my shoulder. "We're lucky to have you. It's like Gabe said, you're part of the family now. You can't get rid of us."

I scoffed, but heat pressed behind my eyes. "You'd be better off getting rid of me. I'm letting you all down."

She frowned. "Of course you're not. Nobody thinks that."

I fought to keep my tears in check. Geraint had told me to open up to the team, but I hadn't dared. Maybe it wasn't so bad. Skylar seemed nice, and I had nothing to lose. If I couldn't get my act together, I'd probably end up on the bench soon anyway. I gathered my courage. "I had a bad breakup before I came here. It's affected my game."

Skylar gave me a knowing look. She peered over my shoulder into the suite. "Do you want to talk about it? I know we can't stay up late, but a cup of tea? We can compare notes on bad breakups. Any ex of yours will do well to beat mine. Sean Wallace has to be the front runner for world's most narcissistic man. You wouldn't believe the crap this guy used to come out with."

I opened my mouth to deliver one of my usual excuses to be alone, then shut it. I'd been pushing everyone away for so long, but company didn't sound so bad. A cup of tea with my captain beat spending the night missing Geraint and feeling miserable.

I stepped aside to let Skylar in. "Whatever your ex did, I think Bryce would be stiff competition for the world's greatest narcissist."

She stepped over the threshold. Curiosity painted across her face. "Oh?"

I hadn't told a soul this side of the pond about what had happened in that church. Gabe knew, but no one had ever mentioned it, so I assumed he'd kept it to himself. I took a breath. "My fiancé jilted me at the altar on our wedding day."

Skylar's sympathetic eyes traveled over my face. "I'm sorry. That must have been awful."

Regret piled on top of me. Perhaps it had been a mistake to be so open. I braced myself, waiting for the pity and worry that everyone heaped on me back home.

Skylar flashed a small smile. "This is some stiff competition for Sean. I think I might have to let Bryce win that round. What else have you got?"

I bent down to open the hamper full of goodies that my team had bought. The team that I'd been pushing away. The team that I wanted to be a part of, but I'd been too scared to let myself cozy up to for so many reasons that didn't seem to ring true anymore. I'd found friendship and acceptance in Wales. There was no reason that I couldn't find it here, if only I let myself try.

I pulled out the Milk Duds from the hamper and presented them to Skylar. "Wait till you hear about Bryce's amateur photography ambitions. He has an Instagram full of crappy food photos. An eight-year-old could do a better job."

She let out a bark of laughter. "Well, don't just stand there. Let's have a look at it." She rubbed her hands together with glee. "Sounds spectacular."

Chapter 40

MADISON

We lined up next to our rivals in the tunnel. I glanced at my opposing number but her gaze was fixed firmly ahead. These women meant business. The roar of the crowd in the stadium echoed in the tense silence that wound between us. Skylar stood poised and confident in her position as captain at the front of the line, and I stood behind her. We'd stayed up later than we should, but it had been fun. We had so much in common. Once we'd got talking about LA, the time had flown.

Skylar threw a glance over her shoulder. "Feeling okay?"

My heart pounded. A rush of adrenaline made every sense too sharp.

Yes. No. Maybe.

Skylar's eyes shone with determination. She lowered her voice. "Whatever happens, this is not all on you. I've got you. Breathe. Try not to get in your head. Just take it all in."

A memory hit me. Dad's words as we'd driven to the chapel drifted through my mind.

Just breathe, and take it all in.

The walls pressed close, as though they wanted to swallow me, and I was back, stranded at the altar. This would be the same. Another spectacular humiliation. Skylar turned to face ahead, and the ref led us forward in two purposeful lines onto the pitch. The stadium's roar grew so loud it blasted my ears. Fans crowded the stands. An icy drizzle hit me, and a bitter wind howled in my ears.

I took my position while the captains met with the ref for the coin toss. The pitch-side cameras burned into me, making me feel hot and self-conscious. I tried to turn away from them, but whichever direction I faced, there was no escape. Everyone back home would watch over breakfast. With any luck, their alarm clocks had failed, and they were sleeping through it. Maybe Geraint would be watching. Tightness blazed through my muscles as I stretched my hamstrings. My body couldn't let go of the tension that plagued my mind. I missed Geraint. I longed for his melodic voice, the warmth of his powerful arms around me, his scent of wood shavings and winter pine.

Despite the anxiety rippling through my body, I tried to take deep breaths. If only I could have one good game. One goal for confidence. Just one damn thing to justify my place on this team. I tried to stand tall and look confident, although my knees quaked. A flash of yellow in the crowd caught my eye. A home-made banner unfurled in the wind. It was a bedsheet, with a funnel-shaped cloud scribbled in gray next to a vibrant lightning bolt. Two adolescent girls wearing LA Halos jerseys, but with Calverdale scarves wrapped around their necks, held the sheet proudly aloft. The words were printed in Calverdale blue.

Unleash the Thornado. We love you, Maddie!

A wash of emotion welled inside. Despite my shoddy performances, these young women in the crowd were rooting for me. They weren't the only ones. I scanned the stands to see more banners with my name on. So much expectation. I felt my knees buckling under the weight of it. I wanted to be the old me. The player who gave everything to the game, and was worthy of the fans' loyalty. Once, I'd been a tornado, powerful and determined, but the winds had become too chaotic. A vortex had swallowed me.

England had only ever been an escape from my disaster of a life. I'd had my head stuck up my ass for so long. I could have embraced this opportunity, and I hadn't. The team and the supporters had welcomed me with open arms, but I'd had nothing to give in return. Bryce had consumed so much of my energy.

The banner flapped in the breeze, and I couldn't take my eyes off it.

We love you, Maddie!

The fans still believed in me. Gabe was right. This is why we played. Soccer brought the community together. Geraint had said the same thing about rugby. It was about the fans. I owed it to them to perform. I couldn't let Bryce devastate me like this.

Enough.

I wasn't the first woman in history to be screwed over by a man, and I wouldn't be the last. Listening to the stories of Skylar's nightmare ex had assured me of that. Skylar had healed, and moved on. She was happily married, and flourishing in her career. I couldn't live like this anymore, weak and afraid. There would always be storms. I couldn't stop the winds from buffeting me, but I could stop myself from being swept away and destroyed.

Bryce had humiliated and hurt me, but anyone in my life who mattered wouldn't judge me. The women holding that banner couldn't have cared less about what Bryce had done. They were here to see me play soccer. That's what I did best. That's what I'd always done best. Form on the pitch would wax and wane, but no one could take away what I'd worked for my whole life. Bryce had abandoned me, but soccer never would. It was in my blood.

There were so many people who didn't get to do the thing they loved. Geraint had loved rugby, and he'd had to give it up. I still had my chance to be on this pitch. To play with these incredibly talented women in front of this crowd who had paid money to support us. It was a gift, and an honor. I couldn't take it for granted. The clouds parted, and the December sun broke through, streaming across the pitch in pale golden beams. I had the sudden sense that I'd come home.

Everyone I knew would be watching, but not because they wanted to witness my humiliation. They were cheering me on. My family and friends had always been cheering me on. The banner flapped in the wind, and it was as if those words had got to the core of me.

We love you, Maddie!

I tilted my chin upward to feel the December sun. I hadn't given enough to this team. It wasn't fair. I'd change that now. I'd give them everything. With my brightest smile fixed in place, I turned to the nearest camera and waved. Maybe this match, I'd live up to my reputation as the "Thornado", or maybe I wouldn't. Maybe I'd just be Maddie, a player trying her best at the game she loved.

Either was fine.

Either way, I was home.

Rain blasted my face as I sprinted the length of the pitch. What was it with this country and the weather? Eighty minutes of play, and neither side had scored. My lungs burned and my muscles blazed with fire. I'd played my heart out, but it wasn't enough. Exhaustion was creeping in. The opposition met us at every turn. Our rivals were the best in the league for a reason.

The opposition striker lined up a shot on goal, but Lana intercepted, winning the ball back in a crunching tackle. The crowd roared in response. Lana brought the ball out of defense, moving at a pace, and passed to Skylar. Skylar spun in one fluid motion, turning on the ball and dragging it to run with. She made swift progress up the field toward the goal.

Adrenaline spiked through me. This was it. The pattern of play we'd been practicing in training to get the ball from one end of the pitch to the other. It depended on each one of us being on our mark at the right time. Miri was already running into position with her head up, searching for an opportunity to make space. I had to get ahead of her so I could get the shot on goal. This was why Gabe had brought me here. I had the speed to do it, but this pattern relied on one-touch passes and quick transitions. It had to be perfectly timed, like a well-choreographed dance between the four of us. One misstep threw everything out.

Skylar flicked the ball to Miri, who received it and dashed down the line. Miri's head lifted, and I was ready. We'd moved so fast, half the players on the pitch hadn't caught on to what was happening, but the crowd had. Cheers filled the stadium. People were on their feet. This was the joy of soccer. When a team worked in synchrony, they created order from chaos. We were an orchestra in perfect harmony. These moments of grace were when soccer became the beautiful game. Together, we'd taken this pitch by storm.

Miri crossed the ball to me, but it was coming at height. Too low to head, but too high to shoot. Jumping, I allowed the ball to hit my chest, and fall to my boot. This was the part I always fudged in training. I prepared to shoot, but we hadn't been quick enough. Two red jerseys loomed between me and the goalkeeper. With no clear shot, I couldn't go around them. The only way was through.

With the ball at my feet, I dribbled past the first defender and made short work of the second. The goalie was off her mark, closing in on a collision course, her eyes wide and frenzied. She leaped, leaving me with no choice but to take the shot. With every last scrap of energy, I kicked the ball as hard and true as I could before the goalie ploughed into me. The blow shunted me. Bright lights exploded behind my eyes. Roaring blasted me from every angle. Then I was on the ground, gray clouds overhead. Metal and mud coated my tongue.

I had to get back on my feet, but it was so much nicer to sink into the wet grass. To rest somewhere soft and forgiving, like a hug, just for a little while. The clouds spun overhead then everything muted until it faded into a haze. My head filled with Geraint, and the way he'd looked as I'd walked away. If only I'd let him say the words. Darkness pressed at the edges of my vision like curtains closing. I had no choice but to surrender to it.

Chapter 41

GERAINT

My shirt collar felt tight and scratchy around my neck. Ewan readjusted the knot in my tie and smoothed my jacket lapels. "Do you want to go through the presentation again?"

Not again. I'd rehearsed so many times. We were ready.

Aled put a cup of tea on the bar in front of me. "You're going to be great."

Bryn, one of our regulars, lifted his pint. "You have us all backing you."

Heads nodded along the bar. This was the busiest I'd seen the place in a long time. Laughter and chatter filled the air, and it was a glimpse of what the pub had once been. If Dad was here, he would have loved to see it like this. At least when the brewery arrived for the meeting, I could bolster my words with a lively pub.

I rolled my shoulders and calmed myself. I'd been ambivalent about this place for so long, but now I needed to fight for it. This was too important to mess up. Ceri had gone over the business plan to ensure it looked professional. I'd been interviewed by the local paper, and Ewan had made Facebook adverts. Our social media efforts were gaining attention, and we had full sign-up for the cookery courses Ewan had planned. We already had reservations for the tourist season. The next step would be refurbishment, but for the first time, this all felt possible. We had a strong case to convince the brewery to renew the lease.

"It's time." Ewan picked up the remote control and angled it at the new TV I'd mounted on the wall.

I took my seat in the armchair where Dad had once sat and watched my games. On the screen, two lines of women in football kits streamed from a tunnel onto the huge pitch. My heart almost stopped when I saw Madison emerge.

Ewan pulled up a wooden stool next to me. His face lit with a proud smile. "There's our girl."

The ref blew the whistle, and the game commenced.

A groan sounded from the bar. "Change the channel. I don't want to watch English football."

I spoke without taking my eyes off the TV. "It's my pub. You'll watch what's on."

A few regulars grumbled, but I didn't care. They could leave if they wanted. Nothing would keep me from watching this woman. Madison was incredible on that pitch. I'd known she had to be good if she was playing for Calverdale, but she was better than I could have imagined. This magnificent person had been mine for a short time, and I'd let her slip through my fingers. How could I let a woman like this go? How was I supposed to carry on with my life when I knew how it was to fall in love with her?

Ewan threw a peanut into the air and caught it in his mouth. "She looks good on that pitch."

Madison blasted down the field, her ponytail bobbing. "She's brilliant."

He glanced over his shoulder at the queue at the bar. "We're getting busy."

Nothing would make me get out of this chair. I flapped a hand. "They can wait."

"Jill is going to be here soon."

"She can wait, too."

Ewan chewed his lip and shot me a tentative glance. "You could have gone to watch this."

My heart sank. "She didn't want me there."

"She told you that?"

"Madison was clear that she didn't want to see me again."

"And you're not going to fight for her?"

No. I'd promised her I wouldn't cause her bother. Madison knew it had been more than a fling to me, and she'd left anyway. I had to respect it even if it was really hard, even if it cut me to the bone. Sometimes, love was letting go.

"I'm going to do what she asked me to do."

Ewan nodded, woodenly.

The game was fast-paced and physical. Calverdale were good, but their rivals dominated the pitch. The opposition had so many chances on the goal that Ewan could only watch from between his fingers. Then something magical happened. A Calverdale defender won the ball in a tackle and passed it down the line to the captain. A fraction of a second later and the ball was at the feet of a blonde striker. The camera panned to Maddie, who leaped gracefully into the air to receive a swift pass. They'd moved so quickly and with such finesse that half the pitch looked confused. Maddie struck the defensive line like a lightning bolt. She weaved with breathtaking skill, storming through two defenders.

Suddenly, Maddie's moniker made perfect sense. She'd touched down here like a tornado—awesome, powerful, and completely without warning. She'd swept my heart up, and taken it away with her. It had devastated me to let her pass through. I wanted her back. I'd never not want her, but she'd also cleared a path for something new. She'd energized me and helped me take back control of my life.

"Oh my God." Ewan leaped to his feet. "She's going to score."

My heart pounded. A tense silence fell over the pub. It was so near the final whistle. This goal would surely give them a win. The keeper barreled into Maddie in a vicious collision, but somehow she kicked the ball toward the goal. The camera panned to the ball hitting the back of the net. A cry of excitement went up.

Ewan punched the air. "Goal!"

Madison had done it. My heart swelled with pride, and I was on my feet clapping and cheering with the rest of the pub. Simon barked excitedly and jumped into my arms, wagging his tail. Then the camera panned out to a wider angle. Madison lay on the pitch, motionless. The goalkeeper had completely wiped her out.

Ewan's jaw fell open, and he paled. "Shit."

A deathly silence enveloped me. Medics carrying stretchers rushed toward Madison.

"Get up, Maddie." Ewan's voice was a breathless whisper.

Her team gathered around her, but still she didn't move a muscle.

Ewan grabbed my arm. "Why isn't she getting up?"

All that mattered was Madison. I was out of the door so fast my feet barely touched the ground.

Chapter 42

MADISON

A spectacular panorama of snow-tipped mountains surrounded me. A freshwater stream trickled down the rocks. The patter of melting ice filled my ears. Everything inside of me relaxed. It was peaceful here. Nowhere to be. Nothing to worry about. Only the climb. Thick snow-flakes swirled, their intricate patterns like lace.

Geraint appeared next to me. He held out his hand to pull me higher.

"Why are we climbing?"

His smile enveloped me in warmth. "It doesn't matter. Just keep going."

"I don't think I can."

"You can. Come back to me. Keep going."

My breath moved sharp in my lungs. I had to rest here on the mountain, just for a minute. A little red cardinal perched next to me. Its low whistle thrummed in my brain. A terrible pounding pain in my head made me groan. "I don't think I can."

Pain radiated through my skull, pulsing into intense blinding agony. My fingertips burned where I held on to rock. "I can't do it."

"You can." Geraint opened his arms. His smile relaxed every part of me. "Come home."

Chapter 43

Geraint

Fluorescent lights dazzled my eyes as I stepped into the hospital waiting room. The surfaces gleamed, and the seats were empty. It was a complete change from the crowded NHS hospitals full of drunks and hooligans I'd been charging around. My gaze fixed on the small huddle of mud-splattered women in red jerseys and football socks. Of course Madison would be in a private hospital. I should have started here.

I darted to the huddle of women. "I need to see Madison Thorner. Where is she?"

A blonde-haired woman in a smart suit twisted to look at me. Her voice was unimpressed. "Who are you?"

"I'm Madison's . . . friend."

"I'm afraid I'm going to have to ask you to leave."

"I'm not going anywhere. Not until I see Madison."

The blonde woman frowned and beckoned a burly guy dressed in a black suit. "Can we get some security here? No fans. No press."

The security guy eyed me. I had no beef with these people. A wave of fatigue washed over me. My knee still ached from the journey. I held my hands up. "I'm not press. Please. I need to know she's okay."

The blonde folded her arms. "Friends and family only."

Damn it. I'd seen this woman on the side of the pitch. The manager? Hadn't Madison said she was a ball-buster?

I tried to keep my voice calm and level. "She doesn't have family here. Have you called them? Are her parents coming?"

The blonde woman eyed me again. "Go now, or I'll have you removed."

A heavy sigh left my lips. This wasn't a time for arguments. "She shouldn't be alone."

"She has her team. I can assure you, Madison is not alone."

The beefy security guy put a hand on my arm. "Come on, mate. You need to go."

Heat and the overwhelming smell of disinfectant engulfed me. It might have been a fancy hospital, but hospitals always smelled the same. Sickness twisted my insides. The eyes of the women on the team burned into me. Why couldn't someone give me an answer? This was how things went. I'd spent my life with people thinking I wanted to cause fights because of the way I looked. The last thing I'd come here for was an argument.

"I've driven a long way, and I've been around every hospital in this city. I'm not going anywhere until I know she's okay."

The security guy's lips thinned before he spoke into a walkie-talkie. "We've got a big fella down here. I'm going to need some backup."

"I'm not trying to cause trouble." An aching pain speared my knee. It had been in one position for too long. I sank into a hard-backed plastic chair that was far too small. "I'm not breaking any laws by being here, and I'm not going anywhere until somebody tells me how she is."

The security guy's hand clamped on my arm. "Get up. Let's go, mate. Let's do this the easy way."

My heart pounded. They couldn't throw me out of here. I shrugged him off. "Tell me if she's okay and I'll go."

The security guy took a menacing step toward me, but I wouldn't budge from the chair. Even with my duff knee, I could take this guy if I had to. I needed one look at her. That was all.

"Stop. Calm down." A woman with lilac hair and a face full of piercings stepped in front of me. She held the security guy at bay. "Madison is fine. She lost consciousness for a couple of minutes, but she's awake and doing okay. She has a concussion, so they are doing tests and monitoring her. Nothing to worry about."

Relief went through me. "She's awake? She's okay?"

The ball-buster blonde shook her head and muttered under her breath, "He could be press."

"He doesn't look like press to me." The purple-haired woman folded her arms and eyed me with a curious expression. "I'm Skylar, the captain. I'm staying with her. She'll be okay. We don't know who you are, and nobody wants a scene. You can leave your details. I'll tell Madison you stopped by. If she wants to talk to you, she'll call, I'm sure."

I sat in my truck where I could keep an eye on the hospital exit. No matter how many times I looked at the clock, the time didn't budge. Through the shiny glass doors, I watched people coming and going. Most of the team had left, but I hadn't seen the blonde bulldog or the woman with purple hair and tattoos. At least Madison had some support. They didn't seem to like me, but I got it. Madison had a public profile. They had to be wary.

The low rumble of conversation on the radio wrapped around me and I shifted, trying to get comfortable. My knee ached, but there was no room to stretch it in the truck. Maybe it had been impulsive driving down here, but I had to. It had been devastating to see Madison lying on the pitch like that. I knew how it felt to be splayed out on the grass in front of an audience, in pain, not knowing what the future would hold. For me, it had meant an end to my career. It didn't sound that way for Madison. That was a relief. I wanted to be the one to tell her everything was going to be okay. If only it could always be me. Did she want that too? I had to know. I'd been a fool to let her walk away.

My belly rumbled with hunger. I'd missed the meeting with Jill. I pushed it out of my head. None of it mattered. I couldn't think of anything until I'd seen Madison.

Chapter 44

MADISON

Beeping filled my ears. A pulse beat in my head. I shifted and pain shot through my skull.

Skylar's clear blue eyes met mine. "Maddie? Okay?"

I nodded and instantly regretted it. The movement made the room spin. Fluorescent lights blazed overhead, and the small hospital room came into focus. Memories hit me. We'd been on the pitch. I'd had a shot on goal, and then the keeper had clattered me. I remembered a wash of blue lights, and being stretchered out of the ambulance into the hospital. I'd fallen asleep after the scan. The painkillers had made me so woozy. Skylar got up and moved to the door. She called for a nurse from down the corridor.

"Did it go in?"

Skylar twisted to me with a quizzical look.

"The ball? Did we get the goal?"

"Don't worry about that now. All that matters is you getting better. How are you feeling?"

"Did we win? I need to know."

Skylar returned to her seat next to the bed. She rolled her shoulder in a gentle circular movement, as though soothing an ache. "Don't you remember? The medics carried you away on a stretcher, and you were drifting in and out. You were shouting that the match needed to go on, then something about a mountain, then you conked out again." She gave me an affectionate smile. "We played on and won. That goal took us to the top of the table."

I shifted, and pain shot through my head. "I can't believe we actually nailed those passes."

Skylar grinned and sat back in the chair, picking at a patch of dried dirt on her Calverdale jersey. "I know. What a feeling."

"Everyone must be so thrilled."

"We are. Gabe especially. He's got the better of everyone who doubted us. He's insufferable at the moment, actually." She laughed.

Skylar's laugh turned into a yawn, which she smothered with her palm. How long had she been here? I had no idea what time it was. The small hospital bay didn't have a window.

"What time is it?"

She ran a hand over her disheveled lilac hair. "Late. You can go back to sleep if you want."

"You look like you need to get some sleep yourself. Go home. I'll be okay."

"I'm not leaving you. It shouldn't be too long now. Reece dropped off a bag of snacks."

She peered inside the rucksack and rummaged through the contents, pulling out a Thermos and an array of plastic boxes of different shapes and sizes.

I propped myself up on the pillow. "That's a lot of food. He shouldn't have gone to so much trouble."

Examining the grapes inside one of the small tubs, she raised a wry eyebrow. "No trouble. My husband has an incredible collection of Tupperware. I'm sure he appreciates the chance to showcase it. Do you want something?"

A wave of nausea hit me. "No. Thanks. Not yet."

Skylar nodded and zipped up the rucksack. "Maybe later. They are working on the discharge papers." Her voice was gentle and soothing. "You don't have to worry about anything. I've called your parents. They are in the air right now. They can't wait to see you."

My parents couldn't come all this way over a little bump on the head. "I don't want any fuss. Tell them not to come. I'll be okay."

"I couldn't stop them. Gabe's bringing them over in his plane."

A private jet? Well, at least they'd enjoy that. That would fuel Mom's conversations for the next millennium.

Skylar slid her hand along the blanket toward me. "I know not having your family here must be hard for you. If you need anything, just ask me. Okay?"

A cloud fogged my brain, and I let my eyes close. We'd been amazing out there. I'd felt back to my old self on that pitch. My voice sounded sleepy and hoarse. "I'm sorry I haven't . . . integrated as much into this team as I could have done. I've had some stuff going on, and my heart wasn't in the game, but I want a new start. I haven't enjoyed playing that much for a long time, but it felt good. Really good." A rueful smile pulled at my lips. "Playing in England was never my plan, but I'm here now. I promise I'm going to give everything I can to this team."

Skylar beamed. "Glad to hear it. You're one of us. We're lucky to have you." She wrinkled her nose and the smile slipped from her face to be replaced by a frown. "I almost forgot to ask. Don't be alarmed, but there's a guy here. Security have got their eye on him, but he hasn't budged from a truck outside. Are you expecting any male visitors? A boyfriend, or . . . ?"

My eyes flashed open. "A boyfriend? No, I don't have anybody. What does he look like?"

"A big guy. Dark hair. Welsh. He left his details at the reception desk."

My breath caught. Geraint? "Is he still here?"

"He's sat in the parking lot outside. He's been there all night."

Chapter 45

Madison

Skylar slipped her arm around me and guided me into the brightly lit atrium. "You're coming back with me. The doctor said you shouldn't be alone. Reece is picking up your parents from the airport. We've got everything under control."

The daylight dazzled me. I'd expected it to be night. "What time is it?"

Skylar glanced at her watch. "Ten a.m."

I scanned the packed parking lot, and my eyes fell upon Geraint's 4x4 sticking out like a cardinal in the snow. Despite my headache, a warm glow flowed through me.

"Can you give me a minute? I need to talk to this guy."

Skylar's wary gaze met mine, and her body stiffened. "Do you know him?"

What did it mean that he was here? We were done, weren't we? "I know him."

Skylar's shoulders slumped. "Okay, good. We were worried he was some sort of creepy stalker. He's been sat there all night."

"He's not a stalker."

Skylar hooked her arm through mine.

I looked at her in surprise. "What are you doing?"

"I'm escorting you."

"I can walk to a car."

"Nope. The doctor said not to leave you alone." She gave a small smile. "Doctors always know best."

Skylar deposited me at the battered truck, which was sandwiched between a Lamborghini and a Porsche. I peered through the glass at the slumbering flannel-clad giant inside. Sleep softened the rough lines of his face. A swath of dark hair fell casually on his forehead. The shadow of his beard and his disheveled hair gave him an even more rugged manliness. Even asleep, he exuded masculinity.

A tremble ran through me. Geraint was here. I'd pushed him away, but he'd come back. "This is Geraint. I met him in Wales. I didn't expect to see him again."

Skylar's eyes traveled over my face. "Did you want to see him again?"

I answered honestly. "More than anything, but I don't know how to trust anyone again after Bryce. I don't want to make the same mistakes."

"That's understandable. It will take time, but if it's the right person, they'll give you grace."

I traced a finger over the truck door frame. "How do I know he's the right person?"

Skylar flashed a faint smile. "You don't. That's part of it. Love is a risk, but when you find the one, it's always worth it." She squeezed her arm around my waist. "Call me when you're done. I'll come collect you and bring you to the car."

I laughed. "Collect me? I'm not a child."

"I told you." Her eyes were mock-serious as she wagged a finger in my face. "Doctor's orders. You've had a concussion. You need to be looked after."

Geraint stirred in the seat. The dark lashes that shadowed his cheeks flew up, and his soft eyes met mine. An irresistible grin curved the corners of his full lips. My heart melted.

"Thanks, but don't worry about me. I'll be looked after."

Chapter 46

MADISON

I slid into the passenger seat and shut the door. "What are you doing here?"

Geraint's fingers hovered by the bandage wrapped around my head before he dropped his hand. "Are you okay?"

"I'm fine. What happened? I don't understand why you're here."

"I went round every hospital before I realized they'd have you in a fancy one." He flicked his gaze across the parking lot to Skylar as she slipped into her purple Audi. "It wasn't exactly a warm welcome. I don't think I made a good impression."

"The team looks out for each other. They thought you were some crazy stalker."

His eyes sparkled with amusement. "I drove five hours and came running in demanding to see you. I probably gave off the vibe."

A pulse pounded in my head. "Why did you drive five hours?"

He kept his gaze on the windshield and picked at the huge steering wheel. "Honestly? Because I saw you lying on that pitch, and I had to be with you. It was the only thing that mattered."

"What about your meeting with the brewery?"

His gaze traveled over my face and searched my eyes. He took my hand in his. My body relaxed the moment he touched me. "Did you hear me? You are the only thing that matters."

"I heard you, but we can't do this, Geraint. We already said goodbye. You're not being realistic. We only spent two weeks together."

"So?"

I couldn't help my laugh at his unruffled expression. "We don't know each other well enough."

He interlaced his fingers with mine. "We know the things that matter."

His mouth covered mine, smothering my words. The sweet warmth of his lips sent a shockwave through my body. He crushed me to his solid chest, and I kissed him back, lingering, savoring every moment. I didn't think I'd ever get to do this again, but Geraint was right—this was the only thing that mattered.

He drew away and brushed a strand of hair back from my cheek. "I'm sticking around to take care of you, at least until your parents get here. You concentrate on resting and getting better."

"You can't do that. You have a life in Wales, and I'm here."

"We'll find a way to work it out. I want you to be my woman. If you'll have me, then we'll find a way where we can both be happy."

"Your woman?"

"The one I get to love. In sickness and in health. For richer or poorer." He reached into his pocket and pulled out a wooden spoon. "I know you think this is some cheesy thing for tourists, but I made it for you." His rough fingers trailed over the intricately carved symbols. "These two bowls represent togetherness because I want to share my life with you. This wheel means work. I will always work on being the best man I can for you. The horseshoe is for good luck, and the heart is for love." His fingers traced down to the bells, and I watched his throat bob as he swallowed. "The bells are for marriage."

My heart thumped.

"My first marriage broke down. It doesn't mean I don't want that commitment again. It's not time yet, but this spoon is about me telling you how I feel and the direction I want this to go. I love you. One day, I want to make you my wife."

Anxiety pulled at my gut. "I'm not getting married. I'm not walking down an aisle." I took a breath. "I didn't tell you this because I didn't want to make a big thing. I was engaged before, and my fiancé didn't show for the wedding."

He was silent for a long time, staring out the windshield across the parking lot. "I'm sorry."

"I've been so angry for so long. I have this awful rage that eats me up. My ex wants me to forgive him, but I can't. He doesn't deserve my forgiveness after what he did. It's hard for me to trust. I want to let go of all this resentment and move on."

Bryce had never crossed my mind once in the hospital. Ever since I'd left Wales, all I could think about was Geraint. The anger inside me had all but melted. What was the point of hanging on to it? I wanted to be with Geraint, but how was I supposed to take that leap?

I wiped my tears. "I don't want to be angry anymore."

Geraint studied my face. "Then don't be. Don't forgive him because *he* deserves it, forgive him because *you* deserve it. You deserve that peace."

His face broke into a smile, and warmth crept into my body. Joy bubbled up inside me, and for a moment the pain in my head vanished. None of this was part of my plan. I wasn't supposed to be playing soccer anymore. I wasn't supposed to be in England, or with this man. This was all because of that day Bryce had changed his mind. Everything since had brought me here. I could never have predicted it.

Nothing in my life had gone the way it was supposed to go.

Thank goodness for that.

I'd been pushing a ball under water for so long, and it was hitting *me* in the face, not Bryce. It was time to let go. Time to forgive. Bryce was a selfish idiot. The world was full of those, but it was also full of good people. The rotten ones just got all the attention. Bryce hadn't ruined my life. He'd set me on a new path. Geraint's hand wrapped around mine. Everything had set me on this path to Geraint. It had led me home.

Geraint rubbed the back of his neck. "Marriage isn't a deal-breaker for me. We'll do whatever you want. We'll walk down the aisle together, or we won't. We get to decide our future together. It doesn't matter to me. I just want to be with you."

I squeezed his hand. "Fine, so maybe I forgive Bryce. What about you? You expect me to be the better person, and you're here losing your pub rather than swallowing your pride and letting me help you. This isn't the eighteenth century. You don't have to carve a spoon to prove to your father-in-law that you can provide for me. I provide for myself. If you're in my life, I can provide for you, too. It would be my pleasure. I love the Dragon. I can't let it turn into some wellness retreat."

"I appreciate the offer, but we don't need it. We're doing better. I needed to commit to fighting for it. I called the brewery to reschedule the meeting, and told them about my plans. They sounded positive. We're going to be okay."

"I heard you're doing better than okay. Ewan texted to tell me you're blowing up on TikTok."

He gave an abashed laugh, and raked a hand over his beard. "I wouldn't go that far."

"I've seen how many followers you have now. Will you refurbish? Maybe I could be an investor? The Dragon means a lot to me, too. I want to help you. I'd love to be a part of what you're doing. I had this moment on the pitch where everything made sense. I've been pushing everyone away because I was so frightened of getting close to anyone after what Bryce did to me. It has to change. I love you, too. In sickness and in health. For richer or poorer. We don't need a ceremony to promise those things." I brushed his hair back from his forehead. "We can just swear to each other now. We could swear on the spoon."

His face lit with a grin. "That's not really how the spoon works." His intense eyes came up to study my face. His voice was rough with emotion. "But I can go with it. I swear it . . . on the spoon."

My heart filled with warmth. "I'm so excited about what we can do with the place. Maybe we can get Brooke over to give us some ideas for the refurbishment. She's amazing at interior design. We can stay in England during the season and keep the pub for our downtime. You could get a manager to run it in the interim. Then, when I retire, we've got a place to live."

He leaned lightly into me, tilting his face toward mine. "Sounds like you've got it all figured out, Kentucky."

I laughed. "Does it, Wales? I haven't, but I know we'll work it out."

"You're right. We will." He moved in close and whispered the words against my lips. "We swore on the spoon. Tradition is important."

Chapter 47

GERAINT

A knock sounded on the door to Madison's apartment.

Madison paled. Unease flickered in her eyes. "That's them."

She smoothed her hair, and I noticed her fingers were trembling. She'd been worried ever since we got back from the hospital. I'd thought it was the shock of the accident, but I was starting to wonder if it was more than that. Madison didn't seem thrilled by the prospect of her parents' arrival.

She ran her hands over her thighs and moved reluctantly to the door. She pasted a smile onto her lips before she answered it. "Hi."

Madison's parents rushed through the door of the apartment. Feeling awkward to be part of such a tender scene, I took a step back to give them space as they greeted each other. Madison looked just like her mum, with generously curved lips and beautiful lashes that swept down across her cheekbones. She had the same chin as her father, as well as a look about their brows that suggested iron determination. Maybe Mr. Thorner had the same stubborn streak as his daughter. I smiled to myself. The "Thornado" took no prisoners on the pitch, but I could make her purr like a kitten.

Madison's fingers fluttered around the bandage that swathed her head. "You shouldn't have come all this way. I'm completely fine. It was just a bump."

Madison's mum wrapped her arms around her daughter and pulled her into an embrace. "Nonsense. We came the minute we heard."

Madison caught my eye and beckoned. "Mom, Dad, I'd like you to meet someone. This is Geraint. Geraint, this is Robert and Pam. Geraint's my—"

"Fake boyfriend." I offered my hand. "To be drafted in in emergencies."

The unease in Madison's eyes shifted to amusement. "That's right. We met online through a Dolly Parton fan club."

"We did." I put a hand over my heart. "What can I say? Dolly is amazing."

Madison's parents watched us with bemused expressions. A sudden rush of nerves made me tense. Perhaps they wouldn't approve. This had all happened quickly. I didn't want to be in anyone's way. I'd told Madison I'd be happy to make myself scarce, but she'd insisted I stick around.

Pam studied my face with an enigmatic gaze. "You're the man from the photo. We wondered about you. You're even taller than you looked on Instagram."

Madison coughed and rolled her eyes. "Please don't embarrass me."

"Who's embarrassing you? We're allowed to wonder." Pam opened her arms to me. "It's wonderful to meet you. We're huggers. Come here."

Madison raised a rueful eyebrow. "Geraint does give the best hugs. A Welsh hug is different. It's called a cwtch. It means a hug that's a cubbyhole."

Pam raised an impressed eyebrow. "A cubbyhole? How lovely."

Perfume filled my nose as I hugged Madison's mum. Her arms wrapped around my back, and she squeezed me tight. Whatever awkwardness Madison was feeling didn't appear to be reciprocated. Pam and Robert seemed thrilled to be reunited with their daughter.

A wry laugh left Madison's lips. "Okay, you can put him down now, Mom."

Pam released me and returned her attention to her daughter. Two deep lines of worry appeared between the older woman's eyes. "How are you feeling?"

I hadn't noticed the strained edge to Pam's voice before. Madison's parents must have been worried about her. It had been hard enough for me watching her injured and vulnerable on the pitch, and I'd only been a car drive away.

Madison rubbed the back of her neck. "Okay . . . I'm feeling . . . different."

Silence wrapped around us. Better to let them catch up. I cleared my throat. "I'll finish dinner."

Pam transferred her gaze to me. "You cook?"

"Geraint is a chef. You wouldn't believe his food. It's incredible."

Madison's warm palm gripped mine. Robert's gaze followed the movement, and his lips thinned. Maybe he wouldn't approve. I got it. Perhaps he was protective of his daughter. He'd been watching me with an inscrutable expression this whole time, and he'd hardly said a word.

Madison squeezed my hand and gave me an indulgent smile. "Geraint owns a pub in Snowdonia." She gestured toward the couch. "Sit down, both of you."

Pam arranged the cushions and perched on the couch. "Snowdonia? We love it there. Did Madison tell you we got married in Wales? Saint Dwynwen's."

Madison rubbed her arms, stood, and drifted to the window. "He knows. I told him about it."

She gazed outside at the River Thames cutting its dark path through the city. "I've been thinking a lot about the story of Saint Dwynwen. She drank a potion, and it turned her lover into a block of ice."

She drew an audible breath but kept her face turned away. "When Bryce left me, it was like I drank a potion. All that anger and bitterness twisted me up inside. I pushed you both away, and I wasn't easy to be around. For that, I'm sorry. Truly. The thing is, that potion didn't turn him into ice. It turned *me* into ice. My rage made no impact on Bryce, it only poisoned me. So, I'm done with it. I forgive Bryce, but not because he deserves it. He doesn't. Bryce is selfish. Some people are like that, and we have to accept it. I forgive him because *I* deserve it."

She swallowed and turned to look at me. "Geraint helped me to understand that. He's in my life now. I know it's sudden. I know you're thinking this is me being impulsive again, but it's not. This is different. We've fallen in love." Madison's gaze rested on my face, and her voice was tender. "When you find the one, all the things inside you that are hard and twisted up have no choice but to soften."

I felt the same. Madison had changed everything for me.

"I know this is right." Madison's posture was full of determination as she turned to face her father. "This time, I'm really sure."

Robert weighed me up and inclined his head. "And you, Geraint. What are your intentions toward my daughter?"

My heart pounded. This mattered. I had to get it right. Jess had always admonished me for speaking without thinking, but I didn't need to think too hard about this. The answer was obvious because it came from my heart.

"I love your daughter. I can't promise her riches, but I promise I will cherish her and do everything within my power to bring her happiness." My words were for Robert, but my gaze found

Madison's beautiful face. "I will always strive to make sure my arms are a safe place for your daughter to land."

Madison's face split into a wide grin. Her eyes sparkled mischievously. "He's also very skilled at wielding an axe, Dad. He's a strong pair of hands for the farm."

"I see." Madison's father inclined his head thoughtfully before a warm smile spread on his lips. "Then we look forward to welcoming you to the family, Geraint."

Epilogue

MADISON

ONE YEAR LATER

Geraint pulled out a tray of potato dauphinoise to inspect the bubbling cheese. He wrinkled his nose and slid it back in the oven. "The top isn't golden yet. It needs a little longer."

He set to work on the rarebit, humming along to the radio as he gathered the ingredients.

I washed my hands at the sink and surveyed the dishes on the island. Geraint had really gone to town with the food. "Are you sure you don't need any help? This is so much food."

"I'm catering for an entire football team. Athletes like to eat." He kissed the tip of my nose. "Now you have your appetite back, I'm feeding you up."

As if on cue, rippling pops stirred in my belly. The baby was hiccupping. Such an odd sensation, but I loved it. Thankfully, I'd moved past the sickness phase. I just wanted to eat all day and be in bed by 7 p.m. Bedtime would be later than I'd had in a while, but I could make the effort. Not only had my entire team come for their Christmas party, but my family was here, too. Tonight was not a night for pajamas and slippers.

Geraint watched my face. "What is it?"

"She's hiccupping." I took his huge hand and rested it on my belly.

Geraint dropped to his knees and pressed his ear to my midriff. He lifted my T-shirt, his lips warm against my huge bump as he murmured some unintelligible words.

"Are you speaking to her in Welsh again?"

"She's going to be bilingual. Better to start now." He rose to his feet. "Come here, Kentucky. Come and give me a cwtch."

I moved into the warmth of his powerful arms.

A polite cough sounded from the doorway, followed by a low male voice. "Sorry to interrupt. I wondered if you needed any help with the food?"

Skylar stood in the doorway with her bespectacled husband, Reece. I'd grown much closer to my captain over the past year. We'd both played for the Halos, but at different times. It was fun to talk about LA. It didn't hold the same pain for me as it had once. Now I'd moved on from Bryce, I could remember all the happy times in my career.

Skylar wrapped her inked arms around her husband's waist and pressed her chin to his shoulder. "Reece always prefers to be in the kitchen at a party."

Reece's face lit with a wry smile, and he adjusted his scholarly glasses. "That's right. Usually, you find all the best people there."

Skylar planted a kiss on his cheek. Her voice was light and teasing. "It's true. Or you find them in the library."

Geraint shook his head. "It's fine, thank you. I'm managing. I might even find my commis chef at some point, and then we'll get this show on the road."

Reece moved to the sink and washed his hands. "I'll be your commis chef. Tell me what you want me to do."

Skylar's face lit with a broad smile. "Me too. Give us jobs. The cameras are buzzing around out there. We'd much rather be in here."

A flash of guilt made my smile tight. The cameras were my fault. I'd asked the Calverdale PR team to arrange something. We had the famous Gabe Rivers and his entire team in the pub. It was too good a publicity opportunity to miss. After the refurbishment, business was booming. Throw in an endorsement from the Calverdale Ladies, and we'd be on to a winner.

"I'm sorry about the cameras. They'll clear off soon," I said.

Skylar waved a dismissive hand. "I know. It's fine. That's when we can really have some fun."

Music burst into the kitchen from the lounge. A deep, slightly off-key baritone voice drifted to us.

Skylar's laugh rippled through the air. "Oh God. Every time. You can't stop the man."

Geraint's brow furrowed. "Is that supposed to be Tom Jones?"

"It's Gabe. He pretends he hates karaoke, but somehow he's always first on the mic," Skylar said. "He's still on cloud nine that we got to the top."

I reached for a potato chip. "We were there for two weeks."

"It doesn't matter. Gabe wanted his moment. Now he's talking up next season. He's got his eye on winning the WSL, and then the Champions League. This man always has a plan." Skylar gave me a wink. "I can see it, especially when we have you on the coaching side of things."

I was excited about my move into coaching. It was time for a new challenge, and it would be better for family life once the baby arrived.

I chuckled. "Let me give birth, then we'll talk about lifting the FA Cup."

Skylar grabbed a golden breadcrumb sausage. She took a bite and groaned. A huge grin split her face. "What the hell is this?"

"Glamorgan sausage," I said.

Skylar picked up another one. "It's divine."

"I know." I couldn't help my own smile. "I've always been a fan of Glamorgan sausage."

Geraint lifted an amused eyebrow and cleared his throat. "If you're just here to pick at the food, you need to get out of the chef's way." He shooed us with his hands.

Skylar's warm palm grasped mine. "Come on. Leave the men to the cooking. Let's do the next song."

I gave an outraged laugh. "Me? There's no way I'm doing karaoke."

Skylar laughed. "Yes, you are. Come on. I'm not doing it on my own."

My walk was waddling compared to Skylar's smooth strides as we made our way down the hallway. The delicious scent of new carpet filled my nose. Everything still smelled so fresh after the renovation. We weaved our way through huddles of chattering players into the sparkling lounge. A gang of laughing children buzzed past us, heading up the stairs. A young boy leaped out in front of me, swinging a glowing lightsaber over his head.

He thrust it toward me and flashed a disarming grin. "Do you want to be a Jedi?"

Lana, one of the defenders, caught up to the boy, breathless. She ran her fingers through his blond curls and gave him an affectionate smile. "Maddie's too pregnant to be a Jedi." Lana raised her own lightsaber in the air. "But you need to watch out because the Empire isn't done with you. Go. I'll give you a head start."

The little boy whooped and ran off laughing. Simon the border collie trailed at his heels, tail wagging.

Lana rolled her eyes, but her grin turned up a notch. "I preferred the pirate phase to the Star Wars phase."

Before I could reply, she dashed off after her stepson.

Skylar linked her arm through mine. The scents of pine and mulled spices hit my nose, and the fire's golden heat enveloped me. We dodged around my teammate Sophie and her boyfriend, Aiden, dancing in the corner, too lost in their own world to notice us. By the enormous Christmas tree, Gabe Rivers held the microphone in his hand. He was singing for everyone, but his bright eyes didn't budge from his beautiful blonde wife. Miri bounced a chestnut-haired child on her lap and roared with laughter as Gabe tackled the low chorus in a faltering baritone. The lounge burst with sound as more people joined in to sing "Delilah".

"Wait here. I'm putting our names down next."

Skylar disappeared into the singing horde. I drank in the silky atmosphere for a while before Geraint's arms wrapped around me from behind. He held me gently, careful not to crush my bump.

"I'm bringing the food out. Can you help me get everyone together?"

"Of course."

"My dad would have loved to see the place bursting with life like this." His voice was thick with emotion.

I turned and cupped his rough cheek with my hand. "I'm so sorry he's not here."

"Me too." Geraint pressed his warm lips to my temple. "But I'm glad your family could be here with us."

My gaze fell on my parents talking to Daffyd and Young Aled. Aled was pointing to the love spoons on the wall. The pub had been refurbished, but we'd kept the things that made it special. Outside, the snow began to fall in thick, spiraling flakes. Warmth filled my heart. Once Geraint and I had been snowed in together. This place had been my escape from the world. Now the world was here with us. I welcomed it with open arms.

Swaying with the music, I relaxed against Geraint's hard chest. "We should make this Christmas party a tradition."

"I agree." Geraint's voice was soft and melodic in my ear. His lips trailed up my neck to nibble my earlobe. "I love you. Merry Christmas, Kentucky."

My heart melted. Geraint held me lightly, but it was enough to make me feel safe. Even though I had no need of an escape anymore, I would never tire of my Welsh hugs. "I love you, too. Nadolig Llawen, Wales."

THANKS FOR READING!

Thank you so much for joining me and the Calverdale Ladies! I've loved every minute of writing this series, and am so thrilled I got to share it with you. It's farewell for now, but if you'd like to keep up to date with future releases, please feel free to sign up for my newsletter or follow me on my socials.

If you haven't already, you can download the prequel novella, PITCHING MY BEST FRIEND. Sign up to my newsletter here, and get the novella for free! https://BookHip.com/RVXCHSB I send newsletters once a month with book updates and recommendations of other books you might like. I promise to keep the boring photos of my garden and my dog to a minimum.

LET'S HANG OUT!

All I've ever wanted from life is a crew to hang around with so that we can all wear sunglasses, look cool, and click our fingers in an intimidating fashion at rival crews. We can chat all things romance and occasionally you might be called upon to become involved in a choreographed dance fight. I will also be your best friend forever. NB: Dance fighting skills not mandatory (but encouraged).

Join my reader group:
www.facebook.com/groups/979907003370581/
Follow my author page:
www.facebook.com/profile.php?id=61553872688253
TikTok: Sasha Lace Author (@sasha_lace_author)
Instagram: www.instagram.com/Sasha_Lace_Author

Psst! Hang on! I'd love a review if you've got a sec? If you enjoyed this book, please consider leaving a review wherever you like to leave them. Amazon, Goodreads, or BookBub. Reviews are the lifeblood of authors, and are very much appreciated! Thanks so much.

ACKNOWLEDGMENTS

This is my second run at writing these acknowledgments. The first time, I was a fresh-faced indie author leaping into the unknown. I had no idea if anyone would pick up my story, or whether (more likely) it would be lost in a pile with a million others. What I didn't expect was to find so many people willing to take a chance on an unknown author.

Writing has brought so many wonderful women into my life. Thank you to all the readers who have supported me, whether it was taking the time to message with words of encouragement, leaving a thoughtful review, or shouting about my books. You helped me find my confidence as a writer. You made me feel like my words have value. It means the world, truly.

Thank you to everyone in the Montlake Romance team for all of your hard work on these books. It has truly been such a brilliant experience, and I've loved every moment. I'm so excited to relaunch these books with an amazing team of professionals. Thank you to Victoria Oundjian for giving me this chance, for your passion and enthusiasm for the series, and for making my lifelong dream to be traditionally published a reality.

Thank you to Victoria Pepe for taking this series on and bringing so much energy and enthusiasm to it. I feel so confident that it is in wonderful hands, and I'm so grateful. Thank you to Lindsey

Faber for your brilliant development editing insight, and for helping me to dig so much deeper with these characters. To Jenni Davis, thank you for giving these books such a beautiful polish, and helping me to banish the word 'quirked' from my vocabulary. I don't know how many books it will take before I can rid myself of it completely, but I live in hope.

Thank you to Laura and Clare at Liverpool Lit. You are amazing agents and lovely human beings. It is genuinely an honor to be represented by an agency so committed to breaking down barriers in publishing.

To my beta reader/editor/mentor Angela, I sent out a plea for help with my first story and the universe overshot the net and sent me you—the best friend I've never met! You have always been so accepting, so generous, and so insightful. You understood what I was trying to say with that weird first story (better than I did) and you helped make sense of it. Not only did you help me become a better writer, but you showed me that people can be miraculously kind.

To my lovely writer bestie, Heather G. Harris. I have long suspected the 'G' stands for genius. You've always believed in me, and encouraged me, and you've been so generous with your time and knowledge. Thank you for being my very first beta reader, and for giving me the confidence to go for it with this story. I appreciate you.

To Jo, Tamymanne, and Kat. You are a wildly accepting bunch of fellow smut-butts. Thank you for all the laughs, and the log-ins. Jo, seriously, thank you. What would I do without the log-ins!? Please don't ever change your password, or this is all over for me.

To Helen, I'm so grateful to have a lovely friend to share this writing and publishing journey with. I really appreciate your talent for finding the perfect shocked-doll expression for every occasion, and your dedication to uncovering Rhysand fan art. Whatever happens, we'll always have the Willywahs and that street team of Ken dolls from Sainsbury's.

Thank you to my precious friend Katie. You have always brought so much joy into my life. Whatever I'm doing, no matter the hour, I'd always rather be on a boat with you, playing table tennis, and stuffing my face with free sushi and peanut M&Ms at 5 p.m., directly before our five-course meal is about to be served.

To Ruchi, my twin flame, all my literary aspirations began with you. Your West Midlands project spoke to me of beauty. The letter to Thom Yorke helped me to refine my prose. All that time spent doctoring BT phone bills honed my attention to detail. The environmental rap taught me how to dig deep. The hole in the ozone layer isn't even an issue anymore. Coincidence, or the power of rap?

Thank you to my mum for always encouraging my passion to read. Even when we had so little, you made sure I always had books. Thank you for your unconditional love and support. The past couple of years have been tough, but your selflessness and strength leave me in awe. Better times are coming, I know it. Thank you for being you. I love you.

To James, your support makes my writing possible. Your support makes everything possible. You've made me laugh every day for the past twenty years. The best part of writing about football is that I get to talk about these books with you. Why are you so randomly good at plotting? It's like that time we went windsurfing and you just knew how to stand up and do it straight away, and I was covered in goose shit and crying. It makes no sense, but I'm into it. You're better than all the book boyfriends put together. They should make a trope about you.

Last, thank you to my kind, beautiful, bright, funny, smart, wonderful boys. I became a writer when I became a mother. You gave me the will to be the best version of myself. Please know that you are the greatest joy in my life, and I love you more than anyone has ever loved anyone EVER. Now get out of here. Go on. Clear off! Do not read these books. Not even when you're grown-ups. I cannot afford the therapy you will need from reading your mother's sweary, spicy books. I have given you fair warning.

ABOUT THE AUTHOR

Sasha Lace used to be a very serious scientist before she ditched the lab coat and started writing kissing books. Sasha lives in the North of England and is a mom of two young boys. Everyone in her family is soccer mad, so she knows way more about soccer than she ever wanted to know. As a scientist and mom, her hobbies include: mulling over the complexities of the universe, treading barefoot on Lego, chipping dried Play-Doh from fabric surfaces, dried flower arranging (because you can't kill something twice), and writing about herself in the third person.

Follow the Author on Amazon

If you enjoyed this book, follow Sasha Lace on Amazon to be notified when the author releases a new book!

To do this, please follow these instructions:

Desktop:

1) Search for the author's name on Amazon or in the Amazon App.
2) Click on the author's name to arrive on their Amazon page.
3) Click the "Follow" button.

Mobile and Tablet:

1) Search for the author's name on Amazon or in the Amazon App.
2) Click on one of the author's books.
3) Click on the author's name to arrive on their Amazon page.
4) Click the "Follow" button.

Kindle eReader and Kindle App:

If you enjoyed this book on a Kindle eReader or in the Kindle App, you will find the author "Follow" button after the last page.